THE GRYPHON'S LAIR

KELLEY ARMSTRONG

PUFFIN CANADA

an imprint of Penguin Random House Canada Young Readers, a division of Penguin
Random House of Canada Limited

Published in hardcover by Puffin Canada, 2020

Published in this edition, 2021

1 2 3 4 5 6 7 8 9 10

Cover design: Kelly Hill
Cover art © Cory Godbey

Manufactured in the U.S.A.

Library and Archives Canada Cataloguing in Publication

Title: The gryphon's lair / Kelley Armstrong.
Names: Armstrong, Kelley, author. | Daumarie, Xavière, illustrator.
Description: Illustrations by Xavière Daumaire. | Previously published: Toronto:
Puffin Canada, 2020.
Identifiers: Canadiana 2020021621X | ISBN 9780735265400 (softcover)
Classification: LCC PS8551.R7637 G79 2021 | DDC jC813/.6—dc23

Library of Congress Control Number: 2019955436

www.penguinrandomhouse.ca

Penguin
Random House
PUFFIN CANADA

ACCOLADES AND PRAISE FOR
A Royal Guide to Monster Slaying

Shortlisted for the OLA Silver Birch Award

A *School Library Journal* Best Middle Grade Book of 2019
An Ontario Library Association Top Ten Title of 2019

"A fast and fun read, [and] a great read-a-like
for Tamora Pierce's Tortall series."
—Starred Review, *School Library Journal*

"A fresh take on familiar fantasy creatures and situations."
—Starred Review, *Shelf Awareness*

"A rousing romp for monster hunters and monster lovers alike."
—*Kirkus Reviews*

PRAISE FOR *The Gryphon's Lair*

One of CCBC's Best Books for Kids and Teens Fall 2020

"A fun and fiery follow-up."
—*Kirkus Reviews*

"An enjoyable follow-up to its rollicking predecessor."
—*School Library Journal*

"*The Gryphon's Lair* is an entertaining novel that speaks to today's
awareness of social difference and ecological protection."
—Highly Recommended, *CM Reviews*

To my nieces: Elena, Tesfanesh and Mya.
May you slay all the monsters.

CHAPTER ONE

I have a way with monsters. Unfortunately, this chickcharney seems immune to it.

When I was three, my dad captured a chickcharney
and brought it home for me. I tried to hug it. You can't blame
me. Chickcharnies look like owls on stilts with amazing
monkey tails. Adorable.

Anyway, the chickcharney, shockingly, did not want to be
hugged, even by a princess. For a flightless bird, it tried very
hard to take flight. Finally, Dad whisked it away and promised
me a more huggable version. I still have the toy, which has had
both eyes and a leg replaced due to over-cuddling.

Now, nine years later, I'm trying to capture a live chickcharney, and I swear it knows how much abuse its stuffed
twin endured. It is not falling for any of my tricks, despite the
fact that I am offering mealworm-and-hazelnut suet, which
chickcharnies love the way I love honey cakes.

I'm crouched behind a rock, watching the chickcharney bob around, totally ignoring the suet. Finally it stops, as if catching the scent.

When the chickcharney turns toward me, my inner toddler squeals. It is truly the most adorable of the bird monsters, all huge eyes and fluffy feathers and those ridiculous legs. Its fuzzy body bobs as it walks to the first nugget of suet. To reach it, the chickcharney has to bend almost in half, like a human touching their toes. It swings down, grabs the nugget and levers up. As it chomps the treat, it squeaks in delight. Then it spots the next piece.

When the beast heads my way, I suppress a shiver of glee. I've chosen my spot perfectly. I am the royal monster hunter, after all. Well, royal monster hunter *in training*, but I do carry the ebony sword.

As Clan Dacre, I'd been raised to be a monster hunter. Yet my training doubled when I took the sword, and today I can see how it's paid off. Chickcharnies are nervous beasts, but this one is heading straight for me, not suspecting a thing. I'm downwind and hidden behind long grass, wearing a tunic and leggings that blend with the green fronds.

The chickcharney keeps bobbing toward me. When it hears a sound, its head swivels all the way around to look behind it. I tense, certain it's about to bolt. But it only peeps twice and then continues toward my hiding place as it scoops up the suet-chunk trail.

It's five feet away. Four. Three . . .

Dry twigs crackle and paws thump the hard earth as something plows through the grass. A flash of brown fur.

Then jagged teeth flash as the intruder squeals in rage . . . and charges the chickcharney.

"Jacko, no!"

The young jackalope pretends not to hear me. He's running at the chickcharney, I'm running at him, and the chickcharney is running as fast as its wobbly stilt-legs will carry it. It's not fast enough, though, and Jacko leaps with a squeal of victory that turns to a grunt of surprise as I dive and grab him.

I land flat on my face, outstretched hands clutching Jacko's furry body. Once caught, he only gives a chirp of confusion. Then he sees me facedown in the dirt, and his chirp turns to an alert cry as he wriggles free and nudges me with his antlers.

I groan and lift my head. The chickcharney is long gone. There's just my half-grown jackalope companion, chattering at me. With long, powerful hind legs and a slender body, Jacko looks like a hare . . . if a hare had striped fur, pointed teeth and tiny antlers.

Jackalopes are predators and a full-grown one could take down a chickcharney. At half size, though, Jacko is just dangerous enough to spook the poor beast.

"I was not being attacked by a chickcharney, Jacko," I say.

His chirrup says he's not so certain. In fact, he's quite sure he's just rescued me from a terrible death at the talons of a deformed owl, and he nudges my hand, looking for the petting he so richly deserves.

I give him a pat. He did think he was protecting me, and despite our training, he's still too young to grasp the difference between threats and targets. Which is why *someone* was supposed to be watching him.

When a giant black wolf charges from the brush, I don't pull my sword. I don't even scramble to my feet. I just skewer the warg with a glare.

"Hello, Malric. Great job taking care of Jacko."

People say that Clan Dacre can understand the speech of monsters. Not exactly. We just learn to interpret their body language. Yet the more time I spend with beasts, the more I suspect they understand a greater portion of *our* speech than we realize.

Malric's snort insists that caring for a jackalope is beneath his dignity, but I don't miss the sheepish look in his eyes. He stalks over and grabs Jacko by the scruff of his neck. Jacko hangs there, limp, even when Malric gives him a shake and a growl.

A shadow passes over us. I squint up as a white cloud floats down to land on four roan-red hooves. The pegasus filly looks at Malric and Jacko and then tosses her red mane with a whinny of annoyance.

"No, you didn't miss the party invitation, Sunniva," I say. "Thank *you* for staying away while I hunted. Unfortunately, your fellow beasts weren't as patient. So much for catching a chickcharney."

Leaving my beasts at the castle hadn't been an option. Jacko needs a steel cage to keep him from coming after me, and even then, he's been known to squeeze through the bars. I refuse to corral or bridle Sunniva—staying with me must always be her choice. As for Malric, well, this isn't exactly an authorized hunt. Mom thinks my brother and I are off enjoying a picnic, which means we need my personal bodyguard, and that's the warg.

I push to my feet and look around. "I'm sure Rhydd won't catch one either, so—"

Malric woofs. It's a deep chuff, and I follow his gaze to see the chickcharney perched on a rock fifty feet away, watching us.

Maybe I haven't lost my chance after all.

"Malric—" I begin.

Before I can finish asking, he pins Jacko under one massive paw. The jackalope grumbles but lies still. I thank Malric with a nod. Then I pull an apple from my pocket and give it to Sunniva, while politely asking her to stay here. Her whinny agrees.

Beasts under control, I leave the chickcharney watching them with interest while I creep through the long grass. On all fours, I make my way toward the monster, ease behind it and toss a suet pellet over its head. It peeps and gives a start. Then it smells the treat. As it gobbles up that one, I toss another into the space between us. The chickcharney trots over and—

Hooves pound the earth, the very ground vibrating beneath them.

A massive black horse leaps out from the forest. A steed with an iridescent horn. The unicorn charges, a rider clinging to his back. Rhydd grins and lifts his net as his unicorn, Courtois, bears down on the chickcharney.

My chickcharney.

CHAPTER TWO

I stand my ground as my brother gallops straight at me. For twins, we don't look much alike. We share the same honey-brown curly hair, though he now keeps his short. His skin is the color of his hair; mine is a little darker. I have our mom's heart-shaped face and our dad's green eyes; Rhydd has Dad's square face and Mom's brown eyes. Those eyes dance as he whips past me.

"Hey! That's my chickcharney," I shout as the bird monster runs for its life.

"Nope!" Rhydd yells back. "You set the rules, Rowan. Remember?"

The last time we hunted, Rhydd had found the target—a hoop snake—first, but then he'd lost it, and when I captured it, he cried foul. So this time, I'd made a rule that being the first to find a monster did not mean it was yours. I'd meant that you couldn't claim a target after you'd lost it. Apparently, I hadn't been specific enough.

"You can still catch this one," Rhydd calls. "Just beat me to it. You've got a pegasus."

I grumble under my breath. He knows I can't ride Sunniva yet.

"I'm sure Malric will give you a lift," Rhydd shouts as they disappear in a cloud of dust.

The warg fixes me with a look that dares me to try it.

"Thanks," I mutter.

Malric lifts his paw from Jacko, who leaps up and stands, poised on all fours, back straight, looking at me and chirping, as if offering his services as a mount. I chuckle and scoop him up.

Rhydd's right—I made the rules—and this is just a game. He'll crow over his victory, but the next time we hunt, he'll be the one who adjusts the rules to be more fair.

I really shouldn't have wagered that the loser had to attend the boring state luncheon tomorrow. I *wouldn't* have agreed if my fellow monster hunter in training, Dain, hadn't sworn he had a foolproof method for capturing chickcharnies. Now Rhydd and Alianor will catch a chickcharney first, and I'll be stuck at that luncheon. I could get my revenge by insisting Dain join me, but the only thing worse than sitting through those speeches would be sitting through them with Dain grumbling beside me.

A horse tears past to my left, on course to help Rhydd. The rider is a girl with light-brown skin and braided light-brown hair, her blue eyes glinting. It's Alianor, my friend and Rhydd's partner on this hunt.

Alianor waves as she passes.

I sink to the ground. "At least someone's partner stuck around."

Jacko hops onto my lap, looks into my face and chirps. I scratch behind his antlers. "Yes, you stuck around. Dain, however, did not."

When Jacko hisses, I twist and notice Malric staring behind me, his narrowed gaze fixed on something that requires his attention, but not his concern.

A boy creeps through the long grass. He's my brother's height but thinner. His ebony hair is tied at the nape of his neck and his skin, a shade darker than mine, almost blends with the shadows cast by the long grass.

"Trying to sneak up on me?" I say to Dain.

"No point with those two glaring at me."

"Malric's just watching you. It's Jacko who's glaring. They're my bodyguards for when my human partner doesn't stick around. I'm teaming up with Alianor next time."

"Oh, so I guess that means you don't want this?" He lifts a burlap bag. Inside it, something peeps in alarm.

I scramble to my feet. "You caught a chickcharney?"

He carefully lowers the bag around the bird, holding it in place. I see a familiar black spot on its beak.

"You caught *my* chickcharney," I say. "The one I was hunting."

"The one we were both hunting. You were luring it in while I was setting a trap in case it got spooked. Or in case your blasted bunny tried to *attack* it."

Jacko chitters at him, teeth flashing.

"First your jackalope, and then your brother," Dain says. "It was pretty much a guarantee that something would spook your chickcharney, princess."

I squint out over the long grass. "So if you caught my target, what are Rhydd and Alianor chasing?"

"I have no idea."

I laugh and crawl over to examine the chickcharney. Dain crouches over it as we study the specimen. Dain might not seem excited by the creature, but his dark eyes gleam with interest, and he lets strands of hair fall into his face without impatiently shoving them back. We study the beast and discuss it, and I sketch it for my journal as Dain holds it without complaint.

Then we prepare to release it. Alianor will grouse about us not proving we caught it—being from a bandit clan, she always expects a trick. Yet Rhydd knows I wouldn't lie, and a training exercise is no excuse for traumatizing a beast.

I carry the chickcharney a reassuring distance from *my* beasts. I may also give it a cuddle. A very small one, and only because it's already snuggled into my arms. I bend and set it down with murmurs and feather-strokes. It peeps, running its tail along my arm as if petting me back. I give it one last suet pellet for the road. Then I rise and step away.

The chickcharney tilts its owl head, looking at me. Then it peeps, hops closer and wraps its tail around my leg.

"No, princess," Dain calls.

I glance at him, my brows rising.

"No, you do not need a pet chickcharney," he says.

I roll my eyes and give the beast another pat before I try to back up again. That delicate but strong tail tightens around my boot.

"Absolutely not," Dain calls. "You're a monster hunter, not a monster collector. Stop taking them home."

I glower his way. "I have never taken a beast home. They follow me willingly. Well, except that one." I hook my thumb at Malric, who watches us with baleful yellow eyes.

"And the gryphon?"

I straighten indignantly. "That is not the same, and you know it."

Before I could become the royal monster hunter–elect, the council insisted that I hunt down the gryphon that killed my aunt and wounded my brother. While I was training for that, the gryphon found us. I hadn't trusted the council to believe I killed it, so we brought it back to the castle alive, where we'd discovered it was pregnant and decided to let it live so we could study both mother and baby.

So, yes, technically, I brought the gryphon home. Still . . .

"It's not the same thing," I say again.

Dain shrugs. "If you insist, princess." His face stays serious, but I don't miss the amusement twinkling in his eyes. I huff and turn to the chickcharney.

"I'm not taking it home," I say. "Now, if it were an orphaned baby that wanted to follow me, then it would be an excellent opportunity to study—"

"No."

I glare at him. "I said *baby*, which this is not." I crouch and unwrap the chickcharney's tail from my leg. "You're fine.

— 10 —

If you ever see me again, feel free to say hello, but you belong out here."

I scratch behind its owl-like ear flaps, and it rubs against my hands.

"Princess . . ." Dain growls.

I straighten. "I was saying goodbye. Now begone, tiny monster. I have no more suet—or petting—for you."

The beast peeps up at me. Then the grass swishes, and the chickcharney startles in alarm. Dain steps toward us, his face fixed in a look that has the chickcharney toddling off, flapping its useless wings.

I chuckle. I don't interfere, though. Part of being the royal monster hunter is doing what's best for the beasts, which is to leave them alone unless they are injured or orphaned or otherwise unable to care for themselves. As I watch it go, something tickles my attention.

I glance around, frowning. I'm not sure what I picked up—a sound, a smell, a flicker of movement? Dain's chasing the chickcharney away. Jacko's napping in the grass. Malric is watching us with his annoyed-babysitter stare and Sunniva . . .

Sunniva had been eating when I glanced over. Now she's stopped, her head up. With a whinny, she races to my side and presses tight against me, a solid wall of white horsehair.

When I found Sunniva, she was alone. She shouldn't have been. Even full-grown mares live with a herd. While Sunniva *seemed* fine, she still wanted her herd, and now she has it with us, so when she's frightened, she runs to me.

As I scan the sky, I get that feeling again—a ripple in the air, stirring the hairs on my neck.

"Princess?"

Dain follows my gaze and shades his eyes. Then he backs my way, reaching for his bow as I withdraw my sword. It's heavy in my hand, polished steel and ebony wood with an obsidian blade.

"Your bow," he says, without turning, hearing only the *thwick* of my blade leaving the scabbard. I'm more comfortable with my sword, but he's right.

As I switch to my bow, I call, "Jacko!"

The jackalope races over, and I point down, a command that tells him to take cover at my feet. Well, no, I think he believes it means "protect Rowan's feet," but the end result is the same.

I nock an arrow just as Sunniva bumps me. Jacko chitters at her, and she two-steps, her dainty roan-red hooves coming too close to the jackalope for my liking. I give her a hard look, and she tosses her mane, hot breath trumpeting from her nostrils.

I try drawing my bowstring, but she's still too close. Malric lumbers over and nudges Sunniva aside to let her huddle against him.

"Thank you, Malric," I say.

His grunt says we're all overreacting. He doesn't see or smell a threat.

He might be right. Still, I keep scanning the empty sky.

A distant shout makes me jump, but it's only Alianor, her triumphant cry suggesting they've caught their quarry. As for ours, the chickcharney watches us, unconcerned. Then it realizes Dain is distracted and makes a tentative hop back in my direction. Dain stamps his foot at the beast, and I open my mouth to say something just as a thin gray shape shoots from the nearby forest.

I catch a glimpse of a fox-like head with tufted ears and a long muzzle opening to reveal rows of razor-sharp teeth. Bat-like wings flap twice, and the beast dives straight at Dain.

CHAPTER THREE

"Wyvern!" I shout.

I spot an outcropping of rock we can use for cover, but it's too late for that. I run at Dain. He's a dozen feet away, and that seems to be where the wyvern is aiming, but just before I reach him, I see it's actually going for the chickcharney, who's bobbing in confusion at my shout. I swerve and leap onto the chickcharney instead. The beast gives one bleating cry of alarm before huddling under me, cheeping in delight, as if I'd tackled it in a hug.

"Rowan!" Dain shouts, just as the wyvern's claws scrape my back. My hardened leather tunic protects me, but I still feel the impact. I let out a grunt and roll, throwing the startled chickcharney aside. It keeps rolling, long legs pumping uselessly, as I leap to my feet and pull my sword.

The wyvern dives at me again. An arrow hits its wing and

it aborts course, veering up, screaming. As it wheels on us, a second wyvern appears above it.

"Cover!" I shout. "Take cover!"

I grab Jacko, run for the outcropping of rock and dive into it. Dain follows, slamming into me, and at a peep of alarm, I turn to see him holding the chickcharney. He looks down at the bird monster as if to say, "How'd that get there?" before shoving it aside.

We crawl into a spot where an overhang of rock protects us from aerial attack. Malric barricades us, snarling and snapping as the wyverns scream. I catch sight of one. It's purplish-blue, which means it's female. The other is brownish-orange—male. A mated pair.

The female is as large as Sunniva, with a long, whipping arrowhead tail and clawed back feet. Her shadow passes over us, reminding me of the gryphon, and my blood chills at the memory.

While the wyverns aren't eager to tangle with Malric, they will. I know that. They're sizing up the situation, and they'll soon realize that the two of them can take him on.

"We need to . . ." I trail off as I look up at the rocky overhang.

"Yeah," Dain mutters. "They can't attack us, but we can't attack them either."

I wriggle to the left, past the overhang.

"Princess," Dain warns.

I keep wriggling. I'm still protected enough, and the wyverns are busy with Malric. Another two inches gives me an arrow-sized gap. Every few heartbeats, one of the massive beasts flies overhead.

I hesitate, hand on my bow. Then I say to Dain, "There's a spot here. You're better. You should take it."

As I edge away, he eases into the spot. He peers out and then grunts. With Dain, grunts and scowls are a language all of their own. This particular noise is satisfaction, acknowledging I've found a spot he can indeed use.

When he grunts again, I translate that one to surprise. Concerned surprise. Something's not right.

That's when I realize I don't hear the flapping of the wyverns' leathery wings.

I cock my head to listen. The chickcharney peeps, and Jacko growls like an older child warning a younger one to be silent.

I can detect the sound of the wyvern wings, but they're moving away. I exhale, rocking back against Dain, opening my mouth to say—

Sunniva screams, and I bolt out from the rocks so fast I bash my head. I reel, and Dain catches my arm to pull me back, but I wrench free and run.

Sunniva is twenty feet away, rearing onto her hind legs as the female wyvern snaps at her. Shouting, I bear down and pull my sword, Malric at my heels. An arrow hits the wyvern in the flank, but the beast barely seems to notice. The wyvern snaps again at the filly, catching her behind the neck.

"Sunniva!" I scream. "Run!"

The pegasus breaks away, blood flecking from her wound. She doesn't run, though. She wheels and batters the wyvern with her hooves. Another arrow passes, this one missing its target. A dark shape blocks the sun. The male wyvern. He shoots straight up into the air. Then he hovers there, and I know what's coming. I know exactly what's coming.

"Sunniva!"

I run so hard I can't breathe. Can't see either, the world tinged with red. In that red, I make out Sunniva, rearing, her hooves slashing as she fights the female wyvern, unaware of the male plummeting toward her. I reach her and . . .

I don't think about what I'm doing. I react as I have been trained, my aunt Jannah's voice sounding in my head.

Protect your mount, Rowan. Always remember that it's a prey animal. If your mare is attacked, don't fight alongside her—you risk being trampled. Get onto her back. Fight together.

I shove my sword into its scabbard, and when Sunniva comes down, front legs on the ground, I grab her and swing onto her back. That's when I realize my mistake. This isn't my mare. It's an unbroken pegasus filly.

Sunniva screams as if this is a fresh attack. She rears, and I wrap my hands in her mane, clinging for dear life.

"Sunniva!" I shout. "Hold on! I'll get off!"

She doesn't seem to hear me. I clutch her neck and keep talking, babbling, my mouth by her ear as she writhes and bucks.

Get off. Just get off her.

I can't. I see the ground below and those flashing hooves, and I know I cannot jump off. Before I found her, she'd struck my trainer, Wilmot, with one of those hooves, and it addled his mind. He's slowly recovering, but he's said many times that he's lucky to be alive.

If I drop from Sunniva's back, she'll trample me.

"Run!" I shout, knocking my heels into her sides. "Just run!"

Please run. We can do this. Run, and I'll keep you safe.

Instead, something bumps my leg, and I twist to see her wings extending.

"No!" I shout.

She can't take off with me on her back. Her wings won't support the two of us.

Teeth flash beside me. It's the male wyvern, with his huge jaws and triple rows of teeth. Leaping onto Sunniva caused enough commotion to thwart his dive, but now he's trying to grab me as Sunniva writhes.

Sunniva flaps those beautiful white-feathered wings. One smacks the wyvern, and he drops. Then the filly lifts off. She manages to get a few feet from the ground only to falter, wings beating madly.

I need to get off her back, let her fly. I have no idea how high we are, but I roll to the side and drop. I hit the ground hard, pain rocking through me.

Something catches my leg. I look to see the female wyvern's jaws clamped around my boot. She swings me into the air. As I dangle aloft by one leg, the ground thunders and a voice screams, "Rowan!"

I catch a glimpse of Courtois charging across the grassland. Then my sword starts to slip from its scabbard. I yank it out as I hang there, the wyvern hovering with me in her jaws. She whips her head, and I sail upward, but I keep my hand on my sword and I slash. The tip catches her in the throat.

The wyvern drops me. As I hit the ground, I clamp tight on my weapon. It stays in my hand, *and* I manage not to land on the blade. I leap to my feet and slash at the wyvern as she dives. She sees the blade, lets out a terrible shriek and tries to divert course. I follow, twisting around as my blade whirls. It strikes her neck again. She screams. Then she hits the ground with an earth-quaking thud.

My gaze shoots to the sky. Sunniva is in flight, hovering as she watches us. To my left, Courtois swings toward me with surprising grace for a creature the size of a draft horse.

The unicorn charges at the fallen wyvern. On his back, Rhydd has his sword out, ready to strike the killing blow. Instead, at the last second, Courtois ducks, nearly sending Rhydd flying over his head. The unicorn's horn impales the wyvern. Still galloping, Courtois lifts the beast aloft and throws it aside. Then he wheels and slows, snorting, his front hooves pounding the ground, ready to trample the wyvern if it stirs.

It does not stir.

"Prince Rhydd!" Dain shouts.

Rhydd and I look up just as a shadow passes over. The male wyvern hovers above my brother. Then he dives.

Rhydd doesn't need to command the unicorn. This was my aunt's steed. Courtois hears Dain's shout, and he moves even before he can see the reason for it. He plows forward . . . and almost mows me down.

As I scramble away, Malric charges, snarling at Courtois. Malric turns that snarl on the wyvern as he veers my way. Seeing the massive warg, the wyvern feints to the side.

I swing at the wyvern. My sword slices into his leg. He screams. An arrow hits his wing, then another in the same spot, tearing the leathery skin. The beast lands and rears up. He only has two legs—back ones. I've injured one of those, and he teeters before finding his balance.

The wyvern's tail whips, its arrowhead slicing through the air. Malric stands beside me, growling. We face off against the male wyvern. We're close enough for me to see his fox-like head covered in fine red hair. His eyes are reptilian, slitted pupils fixed on me. When his jaws open, I get far too close a look at those triple rows of razor teeth.

A thump sounds behind me, with a quick, "It's me," from Rhydd, so I'm not startled.

My brother moves up beside me. Malric growls, telling Rhydd that we have this under control and he is interfering. I shoot Rhydd a glare, but only because he should stay mounted and protect his leg, still healing from the gryphon attack.

"Courtois stole my quarry," Rhydd murmurs with a smile. "I can't let you take down *two* wyverns."

The wyvern snaps at us but stays back, facing us as his head bobs, surveying the situation.

From behind us comes a whinny and the *thomp-thomp* of hooves over hard ground.

"Took you long enough," Rhydd yells without turning. "You missed all the fun."

"Looks like you're still having it," Alianor says. "If your idea of fun is facing off against a wyvern the size of a small house."

The wyvern rears and unfurls his wings.

"He *is* kinda big," Rhydd says, as the shadow of those wings plunges us into darkness.

"Not quite the size of a small house, though," I say.

"Still, really big." His voice quavers so slightly that no one else would notice.

"I'd like to drive it off if we can," I say, raising my voice as the wyvern shrieks. "They were only looking for dinner."

"Agreed."

"On the count of three, we'll charge. Make a lot of noise. Brandish your sword and—"

The wyvern strikes with the speed of a cobra, that snake-like neck springing. I'm mid-word when there's suddenly an open pair of massive jaws coming straight for my head.

I fall back, sword slashing up. The broadside strikes the beast just as a tooth rips into my cheek. Pain, sharp and fierce. Jaws clamp on my shoulder but are stopped by the hardened tunic, and I slam my sword into the beast's head.

The wyvern screams and falls back. Blood streams from its side and flecks spatter from Rhydd's sword. Malric has hold of the beast's leg. The wyvern wheels on the warg, and I raise my sword to strike. A stone *thwacks* against the side of his head. The wyvern lets out a terrible cry as he spins on Dain, now holding his slingshot. It's then that I see Jacko . . . *on* the wyvern's back, his teeth clamped onto his neck. The wyvern's wings extend, ready for takeoff.

"Jacko!"

I run, but Alianor is there first, plucking Jacko off as the wyvern crouches for flight. The huge beast doesn't notice— he has just spotted his mate, lying dead on the ground. As the wyvern flaps over to land beside her, we stand guard, everyone brandishing their weapons. Jacko is in his shelter spot at my feet, and Malric stands beside me. Sunniva has taken cover in the forest. The wyvern hisses our way a few times but stays with his mate, nudging and licking at her.

My heart twists as I whisper, "I'm sorry." I *am* sorry that we had to kill this beast's mate, and yet *had to* are the key words there. Even if we'd given up the chickcharney—which I'm not sure I could ever do—the beasts wouldn't have been content with that small meal. We had no choice but to fight.

"Let's back up," I murmur. "If it will let us leave, we should do that."

"Are you okay?" Rhydd asks, glancing over.

Hot blood trickles down my cheek, and my shoulder aches, but I'm fine and say so.

We start our retreat, gazes fixed on the wyverns. Malric stays in place to give us cover. Once we're about twenty feet away, he allows himself to retreat. Two more steps and I hear a peeping, and look over to see the chickcharney running after us as fast as its stilt-legs will allow, tail whipping as it chirps, as if to say, "You forgot me!"

Dain sighs. Then he pockets his slingshot, jogs over and scoops up the chickcharney, which peeps in alarm. Dain runs back with it under his arm like a ball.

"Looks like you have a chickcharney after all, princess."

CHAPTER FOUR

We're back at the castle. On the way, Alianor—
who's training to be a healer—tended to
Sunniva's and my injuries. Now I've been
double-checked by Dr. Fendrel. The filly is cut and sore.
My shoulder's bruised, and there's a sticking plaster on my
cheek. Superficial wounds, which won't spare me from my
mother's wrath.

Rhydd and I are in her chambers, waiting as she paces.
The captain of the guard, Berinon, stands at attention. His
face is unreadable, shoulders stiff. Berinon is a head taller
than Mom, his shoulders nearly twice as broad. His shaggy
black hair is tamed into a braid today. His dark skin shines
with sweat, though the evening chill has set in and the fire
hasn't been stoked. That sweat is the sole sign that we aren't
the only ones braced for Mom's anger. Berinon isn't in any
trouble, though—his concern is for us.

Berinon was my dad's bodyguard and best friend, and my mom's friend, too, the three of them growing up together. At one time, we thought of Berinon as our uncle. Since Dad's death, he's become the closest thing we have to a father, guiding and mentoring us while leaving the discipline to Mom.

She paces, looking out the window as she passes it, her jaw set. She's wearing a morning gown—the sort that means she won't be giving audiences today. It's grass-green, and each time she pivots in her pacing, the gold threads shimmer. So too does the ebony pin that holds up her hair. That sword-shaped pin reminds everyone that she is a trained monster hunter, like all Clan Dacre monarchs. I watch that tiny sword flash and feel the weight of the one on my back, and all the responsibilities it carries . . . including the responsibility to keep my brother and friends safe from monsters.

I glance around the room. Mom's sleeping quarters are the size of mine, but she has this room, too, for working and meeting family away from the prying eyes of staff. Furs cover the stone floor—furs from my father, who'd stayed a monster hunter even after he married my mother.

Tapestries hang from the stone walls as both decoration and insulation. Each bears a scene depicting my parents' favorite beasts. A pegasus and a warg for my mother. A firebird for Dad. As I study the hangings, I avoid looking at the spot where my father's other favorite had once hung: the tapestry of a gryphon. In its place is my father's sword; below it, my mother recently added my aunt Jannah's secondary blade.

When I was seven, a gryphon killed my father before Jannah slew it. Then, six weeks ago, another gryphon killed her. Rhydd should have been the one to inherit her ebony sword. He's the younger twin—if only by two minutes—so I was in line for the throne while he was meant to be the royal monster hunter. Except the gryphon also badly injured Rhydd's leg, and that gave us the chance to switch places, which we'd always wanted.

I feel the weight of what those swords on the wall signify. Mom's husband and her beloved younger sister were both killed by gryphons. And now her only children stand before her, having admitted to sneaking off and being attacked by wyverns.

"It was my fault," I blurt, unable to bear the silence any longer. "The game was my idea."

"It wasn't a game," Rhydd says. "It was a hunting exercise."

Mom wheels on him. "Was it?"

He swallows visibly and then straightens. "Yes, Your Majesty. Rowan has been thrust into the role of royal monster hunter four years before she should have had to wield the ebony sword. She needs experience. No one forced me to go with her. In fact, when we faced off against the wyvern, she wanted me to stay back."

Mom pales, the same look she gets every time someone mentions our encounters with the gryphon. I've learned what that look means—she's picturing her children in front of a beast big enough to devour them.

I hurry on. "We were fine. It was the four of us, plus a warg and a unicorn, against a wyvern."

"Jacko helped," Rhydd says with an easy smile, trying to distract Mom.

Mom doesn't even seem to hear him. She just meets my gaze and says, "Two." When I fumble for a response, she goes on. "*Two* wyverns, Rowan. Either of them could have killed you. Rhydd, you say it was a training exercise, yes?"

"Yes, Your Majesty."

"To hunt a chickcharney," I add quickly. "Not a wyvern."

"So there was no wager?" Mom asks. "No competition?"

Neither of us answers. We don't need to. She's our mother. She knows.

"If it was truly an exercise," she continues, "you would have taken an adult hunter to oversee it and ensure you didn't—oh, I don't know—attract the attention of a pair of wyverns."

I open my mouth.

She keeps going. "You left under false pretenses. You said you were going on a picnic to Valles Meadow. You behaved like children. You are not children. You can no longer be children. This was breathtakingly irresponsible, and for the next week, when you are not in lessons, you will both be confined to your quarters."

I'm in the hall outside Mom's sitting room, slumped on the floor, petting Jacko. My mother and Berinon think I'm back in my room while Rhydd is off doing his rehabilitation exercises. Instead, I'm here, listening to them and feeling worse with each word.

"We did the same things when we were their age, Mari," Berinon says.

"Did we?" Mom snaps. "I don't seem to recall any wyvern encounters in our games."

Berinon's voice drops. "I know you're upset, but this . . . it's Rowan's . . ."

"It's her life? Is that what you're going to remind me, Ber? That my daughter's life will be spent facing beasts that can kill her? Because that is exactly what I need to hear right now."

After a moment, Berinon murmurs, "They're children, Mariela. Twelve years old. If they weren't getting into trouble, we'd be worried that they weren't the kind of rulers Tamarel needs. They must experience the world for themselves and play . . . just play."

"Do you think I don't know that?" My mother's voice cracks. "Do you think I am not very aware of how unfair this is to them? You're right. They should be playing. Enjoying the last of their childhood. Instead, Rowan already carries a sword that barely fits on her back. Do you think my heart doesn't break when I see that?"

Berinon murmurs something I don't catch. There's a scuffle inside, as if he moved to comfort Mom and she backed away.

"No," she says sharply. "I hate this, Ber. Hate it with every bone in my body. Yet what is the alternative? Let Heward's children take the throne and the sword?" They may be next in line, but we know who would truly wield the power. Heward.

Mom continues. "A man who will plunder our kingdom the way he plunders his own lands. Overtaxes and overworks the people who depend on him, and I cannot do a blasted thing about it, despite the fact that I am queen. *Queen.*"

This is the way our country works. Tamarel was once a land of clans, with no single ruler. We lie between the sea and the mountains, both of which are rife with monsters. Clan Dacre always had the best monster hunters, so our ancestors made a deal with the other clans. If Clan Dacre drove the monsters back to mountain and sea, the clans would unite under our rule, and in return for the throne, we would keep the land safe.

I am descended from the first king, whose sister was the first royal monster hunter. However, it wasn't just those two who cleared the land. It was the entire clan. So we rule with their help . . . whether we want it or not.

Mom is the head of the royal council, with four other clan members who vote on all major decisions. In the event of a tie, Mom casts the deciding vote. If they vote against her, though, she cannot veto their decision. She also can't interfere with the holdings of other ranking clan members, like Heward.

The restrictions on a monarch's power do serve a purpose. For a good ruler, like Mom, those constraints are frustrating, especially when she sees parts of her land being mismanaged. However, if we ever did get a bad ruler, like Heward, then we'd be grateful for those constraints.

When Berinon does speak, I hear only the low rumble of his voice. He's calm, as always, reassuring her.

"I just want my children to be children," she replies. "That is the one gift every parent should be able to give."

Except Rhydd and I can't be children anymore. The country needs us to take the two most important jobs in Tamarel, which means *not* running off to play hunting games that could get us both killed.

When footsteps pad my way, I leap up. Alianor rounds the corner. She has been living at the castle for the past month, part of a peace treaty between my mother and her father.

Seeing her, I tense. It's one thing for me to eavesdrop on Mom and Berinon, but Alianor shouldn't hear their private discussion.

Still holding Jacko, I jerk my chin to say that we should move. She hesitates, glancing toward my mother's room. I shake my head sharply and motion her away.

When we're far enough down the hall to speak, she says, "Your mother's with Berinon."

"He's her bodyguard."

A few more steps. "I've heard rumors—"

"And you won't spread them," I say, as evenly as I can.

"You know what I mean, then. People say there's more than friendship between them."

"I have seen and heard nothing to suggest that," I say stiffly as I head toward my room.

"Your father has been gone five years. If your mother found someone—"

"Then I would accept it. I'm not a child who expects her mother to live alone for the rest of her days. I'm saying that I have seen nothing, and if you spread that particular bit of speculation, we will no longer be friends."

Her eyes flash. "You're threatening me over a silly romantic rumor?"

"No, Alianor, I'm threatening you over a story that jeopardizes my mother's throne. While some people might think it's romantic, others spread the rumor to undermine my mother.

A romance with her *bodyguard?* That is beneath her. And the fact he was my father's best friend is a betrayal of his memory."

"He was your mother's friend, too," she says softly.

"That doesn't matter to those who wish to make trouble. Jannah always said that we might allow women to hold the throne and the sword, but they are still treated differently. No one would think twice of a widowed king seeking romance. A queen, though? She'll neglect her duties, too busy with her new love."

Alianor snorts. "That is ridiculous."

"Yes, but unless you have a problem with my mother's reign, I'll ask you not to talk about her and Berinon. If you choose to, I'll presume you *do* have issues with her reign, and at that point, we can no longer be friends."

She goes silent.

"*Serious* issues with her reign," I correct. "Obviously you have minor complaints. Mom always says that any subject who claims to agree with everything their queen does is either a liar or a fool. You are not the latter, and you don't need to be the former around me."

She chuckles softly at that. Then she sobers and says, "I'm still getting used to court life. Back home, I wouldn't have thought twice about spreading romantic gossip. If they aren't married, what's the harm?" She looks at me. "I see the harm now. If anyone asks me about them, I'll say I know nothing of it."

"Thank you."

I push open my bedroom door. Jacko zooms past and hops to the fire, where Malric sprawls. Eyes closed, the warg curls his lip in a low growl that has Jacko skidding to a halt.

They play a game then, one I call "how close can Jacko get to the fire?" Jacko takes a step in one direction. Malric allows it. Another step. Growl. When Jacko finally settles on a spot, it's just *past* the point where Malric growled. Jacko must always push that boundary, and the fact that Malric doesn't toss him across the room suggests the warg respects that.

I'm still stepping through the doorway when a peep startles me, and I look over to see the chickcharney on my bed.

"What are you doing here?" I ask as I walk to it—to *her*, actually. I'd checked that on the way home. The last time I saw the beast, Dain was offering to take her as Rhydd and I went in to confess to our mother. I'd told him *where* to take the chickcharney, too.

"Does this look like the chicken coop?" I mutter.

"Kinda does," Alianor says as she bounces on my bed. "A menagerie, at least. Between the live beasts and the stuffed ones and your sketches . . ." She sweeps a hand around my room. "I get the feeling you're, like, the royal monster hunter or something."

I sigh and pick up the chickcharney. She settles onto my lap, which is kind of awkward since she can't bend her legs.

"Thank you for not eating the chickcharney, Malric," I say.

He grunts without opening his eyes.

"Thank Dain," Alianor says, "for filling the warg's food bowl when he dropped off the bird."

"I'd thank him more for not dropping off the bird at all."

"She can keep you company, since you'll apparently be spending a lot of time in here, having not taken my advice."

"Rhydd and I don't lie to our mother."

"But it would have been a *good* lie. Helped you and helped your mother. That's lying for the best possible reason."

I shake my head.

She twists to look at me, her light-brown hair falling over one shoulder. "No one was seriously injured. You could have said you and Sunniva hurt yourselves goofing around. Dain would have kept your secret."

"Right, Dain would have had to lie to Wilmot . . . and anyone else who asked. Then, if someone did discover the truth, Mom would have had to admit that she couldn't control her children. That the future king and royal monster hunter aren't just mischievous kids who get into trouble hunting chickcharnies. That they're untrustworthy brats who lie about it to their queen. It'd be one more thing for Heward to use against her. She's a single parent, still grieving over her sister, and paying no attention to her wild and irresponsible children, probably because she's busy cuddling with her bodyguard."

"Have you ever *seen* her cuddling—?"

"*No*. Stop that."

She thumps back onto the bed. "It's just so romantic. The queen and her bodyguard, thrown together by the death of her beloved husband and his beloved friend, finding solace in their grief . . ."

I reach under the bed and shove a book into her hand.

"What's this?" She turns the pages, and her eyes light up. "*The Ballad of Chikako and Reynard*. You read romantic novels?"

"No, but it seems you need to, so you can have that one. My aunt gave me a few, for when I got interested. I'm not yet."

Alianor's eyes got round. "Jannah read romantic novels?"

"Why not?"

"Is it true about Jannah and Wilmot—?"

"Stop. Please, stop. Go read, and if that isn't enough, I'm sure we can find you a handsome stable boy to moon over."

"I don't want to moon over anyone. I just like hearing stories. I'll take this one, with thanks."

She puts it aside and settles in. "I'll be careful about your mom, too. I thought being a warlord's daughter was complicated. It's easy compared to being a princess."

I shrug and pet the chickcharney. "If I were a scullery maid, I'd have fewer responsibilities, but I wouldn't have this room. Or my monster companions. Or my dresses, my jewels, my books, my weapons, my mare... We are well compensated for our hardships."

"You would have made a good queen, Rowan."

"I'll make a better royal monster hunter."

"True. And while you will not like being confined to your room, you do have something to look forward to. The gryphon will give birth any day now." She catches my stricken expression and stops. "Surely your mother will lift your punishment for that."

I hug the chickcharney tight enough to make the beast squirm. "She can't."

Alianor considers and then nods. "Because if she grants an exception to your punishment, it can be seen as weakness." She sighs and leans against the headboard. "The next time we go hunting, Heward should come along. For the experience. It's not our fault if you attract monsters. Not our fault if a wyvern thinks Heward smells delicious. *Definitely* not our fault if that's because someone substituted beef tallow for his shaving cream."

She grins my way, but I barely notice, my stomach roiling at the thought of missing the gryphon birth.

"Maybe I can convince Mom it's a lesson," I say. "When else will I get a chance to watch a gryphon give birth?"

I expect Alianor to jump on this. Instead, she goes quiet, and when I look over, she says carefully, "But if you ask and she has to say no, that's going to upset her, right? She's already upset about having to punish you."

I sink back onto the bed. I could argue, but doing the "right thing" isn't really in Alianor's vocabulary. If even *she's* suggesting I shouldn't ask . . .

This is part of growing up. Of being mature and responsible. A child can think "there's no harm in asking." But it will hurt Mom to refuse something I want so badly, and I'd be putting her in a difficult position if I asked.

I messed up. This is my punishment. I need to accept it.

CHAPTER FIVE

Two nights later, I'm woken by Malric's growl. I leap up, sending Jacko tumbling off me. Chikako—the chickcharney—peeps from her night cage, where she sleeps with my stuffed chickcharney.

Malric is nowhere to be seen, and I exhale with relief. My aunt's dying command tasked him with my care, and I've been unable to persuade him to abandon his post, however much he hates it. This isn't the first time I've woken to his growl and had this sudden image of the warg ridding himself of me with one clamp of his powerful jaws.

He is not, however, looming over my bed, slavering on my helpless sleeping form. Jacko chitters in mild annoyance at being woken, which suggests I'm the one who woke both him and Chikako. In other words, I must have dreamed Malric's growl. Before I close my eyes again, I can't help but glance over at Malric's bowl . . . in case my dream was suggesting I'd forgotten to refill it.

His bowl holds only bones, meaning Malric has eaten. However, the warg himself is not in his spot by the smoldering fire.

"Rowan?" an unsteady voice says. "Could you please remind him I'm a friend?"

I look to see Alianor just inside my door . . . with Malric blocking her, a silent growl rippling his sides.

"Malric?" I say. "I'm awake now. But thank you for your concern." I turn to Alianor. "He knows you're a friend. That's why you're still in one piece."

She lets out a wavering laugh.

"I'm serious," I say as I swing my legs out of the bed. "His job is to protect me from anyone who comes in here at night. He'd block even Rhydd. He won't hurt you, but he'll make sure you stay back until I'm awake."

"Wow. That's some watchdog."

"Bodyguard," I correct. "Monsters aren't animals."

She walks over to where I sit on my bed. "You need to teach me more about monsters. All Clan Bellamy cares about is how to avoid them in the mountain passes, but I'll need more if I'm going to be a monster healer."

I arch my brows, and she bounces onto my bed with a grin.

"Yep," she says. "I've decided to change professions. The kingdom is in need of a proper monster healer, because your current animal healer can't do the job."

"Doctor Tyesha does just fine," I say. "Yes, her specialty is animals, but she's learning to treat monsters, too."

"Not fast enough. There's a reason I'm waking you at two in the morning, Rowan, and it isn't to tell you that I want to be a monster healer. The gryphon is about to give birth."

I scramble up. "What?"

"Well, according to your Doctor Tyesha, it'll be another week. But I've been telling her all day that she's wrong—my healer training tells me the baby is coming much sooner. She's been treating me like a silly child. Guess who's right?"

"The baby is coming now?"

She nods. "I've been sneaking in and checking every hour. Doctor Tyesha is there, but she shooed me off and tried to say it'll still be days, even when I could tell the gryphon had started her labor. It'll be tonight. So I came to get you."

"We already talked about this. I knew better than to ask Mom."

Alianor grins. "Exactly. You never asked . . . so you aren't disobeying. Realizing the gryphon was about to give birth, I ran to get your help. You're the royal monster hunter, and this is a monster birth. Naturally, you should be there. Woken from sleep, you can't be expected to stop and consider whether this breaks your punishment. It is an emergency, after all."

"This is why you didn't want me *asking* earlier, isn't it? You planned this."

"You get to see the birth of a *gryphon*. Are you actually arguing?"

I hesitate.

"Doctor Tyesha can't handle it," Alianor says. "She's proven that. So I really do need your help. If the gryphon has trouble birthing, I'm not sure the doctor will know what to do."

I push to my feet. "All right, let's go."

We tiptoe through the silent hall, stone floors icy under our bare feet. Malric pads along after us. Alianor grumbles about that. "How are we supposed to sneak around with a two-hundred-pound wolf following us?" Honestly, though, Malric makes less noise than we do. Leaving him behind wasn't an option. During the day, I can wander the castle alone. At night, he follows.

As for the jackalope perched on my shoulders . . . well, he's quieter up there than he'd be if I locked him in my room.

The gryphon is being held in the hay barn, which is almost empty in the summer, when the horses can graze. She has a small pasture, too, and we keep those doors open so she can walk outside. She can't fly, though. A huge steel leg band chains her to a massive stone. This is a gryphon who has already killed my aunt and tried to kill the rest of us. Given the chance, she'd finish the job.

Dr. Tyesha is temporarily living in the head groom's quarters, and I ask Malric to stay outside while I make my way to her room. He agrees with a grunt that warns me not to leave his line of sight. I set Jacko on the ground and ask him to stay, too. He's still considering the request when Malric lifts a restraining paw, and Jacko lies down with a sigh.

Alianor and I approach the darkened rooms attached to the main stables. Alianor whispers that there'd been a candle burning earlier as the doctor read or worked late into the night. I'm about to peek through the window when jackalope paws thump the ground, and I look to see Jacko hopping my way. I lift my gaze to glare at Malric, but he's on all fours, watching. He let Jacko run to me, which means . . .

"Someone's coming," I whisper to Alianor. Before I can pick up Jacko, he runs back toward where Malric waits in the shadows. That's when I see what I'd missed before—light seeping around the heavy hay-barn door.

"That was dark when I left to fetch you," Alianor whispers.

I hurry to the hay barn. There aren't any windows—no need for them in a storage building—but I know a secret way in. The castle is my home, and I know all its secrets, especially those that take me places I'm not supposed to go.

When the barn is full, Rhydd and I like to play in the hay, building slides and obstacle courses. I'm old enough now to realize the grooms can't help noticing their bales are suddenly in the form of a giant ship, but they've never complained to Mom. We don't damage the bales. We just . . . rearrange them.

Rhydd and I aren't supposed to do that, of course. So when we come to play, we need to sneak in. There's a roofline hatch for air circulation, and somehow, there are always stray bales below it outside, which suggests the grooms don't mind our antics. It's been six months since we've snuck in, but the bales are still there. Alianor and I pile them to help us reach the roof hatch. Then I ask Malric and Jacko to stay below as Alianor and I climb our bale-ladder.

At the top, I peek through the propped-open hatch. The smell of gryphon almost makes me gag. It's not a bad smell—their breath is honey-sweet, and otherwise, their musky scent is part-bird, part-beast. But with a monster of that size confined, even in a very large barn, the smell is overpowering.

The hatch opens into a shallow loft. I can hear the gryphon below, shifting and grunting softly. I've never heard the grunting. Shrieks, hisses, beak clicks, yes—but the grunts are new.

Alianor taps my foot. I heave myself through the hatch as silently as I can. Old chaff swirls around me, and I cover my mouth to stifle a sneeze. Alianor isn't quick enough, but her sneeze is a kitten-like *achoo* that I barely hear.

I crawl and peer through a knothole in the floor. Below, the gryphon lies on its side, its flank heaving. All four legs are bound, and a huge leather band clamps its head to the floor. When Alianor squeaks behind me, I turn to see her staring through a hole of her own, her eyes round with outrage.

We never leave the gryphon bound like this. That would be cruel. It's only tied down for medical procedures, and while we'd discussed doing it during labor, we'd decided it was better not to interfere with a natural process. Instead, the doctor—and Alianor—would be on-hand to assist, and a mild sedative would be administered instead of bindings.

Dr. Tyesha isn't following the plan. That's why she shooed Alianor away earlier, and probably why she claimed the gryphon wasn't close to giving birth.

Someone had to have helped Dr. Tyesha sedate and bind the gryphon. We've been using a sedative dart design that

Dain and Wilmot devised, but Dr. Tyesha couldn't do it herself. Nor could she bind a partly sedated gryphon.

All I see, though, is Dr. Tyesha alone with the beast, touching its belly. Beneath her fingers, the bulge moves, and a thrill whips through me. A baby gryphon is about to be born, and I'm going to be here to witness it.

Alianor motions that she wants to confront Dr. Tyesha about the bindings. I shake my head. The gryphon is already in labor, and I don't dare interfere.

Alianor crawls over and whispers, "This isn't right."

"I know. My mother will deal with it later. For now, I want to help, not argue."

Alianor grumbles but agrees. We start toward the ladder. Whenever we pass a crack or knothole, I look down. The doctor is off to the side now, preparing another syringe. There's no reason for a second dose. She must just be getting it ready in case of an emergency. The gryphon is already as sedated as you'd want it to be during birth.

Dr. Tyesha walks to the beast and puts the needle to the gryphon's neck.

"No!" I shout.

I clatter down the wooden ladder. The doctor goes still, needle in hand.

"Princess?" she says.

Her gaze swivels above me, and her eyes narrow.

"I thought I told you to stay in your quarters, Alianor."

"No, you told me there was no need to come because the gryphon wasn't about to give birth. Since she is, then I should be here. I brought the princess to help."

"I don't require your assistance, Alianor. This is not a puppet-show performance for the entertainment of children."

"We aren't children," I say as I stride over. "I am the royal monster hunter. Alianor is a healer in training. You were well aware of our reasons for attending the birth, along with the fact that my mother expected us to witness it." I look at the gryphon. "You were also aware that we had decided against restraints and sedatives."

"*Unless* necessary, your highness. That was my call to make. The beast was in distress, and I took the proper steps."

I glance around. "Where are the guards who helped restrain her?"

"I sent them away. A birth is a very private matter, fit only for the eyes of women."

I snort. "My father attended my birth."

"As did mine," Alianor says. "He passed out, apparently, but he attended."

"In my village, childbirth is for women only," Dr. Tyesha says.

"That wouldn't exclude myself or Alianor," I say. "Nor any of the castle's female guards."

I wave off her excuses as I approach the gryphon. I may no longer be in line for the throne, but I still remember how to act like a queen.

I ignore Dr. Tyesha's protests as my gaze sweeps the beast. We've had it for a month, yet I can never repress this first moment of awe. It's not simply the beast's size. It is ... majestic. There is no other word.

A gryphon looks like a cross between an eagle and a cat.

It has a raptor's head and forequarters, with its front legs ending in talons. Its back half is feline, with clawed hind legs and a tasseled tail. It also has an eagle's wings and a cat's ears. For a creature that nearly fills the barn, it is both beautiful and terrifying.

"You won't need to administer that second sedative," I say as I touch the gryphon's chest, feeling her shallow breaths. "You've given her quite enough already."

"Rowan . . ." Alianor says.

I lift a finger. I move to the beast's head. Its huge amber eyes are closed now. They'd been open earlier, and I nudge her, frowning.

"Rowan . . . ?" Alianor repeats.

I look over to see her pointing at the second syringe, still in the doctor's hand. It's empty.

I quickly touch the gryphon's chest. When it moves, I exhale in relief. Then I realize that what I'm feeling is the *baby* moving. The gryphon's actual breathing is very shallow, its lungs barely fluttering.

"You've given her too much sedative," I say sharply. "She needs to be awake for this."

Dr. Tyesha shakes her head. "That is what I was going to explain, your highness. The baby is in the wrong position. The gryphon is being sedated for surgery. I need to extract the baby, and that is not something you need to see. Either of you."

"I'm a hunter," I snap. "I'm hardly going to faint at the sight of blood."

"As a healer, I've attended many births," Alianor says. "I've also assisted in the surgical removal of two babies."

I channel my queenly lessons. "We appreciate your concern, doctor, but we are ready and able to assist with the surgery."

"That won't be necessary."

I open my mouth but behind Dr. Tyesha, Alianor waves me to silence. She's pointing at the table, though I can't see why that's important.

Alianor clears her throat. "Perhaps Doctor Tyesha is right, Rowan. This is more than the birth of a human infant. We should leave her to it."

Alianor's obviously up to something. I go along with it. Not too fast—that'd seem suspicious. I grumble, and Alianor argues until I grudgingly agree to go.

"Call us when the baby's born?" I ask at the door.

"I will, your highness."

We slip outside. Malric and Jacko appear as Alianor leads me away.

"There are no surgical instruments," she whispers.

"What?"

"She only has syringes and sedative. You can't extract a baby with those."

"You should have said something," I say as I wheel back toward the barn.

She grips my arm. "She'd have made up another excuse. She's not going to admit what she's doing."

My gut chills. "And what *is* she doing?"

"Slowing down the birth, maybe? I don't think she's ready to handle it, so she's over-sedating the gryphon while she figures out . . . Rowan?"

I'm already striding back to the barn. I yank open the door

to see Dr. Tyesha poised with another needle . . . this one over the gryphon's belly.

"Don't you dare," I say.

She ignores me and starts lowering the needle. Malric charges past me, snarling. He stops three feet from the doctor, but she still stumbles backward like he's lunging to rip out her throat.

"You're right, Alianor," I call over my shoulder. "Our doctor is a lousy monster healer. You can't treat something you're afraid of." I stride to Malric's side and point at the needle. "You were going to sedate the *baby?*"

She straightens. "Just a little. For its own good. The birth process can be traumatic and—"

"You don't *ever* sedate babies in the womb," Alianor says.

"It's a very mild sedative."

"Put it down," I say.

She looks from me to Malric and then straightens a little more. "No, your highness. I have a job to do, one given by your mother, my queen."

"My mother told you to sedate the gryphon?"

"She charged me with this task, to do as I see fit."

"In other words, no," Alianor mutters. "Your mom said nothing about sedating the beast."

Dr. Tyesha sidesteps toward the gryphon, syringe ready. "I am the animal healer, your highness, and you are interfering—"

"Yes. Yes, I am. If you want to administer that sedative, you have two choices. Deal with Malric or deal with my mother. You can try injecting the beast and see how Malric feels about that. Or you can go inside, have my mother woken and ask her."

"I would never wake—"

"Then I will. Alianor will stay with you and the gryphon."

I glance over my shoulder to see Alianor beside the beast, one hand on its chest. She looks at me, her eyes saucer-wide.

"Rowan . . . ?" she says.

I see her face, and I hear her voice, and I don't need to ask what's wrong. I scramble to the gryphon, nearly tripping on Jacko as he zooms out of my way. I press both hands to the gryphon's chest. Its heart is still.

"No," I whisper. "No, please, no."

I race to the gryphon's head and touch its neck. No pulse. I put my hand in front of its nostril, the opening as big as my fist. No breath.

Jacko leaps onto the gryphon, and I'm about to snap at him, but he gently makes his way to the beast's head and pokes a careful paw at its closed eyelid. It doesn't even flicker. Jacko chitters and tries again. Then he throws back his head in a mournful yowl.

I wheel on Dr. Tyesha. "Her heart stopped. You need to do something."

She doesn't move.

I run to the open medical bag, Jacko tearing after me. As I riffle through it, he's up on the table, his nose right in there. I pull out the bottle within.

"This is the sedative," I say. "Where's the reversal agent?"

Dr. Tyesha says nothing.

I snatch up the bag, march over and thrust it under her nose. "You aren't supposed to sedate without having some-thing to reverse it."

"It's too late, your highness," she says. "Once the heart stops in a beast this large, we cannot restart it. That's why I didn't bring a reversal agent. It would be unnecessary."

"No," Alianor says. "You didn't bring it because this isn't an accident. It's what you planned. Kill the gryphon. Kill the baby. Tell everyone the labor went horribly wrong. That's why you didn't want me here to witness it."

I stare at the doctor. I want her to say Alianor's wrong. I want to hear a plausible explanation. Yet even as I gape at Dr. Tyesha, I know Alianor's right. It makes horrible, awful, inconceivable sense.

And it's my fault.

My fault because the doctor couldn't have attempted this if she hadn't known I was grounded. She might have been able to explain why she didn't summon Alianor to the birth. But she could not have explained why she didn't summon the royal princess.

"Rowan?" Alianor says.

Whatever I did, I can't undo it. I can only deal with it now. I wheel on Dr. Tyesha. "The baby is alive. You can remove it."

"What? No. That's not possible."

"It is," Alianor says. "But we don't have much time." She touches the gryphon's belly. The baby kicks back, and Alianor nods in satisfaction. "Keep the doctor here, Rowan. Don't let her inject that needle. I'll be right back."

CHAPTER SIX

As Alianor leaves, Dr. Tyesha makes a move toward the gryphon, but it's halfhearted, testing to see if I'm distracted enough for her to inject that sedative. I'm not . . . and neither is Malric, who feints at her, growling. I walk over, pluck the syringe from her hand and hit the plunger, emptying it onto the floor.

"Do you really think that will save the baby?" Dr. Tyesha says. "If you are a true monster hunter, Rowan, you'll let me put it to sleep, for its own good. Its mother is dead. It's suffocating in there, even now. The best thing—"

"No."

I didn't miss her switch from "your highness" to "Rowan." I'm no longer a princess to Dr. Tyesha.

"Who told you to do this?" I ask.

"No one. I made the decision myself, for the good of my country. You are a spoiled little girl, Rowan. A fatherless child whose mother indulges her. That's bad enough for a normal parent, but it is unforgivable for a monarch. You are willful and selfish, and your mother cannot see that. She let you keep a gryphon that murdered your aunt. Lamed your brother. Tried to kill you."

"This gryphon didn't *murder* anyone." I step forward and look her square in the eye. "It defended itself against my brother and my aunt after it snatched *me* for dinner. I don't bear it any ill will, because *that's* what it means to be a true monster hunter. I understand beasts have a right to feed and defend themselves, like we do."

I move closer still. "My mother agreed to let this gryphon live because it was pregnant, which meant an incredible opportunity to learn more about these monsters. The more we know, the more easily we can deal with them. This gryphon wasn't a pet. It was a research subject who taught our monster hunters more about its kind than we ever imagined. *That* is why we kept it alive, and if it had to be killed, it was supposed to happen after the gryphon had the baby. You had no reason to do it before that."

"No reason except to ensure you didn't unleash another monster on our kingdom. Make sure you didn't decide to add this *baby* to your menagerie. That beast"—she jabs a finger at Malric—"is menace enough."

"Malric was my aunt's companion." I step toward the doctor. "You treat me like a child, but I am not a child. I'm a princess and the royal monster hunter, and I do not for one moment believe this was your idea. You couldn't have secured this beast on your own."

"Those who helped knew nothing of my plans. This was my choice. Mine alone."

I move beside the dead gryphon, palpating its abdomen, making sure the baby is still moving. Some of the sedative will have passed to it, and its movements have slowed.

Am I doing the right thing? Am I being mature about this? Or am I prolonging a beast's pain because I'm not ready to let go?

"It's dying, Rowan," Dr. Tyesha says. Her voice is calm and gentle, but it still raises my hackles. "As a monster hunter, you know what is best, as hard as that might be."

"No."

"Then you truly are a child. A self-centered—"

Alianor bursts in with a medical bag in her hand.

"That's mine!" Dr. Tyesha exclaims. "You stole it from my quarters."

"Yep, I did." She walks up beside me, touches the gryphon's side and nods. Then she turns to Dr. Tyesha. "So—"

A clomping sounds outside the door. It swings open, and there's Rhydd, his bad leg wearing its nighttime brace. Jacko hops in past him, and I look around, as if I'm seeing double. Jacko was right beside me . . .

He *was* beside me earlier, but during the fight with Dr. Tyesha, I must not have noticed that he'd slipped out.

"Jacko scratched at my door," Rhydd says. "I figured that meant you were in trouble, and I should follow." His gaze goes to the gryphon lying on its side. "Is it time for the birth . . . ?" He trails off. Then he puts a hand to the gryphon's cooling body, and his eyes widen.

"She's gone," I say. "We need to remove the baby."

"Remove . . . ?" He pales and then swallows before squaring his shoulders. "Right. Doctor Tyesha, I presume you're performing the procedure. Alianor will assist, along with Rowan and myself. Is there anything you require before we begin?"

When Dr. Tyesha doesn't answer, Rhydd glances at me. I'm beside the gryphon with Alianor, who's running her hand through the fur on the beast's belly, assessing.

"We need hot water and towels," Alianor says to Rhydd. "If you could get those, your highness, we'd appreciate it."

He looks again at the doctor.

"Doctor Tyesha isn't in charge anymore," I say. "She killed the gryphon. Then she tried to kill the baby."

He wheels on Dr. Tyesha. Before he can say anything, I cut in with, "We really are going to need water and towels, Rhydd. Unless you'd rather assist with the surgery."

His expression answers that. My brother is a fine hunter, but there are aspects to it that don't necessarily agree with his stomach. He turns to go and then pauses to face the doctor.

"Doctor Tyesha," he says, his tone formal. "May I escort you to your quarters, please? You will remain there until morning, when you will explain your actions to the queen."

I don't hear what the doctor says. I'm busy with Alianor, who's using a razor to cut a strip of tawny fur just below the bulge that is the baby gryphon.

Once Rhydd and Dr. Tyesha are gone, Alianor murmurs, "On a practical note, at least I don't need to worry about injuring the mother."

"Hmm."

"Which is good, because I've assisted twice, but I've never led the procedure. I need to open her up and take out the baby. Preferably without cutting *it*."

"Preferably."

I want to reassure her that if anything goes wrong, I'll understand. Yet she doesn't need that. I've been raised to act as if I'm sure of my choices and actions. With Alianor, it isn't acting. She sees something she must do, and she does it, and if it doesn't go according to plan, she'll deal with that later.

Jacko has climbed onto the beast and is peering down. He's staying out of Alianor's light, so I let him be. He's curious, like me. Malric is not—the warg stands facing the partly open door, as if guarding, but I can't help but wonder whether, like Rhydd, he's thinking that he doesn't want to see this.

I do want to see it. And, yes, it helps that the gryphon is dead. I hate saying that, but it means we don't have to worry about what damage we cause getting the baby out of the womb.

As Alianor cuts, I hold the baby-bulge in place. Then I need to stretch the incision while Alianor reaches inside and—

"Oh!" Rhydd says behind us, his boots squeaking as he stops short.

"Look away," I say. "Just have the blankets and the water ready, and keep your back to us."

He does, and after a moment, Alianor says, "Pull!" and I need to heave the incision wider. She pulls too, and what she's pulling isn't nearly as small as a human baby. As she grunts with exertion, Rhydd appears at my side.

"You don't need—" I begin.

"Help Alianor."

He takes my place, and I reach inside and touch what feels like a beak. I don't want to tug on that. Nor do I want the head I feel next. I keep going until I'm holding the baby's body with Alianor, and then we count to three and—

The gryphon pops out like a bottled cork and hits me square in the stomach. I stagger, and Alianor yelps and knocks into me, and down I go, flat on my back with something on top of me.

I lift my head to find myself looking into the eyes of a tiny gryphon.

"Hello," I say.

It opens its beak and lets out a gurgling screech.

"You . . . may not want to hug that," Rhydd says. "It's . . . a little messy."

It is. It's also shivering in the chilly barn. I wrap my arms around the baby, ignoring the mess, as Alianor cuts the umbilical cord. I hold the baby tight against my chest and crawl over to the blankets and water. Jacko hops along with me, his ears twitching with interest. When I start cleaning the baby, he sniffs it. Malric looks our way and curls his lips, as if to say, "That's disgusting."

It is not disgusting. It is wondrous. In my hands I hold the first baby gryphon we have ever seen, maybe even the first *anyone* has seen. We only knew they had live births, not egg hatchings. I am looking at something incredible and magnificent . . . and also adorable.

The baby is as big as a medium-sized dog—at least two feet long, not including the tail, which it keeps tucked around its body. It has huge eyes, the nictitating membrane flicking sideways over amber pupils. Its head looks like an eagle's, its ears slicked down, and even when I dry them, they're small and more rounded than an adult's. Instead of feathers, its upper half is golden down, the same color as the wet fur on its body. It has four legs, the top ones birdlike, and the back ones like a cat's. Its small wings stay pressed tight against its body.

I sit on the floor, and I clean the baby gryphon, and it stares at me. When I move, its gaze follows me, head wobbling. Rhydd and Alianor crouch beside me, and they reach to pet it, but it doesn't even seem to notice. It just keeps staring at me.

The door opens, cold air rushing through, and I gather the gryphon to me. Berinon steps in with, "What's—?" Then he sees me holding the gryphon and a huge smile lights up his broad face.

"Well, there's something you don't see every day," he says. "Did it fly out of the womb and straight into your arms?"

"Not exactly."

He opens his mouth to say something else. Then he catches sight of the mother gryphon. His gaze travels over it, from its bloodied belly to its lolling head. He rubs his mouth and shakes his head.

"I'm sorry," he says. "It happens, but I'm still sorry you had to see that. At least the baby survived. Doctor Tyesha did her job well. Your mother will be pleased." He looks around. "Where is the doctor?"

Rhydd pushes to his feet. "That's a long story, and it's Rowan's to tell. We might want to wake Mom to hear it."

An hour later, I've told my tale, and I'm sitting on the floor in the throne room feeding ground meat to the baby gryphon. We weren't sure what it would eat, but I theorized it would be more like feeding an eaglet than a kitten, since the mother didn't have mammary glands. I guessed ground meat, similar to the regurgitated food a mother raptor would use. That seems to be correct, though I'll need to closely monitor the baby to be sure its stomach doesn't reject the food.

I've told Mom and Berinon my story. Heward was there, too—Berinon fetched him as soon as he realized we were dealing with sabotage. Yes, Heward will be a suspect, but Berinon was also making sure Heward heard my story from the start.

I went through it twice, with Alianor supporting everything. Rhydd brought the syringe and the doctor's bag with the sedative, and Berinon posted a guard to watch the gryphon's body so no one could tamper with it.

As for Dr. Tyesha, she's gone. Rhydd had escorted her to her quarters, but we hadn't thought to set a guard, and she slipped away before Berinon could fetch her. She left a note taking full responsibility for what happened and being very clear no one else had been involved, which means someone else almost certainly was behind it, someone powerful enough that she's taken her payment and fled.

Berinon didn't need to track down the guards who'd assisted Dr. Tyesha. As soon as they heard the commotion, they turned themselves in. The three claim they were approached last night by Dr. Tyesha herself, who'd said the gryphon was about to give birth and she needed their help. She'd told them the queen insisted on discretion to avoid curious onlookers. After the gryphon was bound, they'd returned to their quarters, on the doctor's orders.

While their story makes sense, Berinon will assign them to non-castle duties while he investigates. We cannot risk having guards who might be loyal to anyone other than their queen.

I listen to Mom and Rhydd discuss the situation while I feed the baby gryphon. Finally, Mom says, "Rowan?" and I look up.

"You realize that will be a problem," she says, nodding at the newborn. "Whoever is behind the plot will be looking for an excuse to claim that baby endangers us all."

When I open my mouth, she says, "Yes, it's a newborn. But it won't be forever."

"I know. I was just going to say that I understand."

"Do you?"

I nod. "I understand that raising her will be my responsibility. I understand that it might not be possible to raise a gryphon in captivity, and she might . . ." I swallow. "Not survive. If she does, then eventually she will need to be returned to the mountains. We can't keep a full-grown gryphon here. She must be taken far into the mountains, where she cannot return and endanger humans. If that isn't possible, she will need to . . ." Another swallow. "She will need to be euthanized. The kingdom's safety comes first. This is not a pet or a monster companion. She's a research project to help us better understand gryphons and protect ourselves from them."

Mom walks over and bends to kiss the top of my head. "Thank you for understanding that."

"I do."

She lowers herself beside me, sweeping her skirts out of the way. "Then let's enjoy this project while we can," she says, as she reaches for some of the ground meat to feed the gryphon.

CHAPTER SEVEN

TWO MONTHS LATER

"Y ou need to do something about that gryphon."

Mom stands in the pasture, hands on her hips, Berinon at one side, Wilmot at the other. All three look down at me with matching expressions of frustration. I feel like I'm five again, when both my parents and Berinon would cluster like that, a stone wall of disapproval.

I glance at Wilmot. He's about Mom's age, with hair the color of hay and the pale skin of those who live over the mountains. His blue eyes narrow as I glance his way, promising me no shelter there.

"I know," I say. "I'm really sorry. I don't know how she—" The gryphon bumps me from behind. I put a hand out to warn her this is not the time. She only bumps me again, annoyed with this interruption to our play.

"I don't know how she escaped," I say. "I'm sorry she frightened the chickens."

"They won't lay eggs for days now," Wilmot says. "My basans might never lay again after that scare."

"I'm sorry. I really am. She's eating almost half her body weight every day, and she's still hungry, and I honestly don't know how she keeps escaping."

"Are you sure she can't fly yet?" Mom says.

I glance at Tiera, who bobs her head and then flaps her wings weakly, as if they're far too small to lift her body from the ground.

"She . . . hasn't flown for me," I say. "Nor has anyone else seen her fly, but I suppose . . ."

"She might be smarter than you think?" Berinon says. "And keeping her flights a secret?"

Tiera begins cleaning her feathers with her beak.

"She needs to be contained," Wilmot says. "When she's not with you, she must wear a leg shackle."

I shiver at the word *shackle*.

Wilmot gives me a hard look. "Would you prefer we put her into a cage? Or confine her to the hay barn?"

"We cannot confine her to the hay barn," Mom murmurs. "Not unless we want the staff driven mad by her shrieking."

"A shackle with a very long, lightweight chain to provide as much freedom as possible," Wilmot says. "While we make plans to return her to the mountains before winter."

"Before winter?" I squeak. "She's only a . . ."

I turn to the gryphon, and the word *baby* dies in my throat. We had theorized about her growth rate. That's part of science, coming up with theories and seeing if you've predicted correctly.

Predatory monsters tend to have long juvenile stages, to give them time to learn to hunt. In the three months Jacko has been with me, he's doubled his weight, but he's still only half his adult size. In that same time frame, a baby rabbit would be grown. Dogs take over a year to mature, and wargs require twice that. Therefore, it stood to reason that the massive gryphons would take years to reach maturity.

I glance at Tiera. She lifts her head, and when she does, we're nearly at eye level. She's as big as Malric, and getting bigger every day. The problem with my calculations was that I was comparing her to predatory mammalian monsters, like jackalopes and wargs. But she's half bird, and they mature faster.

Tiera no longer looks like a baby anything. She's a miniature gryphon, with powerful beak and talons.

As if reading my mind, Mom says softly, "She's becoming dangerous, Rowan."

"She'd never hurt me," I say.

The gryphon nudges my back, more gently now, making a rasping sound that means she wants petting. I scratch her ears, and she leans against me, rubbing her head against my shoulder . . . and I brace myself against being knocked over.

"She wouldn't," I say. "No more than Jacko or Sunniva would."

"I agree," Mom says. "Which is part of the problem. She's imprinted on you."

"I didn't intend that," I say. "We had no idea that gryphons imprinted, but it's a fascinating characteristic, one that requires further study—"

"Enough," Mom says, lifting her hand. She steps forward and gives me a one-armed embrace. "I know you've made the most of this time with her. You've learned a lot, and I have, too." She looks at the gryphon, and her expression softens. "I've learned that they are more than the terrible monsters I came to hate, and I will always be grateful for that. I also agree that she wouldn't hurt you."

The gryphon reaches her head out for Mom, who sighs and pets her. "You are a beautiful, wondrous creature, but you do not belong in a castle. Nor do you belong with a princess, even if she's the royal monster hunter."

Mom turns to me. "She wouldn't hurt you intentionally, Rowan, but the bigger she gets, the more likely she is to do it by accident. She may also injure someone else. She is . . . less fond of some people than others."

Wilmot harrumphs at that.

Mom's right. She's also being very understanding, given the circumstances. Her husband and sister were killed by gryphons, and now her daughter is raising one that's already big enough to . . .

I look at Tiera's beak and talons.

I'm about to say something else when Dain strides out from behind the barn. He's holding something red in his arms, and his gaze is fixed on me as he marches over.

"Watch—!" I begin.

Too late. The moment he's within reach, Tiera swings around, knocking him clear off his feet with her tail. I hurry over and put out a hand to help him up, but he ignores it and gets to his feet as the gryphon wedges her body between us, hissing.

"As I was saying . . ." Mom murmurs.

It's not just Dain that Tiera doesn't like. She isn't fond of men in general. That seems odd, but when I started asking around, staff mentioned having dogs or cats that preferred humans of one sex or the other. Maybe it's because Alianor and I were the first people to hold her, and my mother was one of the first to feed her.

Whatever the reason, Tiera likes us three, tolerates other women and dislikes the male half of the population, especially when they get too close to me.

I push the gryphon aside, and she allows it. As Mom says, she's imprinted on me as her mother. When I shove, she squawks but moves, and I'm about to apologize to Dain when I see what he's holding, and I gasp.

I hurry forward and take the bundle from him. It's a hen-like bird with red and black feathers and a bright-red comb. One of Wilmot's basans . . . limp and lifeless in my hands. I swallow hard as I turn to Wilmot.

"I am so sorry. I . . ." I examine the bird quickly. "I don't feel any wounds . . ."

"It died of a heart attack," Dain says. "Your blasted gryphon scared it to death."

Tears fill my eyes. Basans are monster birds, and Wilmot was the first hunter to domesticate them. We'd brought the small flock from his cabin and set up a coop here, next to our chickens.

Dain and I had been in a monster-study lesson when Tiera got free. As soon as we'd heard the shouts, we went running to find her lunging at the coop, trying to get her beak through and grab a basan.

I step up to Wilmot, the dead basan in my arms. "I'm—"

"Yes," he says, his tone abrupt. "You're very sorry."

The tears fall then, and he lays one hand on my shoulder, squeezing, as he says gruffly, "No one's blaming you, child. I checked Tiera's gate earlier. She fooled me, too, pretending she couldn't fly. All we're saying is that she's growing up fast, and you won't be able to keep her for as long as you'd hoped."

"I know."

He takes the basan from me. "This one was old. Her heart was already weak. If you want to make it up to me, keep watching those eggs and hope one hatches."

I nod. "You're right about the shackle. I don't like the idea, but it's better than confining her to the hay barn."

Berinon promises to smith the shackle himself, out of the lightest but strongest material we have.

Mom and Berinon leave, and I'm about to say something to Wilmot when a figure rounds the barn and my whole body tenses. It's Branwyne, Heward's daughter, who is next in line for the throne if my mother is unseated.

Branwyne's twenty, already old enough to be queen. I didn't know her well growing up, but since Jannah's death, Heward has brought his children from their own lands to live at their village house, so they can spend more time at the castle. He says he's just preparing them in case of an emergency, but I feel like Malric when Jacko hops too close to his spot on the fire hearth.

Branwyne doesn't even look at me. Her eighteen-year-old brother, Kethan, follows, and he acknowledges me with a strained smile and a nod. I suppose Kethan is the one who should raise my hackles—he's next in line for *my* job—but he doesn't. Sometimes he trains alongside Dain and me, taking advantage of Wilmot's lessons. I never feel like he's competing with me, though. His sister? That's another matter. Even Tiera hisses at her.

"I hear that beast of hers got away," Branwyne says to Wilmot.

"The *princess's* beast, you mean," he replies, his voice deceptively mild. "Since she's standing right there, perhaps you should address her."

Branwyne snorts. "If she's not capable of restraining that creature, I'll address someone who might be."

"Branwyne . . ." Kethan says.

"You need to do something before it kills someone. It's a gryphon. That's what it does, as the queen should know better than anyone. The girl can't handle the beast."

Branwyne turns to Dain, who tenses. She waves at him. "Give it to him. At least he seems reasonably competent."

Wilmot opens his mouth, but Branwyne is already marching away. Kethan leans in to whisper, "Ignore her," before following his sister.

Dain glances at me, mutters something I don't catch and stalks off in a different direction. Tiera butts my shoulder for a scratch, which I give her absently.

"Don't take Kethan's advice," Wilmot says, his voice too low for anyone to overhear. "He means well, but the worst thing you can do is ignore his sister. Do not engage her unless necessary. Do not ignore her either. She will cause you trouble if you do."

I start to respond, but he only clasps my shoulder and says, "Take your gryphon and go play. You could both use the exercise."

CHAPTER EIGHT

A week later, I'm tending to the basan eggs. They were my special project even before the basan died. Now I'm extra diligent, determined to see at least one hatch.

Wilmot has one rooster and five hens. While he's been raising them for years, the fertilized eggs never hatch. My theory is that captivity makes the hens less than attentive mothers. It's not uncommon—some animals don't reproduce well in menageries. So I've been collecting fertilized eggs and experimenting to reproduce a hen's care. Heat is the main thing. The problem is getting the right consistent temperature.

I may actually have it this time. I'm crouched in front of the coal-heated box, and one of the eggs is rocking. Jacko perches on my shoulders, bent over by my head, his face nearly blocking my view as he watches the egg.

"We may be close," I murmur.

Malric bends to sniff the box. With one eye on me, his giant jaws open and begin to close, ever so carefully, around an egg.

Jacko chitters and hisses at him.

"Not breakfast," I say, shooing the warg back.

I hand him an unfertilized egg from the coop. He retreats to eat it. Malric has discovered a fondness for the red eggs. I don't blame him. They're twice the size of regular hen eggs . . . and twice as delicious.

I lift the moving egg. When I cup it in my hands, it knocks against my fingers and I smile.

Chikako appears and awkwardly flaps her wings to hop into the box, where she equally awkwardly lowers herself onto an egg, wrapping her tail around it. She has appointed herself foster mom and regularly sits on them, which doesn't seem to do any harm.

"That chickcharney is going to be very pleased with herself if any hatch," Wilmot says as he walks over from the coop.

"I think this one might." I hand him the egg, and he wraps his hands around it.

The only time I've seen Wilmot smile was when he'd been suffering from his head injury and mistook me for my aunt. While he doesn't smile now, his blue eyes lighten with satisfaction as he cradles the egg.

"There's definitely something alive in there," he says. "Something that wants to come out."

I spot Dain, walking past and glancing our way.

"Come see," I say. "This one seems close to hatching."

"It won't," he says. "You're wasting your time. Time better spent . . ." He touches the bow slung over his shoulder. "Training for your actual job. Hunting monsters. Not playing with them."

"I'm not playing. I'm experimenting with breeding."

"Looks like playing to me." He walks on. "I'll be in the court-yard training with the monster hunters who *aren't* princesses."

As I watch him go, I seethe, and Jacko chitters.

"Tiera has the right idea," I mutter. "If he's a jerk to me, I should be a jerk back. Better yet, drive him off like she does."

"That's one way to handle him," Wilmot murmurs.

I give a start, and my cheeks heat. I'd forgotten he was there. "Sorry. He's just . . ."

"Stubborn. Difficult. Argumentative." Wilmot eases back on his haunches. "I have no idea where he gets that from."

I want to smile at that, but I'm too angry. More than angry. I'm hurt.

"I don't know what I've done," I say. "He was like this when we first met, and then we became . . ." I flail, unable to say the word.

"Friends?"

"Obviously not."

Wilmot passes the egg back to me and I place it back down in the box. Chikako bobs over to settle her rump onto it.

"I should take the blame for his ill temper," Wilmot says. "We share a similar disposition, therefore, I must have made him this way. Yet, at the risk of defending myself, Dain was like this when I met him. Worse, if anything. Sullen. Morose. Getting a word from him was like getting a bone from Malric."

He reaches to rub the warg's ears. The first time Wilmot did that, I'd jumped in, terrified he was about to lose his hand. Even I can't pat Malric. But Wilmot was with Jannah when she found the warg pup, and he helped raise Malric. Sometimes I think the warg would rather be with him. I've tried suggesting it—giving Malric permission to stay in Wilmot's cabin—but he just trudges after me, like I'm dragging him on a chain.

Jacko climbs down and curls up in my lap, making his odd purring sound, as if sensing my mood.

I glance at Wilmot. "About Dain . . . That's not the story he tells. He says he begged to be your apprentice, and you wouldn't have him. So he followed you home, begged again, and you sent him off."

"Begged?" Wilmot makes a sharp sound that may be a laugh.

"Well, maybe he didn't use that word, but it was certainly the impression I got."

"Then his idea of begging was to stand in front of me and say, 'I want to be your apprentice.' And, when I refused, he stalked off without another word. I've been called prickly, but that boy is a porcupine."

"I made progress before," I say, petting Jacko.

"And you will again. You hesitate to call him a friend because he doesn't always act like one. He doesn't know *how*, Rowan. He went from indentured servitude to life with me in the forest. I don't think he's ever had anything remotely like a friend."

"It would help if you let him speak to my mother about his servitude. Let her explain that she had nothing to do with it. I know she didn't."

"As do I."

Frustration darts through me. "Then why allow Dain to believe it? He's grown up hating my mother, and sometimes I feel like he blames me, too."

"He doesn't. He doesn't even blame her. I've explained that if his parents owed taxes, it wasn't to the queen."

"Then whoever they did owe must be punished. Indentured servitude is illegal. His parents lost their farm through no fault of their own, and they were forced to *sell* him to save the family."

"And if that's not true?"

I glance sharply at him. "What?"

Wilmot looks around, and while there's no one within earshot, he still lowers his voice. "That is the story Dain's parents told him. What if I suggested that it isn't true? That they weren't poor farmers beset by troubles, forced to part with their beloved son."

"I don't understand."

He studies my face and nods. "Of course you don't. I remember when you and your brother were born. Your father was ready to burst with joy. Your mother's happiness was always quieter, but she was just as excited. They were deeply in love with each other, and deeply in love with you and your brother before you were even born. Berinon built your cradles by hand. Jannah cured your blankets from monster hides, so many that I told her you'd smother under them ... while I was secretly making some myself. That's the family you know. Anything else? Any other experience?"

He shakes his head and meets my gaze. "There are other experiences, Rowan. Rationally you know that, yet you cannot quite comprehend one that is so far from your own. I might suggest you try to understand a life that isn't filled with people who love you. A life where you only have one crotchety old hunter."

I nod, still stroking Jacko as he purrs.

"Dain changed on your adventure, yes?" he says. "He lowered his porcupine quills."

I nod again.

"And I'll wager he lowers them when you two are alone, on hunts or training."

"He does."

"He respects your brother, but Rhydd still makes him nervous. He is Dain's future king, after all. Alianor . . . he likes her well enough, but they have little in common besides your mutual friendship. You have your brother—a twin, no less—plus Alianor, your mother, Berinon, a castle full of people who've known you since birth. You also have . . ." He waves at Jacko, Malric and Chikako. "Now you even have a gryphon. He has me and a new friend with many others sharing her attention."

"So I need to make more time for Dain?"

"No. In fact, I would suggest that is entirely the wrong thing to do. I know firsthand what happens when you demand the undivided attention of someone who cannot give it."

His gaze slides to the box, and he leans over it, his expression hidden as he touches the eggs, each in turn. "I would strongly suggest that this is Dain's problem to resolve. You've made room for him in your life. It's his job to take that space . . . or decide he's too proud to accept it."

Wilmot lifts an egg and passes it to me. As he does, it gives a violent wobble.

"Oh!" I say. "Another one." I run my hands over the shell, feeling the beast within moving. Then I glance at Wilmot. "I tried to get Dain to help with this project. I thought it was something we could do together, as monster hunters. He refused."

"Probably because he's been trying to hatch basans himself for two years, with no success."

"What?" I look at Wilmot. "Why didn't you tell me? I . . ."

"You wouldn't have done it, for fear of showing him up? That's what you were about to say, wasn't it? Then you realized it would be a lie." His eyes brighten with amusement. "You wouldn't abandon a project to avoid offending him. You just would have felt bad if you'd succeeded where he'd failed. Again, this is his problem to work out, Rowan. You have a gift that he and I both lack."

He glances at Malric. "Do you know what I said when your aunt found this wee orphaned warg pup terrorizing chickens?"

I shake my head.

He scratches behind Malric's ears. "I told her to put him down. That he'd never be anything but a wild beast who would surely turn on her. I told myself I had Jannah's interests at heart. She was my best friend, and I didn't want her hurt. The truth is that I was young, too young to put a proper name to what I was feeling."

He looks at me. "It was jealousy. She had Courtois, who wouldn't let me near him. She had a hoop snake, too, who'd followed her home when she rescued him from a snare. Neither wanted anything to do with me. After she rescued Malric, he nipped me hard enough to draw blood and I . . ."

Wilmot scratches his chin. "I was ready to march to Jannah and show her what he'd done, in hopes she'd return him to the mountains. Then I looked down at him, a ball of black fur no bigger than your jackalope, and I understood what I was really feeling. So I bandaged my finger, and I went to get him some meat from the kitchen, and I resolved to be kind to him instead."

He pets Malric, and I try not to be envious myself, but he catches my look. "You think he doesn't like you much, don't you?"

"Dain or Malric?"

Wilmot's lips twitch. "Both, I suppose. Malric, I meant."

"He's stuck with me, and he doesn't want to be."

"If you feel that way, perhaps he does, too." Wilmot takes another egg from the box. "Malric is a grumpy old man, like me. He's fond of you, in his way. Dain is, too, in his. Both are wary, watching to be sure of their welcome. With Dain, I know his recent foul mood upsets you. Don't let it. Don't tolerate it either. He must find his place in your life, and he must find his place here, in the castle, or he will always feel like an outsider. No one is making him feel that way except himself. Let him resolve it."

The egg then gives a tremendous crack, and a tiny red beak pokes through.

Wilmot hands me the egg. "Your first basan birth, great Royal Monster Hunter. Just try not to let this little one imprint on you."

He winks, and we settle in to watch the basan peck its way into the world.

I'm not sure I really understand what Wilmot said about Dain. I do understand the part about Dain not having experience making friends. To an outsider, it probably looks as if I'm surrounded by friends of my own. While there are dozens of children living both inside the castle gates and in the village just beyond, they're kept on the other side of an invisible wall. If they're the children of castle staff, their parents erect that wall, making sure their sons and daughters don't treat the royal children like equals. If they're the children of courtiers, their parents push them toward us in hopes of alliances, and we must erect the wall. Behind it, there's only my brother and me, a play circle of two.

Even with Alianor, I'm always aware that her father didn't leave her here as an extended playdate. It's fostering, where Alianor stays with us to learn court life and cement her new friendship with a very useful princess. It's also a friendly hostage situation. Mom and Alianor's father—Everard of Clan Bellamy—have come to a peaceful agreement, and keeping Alianor here ensures the bandit warlord will uphold his end of the deal and stop bandit-ing. So while Alianor might be a genuine friend, there's an awkward element to it. Like Wilmot insisting that Malric likes me just fine—even if he does, he's not with me by choice, and that makes things uncomfortable.

So I understand that friendship is new for Dain because it is for me, too. What I don't understand is Wilmot's advice to just leave Dain be and let him figure it out for himself. Isn't friendship supposed to be about helping each other? Being supportive and understanding?

Wilmot's right that if Dain's in a mood, I can't just stand there and be his whipping girl. But if the problem is that Dain's more comfortable alone with me, then shouldn't I try to make time for that?

What we need is an adventure for two. A chance to bond over the thing we have in common: monster hunting. I don't mean luring him into another secret hunt either. This must be an actual queen-approved adventure. And the next day, the perfect opportunity lands in my lap.

When our subjects have monster troubles, they send word to the castle. If they live close enough, they might even come themselves. For two hours each day, Mom meets with subjects in the throne room.

If Mom knows there's a monster on the agenda, she calls me in. Officially, resolving those problems is my job, but Mom isn't going to interrupt my lessons to send me halfway across the kingdom to deal with a single warakin. Since Jannah's death, her troop has handled almost all complaints.

Today, though, a farmer brings an easy one. A khrysomallos has infiltrated his flock of sheep. That sounds dire . . . if you don't know that a khrysomallos is simply a winged golden ram, and no more dangerous than your average sheep. This one has a wounded wing, so it's stuck with the farmer's sheep. I'm sure it would be tempting for the farmer to keep it, but he understands that it's a wild beast and belongs with its own kind.

The mission, then, is to capture the khrysomallos and return it to the castle, where Alianor can fix its wing. The farm is only an hour's ride away. A simple and safe job, and when I glance Mom's way, she nods, giving me permission to handle this myself.

After the audience, I ask to take Dain along. I also ask permission to handle this alone—just Dain and myself, with a guard to watch over us. Mom hesitates, but even she can't see any danger with a khrysomallos, so she agrees.

With that, I have exactly what I want. A queen-sanctioned, totally safe monster-hunting adventure with Dain.

CHAPTER NINE

"Tell me again why we're doing this," Dain mutters as we ride toward our adventure.

"The khrysomallos is wounded and—"

"No, *this.*" He waves a hand around us. "I feel like I'm leading a parade."

I glance at the village children running after our horses. When one reaches to touch Malric, her mother snatches her back. I stop and lower Jacko instead, allowing the girl to pat him while explaining what he is. I also explain that it is never a good idea to pat any animal or monster without getting permission first.

"Malric is a warg," I say. "He doesn't even let me pet him." I lower my voice to a conspiratorial whisper. "He's really cranky."

As the girl giggles, Kaylein—our guard for the day—rides closer and says, "Malric's job is guarding the princess. He takes it very seriously, and if you tried to pet him, he might mistake that for an attack."

The little girl nods solemnly, her curls bouncing. I'm turning to let other children pat Jacko when the girl sees my sword and gasps.

"Can I touch *that?*" she asks.

I chuckle. "You may, and thank you for asking first. It's very sharp. Here, let me take it out for you."

I hand Jacko to an older boy and ask him to hold the jackalope low so others can pet him. Then I climb from my mare and take out the ebony sword. I explain what it represents and what it's made of, and they have tons of questions, which Dain interrupts with, "Do you plan to get to this farm by nightfall, princess?"

"Is that your page boy?" an older girl asks, squinting up at Dain.

Dain mutters something I don't catch.

"Dain is a monster hunter," I say. "He's in training with me." I resist the urge to make a joke about him being as cranky as Malric, but a boy our age says, "If I were riding with a princess, I'd be a lot happier about it."

Dain fixes the boy with a dead-eyed stare. "I would be, too ... if we were actually riding and not entertaining children."

The boy straightens. "Who are you calling a child?"

A man's hand lands on the boy's shoulder. "Easy now. They've someplace to be, and while the princess is being very kind, they do need to be on their way."

That gives me an excuse to sheathe my sword and lift Jacko back onto the saddle. I say a few final words. Then I reach into my pocket, where I carry several wyvern teeth. Wilmot returned to the dead wyvern to fetch them for me, and I brought them along for this.

I hand one to the little girl who'd tried to touch Malric. When I explain what it is, her eyes grow round.

"Did you kill it?" she whispers.

"We had to, unfortunately. We prefer to drive monsters away. When we do need to kill one, we take something to remember them by." I touch the pocket on my tunic, where I've replaced one button with a tooth. "It's a way to honor their death."

She nods solemnly, her fist wrapped tightly around the tooth. The other kids ask to see it, but she shakes her head. As I smile, Dain grumbles. I ignore him. Part of giving her the tooth is kindness—it's a treasure she will remember. Part of it is letting people know that I helped kill a wyvern. That might seem like bragging, but Jannah taught us that a monster hunter should not hide her feats. It proves we deserve our title. Wilmot says that's especially important for me, being so young.

It's Kaylein's job to herd us along, making it seem as if I'd love to linger, but my mean bodyguard won't let me. Kaylein is great at that, even if *mean* isn't a word I'd ever use to describe her. I'd personally requested her. She's the newest guard and the youngest, at eighteen, but she's already capable enough that Berinon agreed.

When some of the children try to stall us further, she shoos them off, her dark face as impassive as a statue, the wind rippling her short curls. Once Dain and I are far enough, she follows.

"Next time, princess, can we take the back roads and avoid the parade?" Dain says as we head out. "I know you like the attention but . . ."

"Actually, I do *not* like the attention. I accept it as part of my position. I took these roads because, whenever possible, I must ride through town so my subjects see me working on their behalf."

He mutters, and my shoulders tighten, a familiar ache starting between them.

"Next time, if you wish to take the back roads, *you* may do so," I say evenly.

"May I, princess?"

The tight spot between my shoulders twitches. "My name is Rowan. And if you didn't want to be here, you could have refused."

"I got the feeling that wasn't an option."

"It's always an option."

"It's an option for you, too, princess. You didn't need to bring me."

"I asked to bring you." *And now I regret it.*

I don't say that part. I just look back at him, meeting his gaze and holding it, my scowl the twin of his.

He looks at me, his dark eyes piercing mine. Then he rides up beside me.

"If you keep twisting to glare at me, you'll re-injure your shoulder, princess."

"Give me less reason to glare at you, and I won't re-injure my shoulder."

He seems ready to snap back. Then he pauses and says,

"Is it bothering you? I thought it had healed after the wyvern, but you make a face when you turn, as if it hurts."

"My shoulder's fine. Just . . ." I reach between my shoulder blades and rub. "It's sore there. I don't know why."

"Oh, I know why, princess. You've been practicing too much archery. Hoping to best me. You won't, but it's nice that you try."

His lips twitch into a near-smile, and I relax, feeling that tension ease.

"Give me six months," I say, "and I'll be as good a marksman as you."

"Care to wager anything on that?"

I lift Jacko and hold him out.

Dain's hint of a smile breaks through. "You keep trying to give me that oversized rodent, princess. One of these days, I'll take him, and it'll be jackalope stew for dinner."

Jacko hisses.

"Keep your bunny," Dain says. "I do have my eye on your firebird arrow, though."

I let out an indignant yelp that makes him smile again, his eyes glittering.

"Not up for the challenge, huh? I didn't think so. You're full of swagger, princess, but when push comes to shove . . ."

"Fine. The firebird arrow. But you need to come up with something to wager yourself. I'm rather fond of your bow, actually."

He lets out a yelp of his own, and we tease and bicker for the rest of the ride, and it finally starts to feel like it used to.

As we reach the farmhouse, I'm reminded of Mom's festival day speeches. Every season, Mom holds a carnival at the castle. My favorite is the midwinter one, which starts at sundown and lasts all night. The courtyard and castle grounds are alight with bonfires, the air perfumed with burning wood and candied apples.

For the first few hours, Rhydd and I get to be regular kids, wearing our masks and buying trinkets and playing games and eating until we're sick. Then, as for all seasonal carnivals, we must don our royal garb and join our mother on the castle balcony, where she addresses the crowd.

Mom's speech is mostly boring political stuff, as she lists recent noteworthy events in Tamarel. Then she always tells a story that demonstrates how wonderful our subjects are and closes with something about how lucky she is to have them.

This year, I'll give my first speech at the harvest carnival, and I'm already preparing to follow Mom's example and use today's adventure as my story. A wounded khrysomallos landed in this farmer's pasture, and instead of rubbing his hands at his good fortune and secretly selling the wool, he asked us to help the poor beast. In the meantime, he's been feeding and caring for it. The very model of how a citizen should treat monsters.

I'm preparing my story even as we arrive at the farmer's home. I don't expect anyone to come out to greet us but . . . Well, it would be nice, wouldn't it? We're riding up with a warg at our side and a jackalope on my saddle. You can't miss us, as Dain has grumbled every time a farmhand or a trader has come running to watch us pass.

Yet there is no sign of anyone at the farmhouse. That's fine—it's a big farm, and the family must be out working in the fields. I hope they don't want to help us capture the khrysomallos. That's always awkward. Too many helpers can panic the beast. I'll follow Jannah's example and give them all tasks . . . ones that keep them from getting in our way.

As I rap on the front door, I'd be lying if I pretended I wasn't trembling, just a little, with anticipation and pride. The farmer expects Mom to send one of Jannah's troop. Instead, someone will open this door to see the princess herself, ebony sword across her back. Dain can mock, but it's exciting seeing their faces and knowing this is a moment they'll tell their grandchildren about.

When the door opens, I flash my friendliest smile, ready to announce myself, because it would be rude to presume everyone knows who I am.

Yet the woman stays half behind the cracked-open door. The one eye I can see narrows warily, as if I've come selling black-market jackalope antlers.

"Hello, I'm Rowan of Clan Dacre," I say.

I wait to flash that smile again, as she falls back in astonishment. Instead, she just says, "Here about the khrysomallos, I take it."

"Er, yes. I'm the royal—"

"It's around back. With the sheep."

She shuts the door. I stare at it as I replay my words. Should I have said *Princess* Rowan, to be clear?

I lift my hand to knock again. Then I feel the weight of Dain's narrowed gaze, and my cheeks heat as I lower my hand. He'd just grumbled about me liking the attention too much. I can hardly reintroduce myself because I didn't get the expected response.

When I turn to go, though, he lifts *his* hand to knock. I catch it.

"What are you doing?" I say.

"The royal monster hunter herself has come to handle her problem, and she treats you like a ratcatcher sent to clear her barn?" He pulls his hand from mine and goes to knock again. "She's going to greet you properly, or we aren't taking that blasted khrysomallos off her hands."

I grab his arm again. "Maybe she didn't understand. Even if she did . . . ?" I force a small smile. "You were just scolding me for liking the attention. Perhaps my ego could stand to be knocked down a peg."

"If your ego was a problem, princess, you'd be sitting on your horse while Kaylein knocked. That woman was rude, and I'm not letting her get away with—"

"It's all right. Please. Let's just do the job."

His face tightens, and I hear his words again.

She treats you like a ratcatcher sent to clear her barn.

Had his master hired him out? I suspect he did, and Dain had been treated like this, if not worse. The woman's behavior stung him, too. He's no longer an indentured ratcatcher. He's a monster hunter in training, apprenticed to the greatest hunter in Tamarel, and he's standing at the side of the royal monster hunter herself.

"It's a misunderstanding," I say. "But she *was* rude to us. I was going to offer them a shearing from the khrysomallos, but now we'll keep the wool ourselves. Save some to give to village children and use the rest to make mittens. Or maybe a scarf." I grin at him. "You'd look very dashing in a brilliant golden scarf."

He rolls his eyes. "You can have a scarf, princess. I'll use my share to knit a new strap for my quiver."

"Which will look equally dashing. Let's hurry and do the job, before she has time to realize her mistake, and I feel obligated to give her the wool."

CHAPTER TEN

I really do expect this to have all been a terrible misunderstanding. We'll come around the back and find the farmer waiting, and when I mention the woman, he'll say, "Oh, that's my wife's sister—she didn't know what was going on" or some such excuse. Instead, the barns are empty except for cows and horses, which should be out at pasture this time of day.

There are also a handful of sheep, and I wonder if the farmer lured the khrysomallos in with them, which would make our job easy, if rather dull. There's no golden-haired ram amongst the white and black animals, though. I'm peering into a dimly lit corner when we hear a strange trumpeting sound from outside and the sheep begin to bleat uneasily.

I glance at Dain, who frowns, tracking the sound. Jacko chatters. I lift the jackalope and drape him over one shoulder. Then we step out. Malric's there, with Kaylein and the horses, so it wasn't the warg that spooked the livestock. When I glance at the animals, they're all gazing at the distant pasture.

"Was that the khrysomallos?" Kaylein asks.

"I . . . don't know."

"It's not," Dain says as he takes the bow from his shoulder. "I've heard them in the mountain pass, and they don't sound like that. I think we've been tricked, princess."

"Do you have any idea *what* it is?"

He shakes his head. I draw my sword, and we set out. We can't see the far pasture—a hillock blocks our view. As we continue toward the fence, that sound rings out again. I glance back at the house to see the woman appear in an upper window. The farmer steps up beside her.

My jaw sets, and I consider marching back to demand answers. But we can hear the beast, so we're forewarned, and all three of us are armed. Plus, we have Malric. Whatever it is, we'll handle it . . . or get to safety and send Kaylein for backup from the castle.

We climb the fence. Malric vaults over it with a grace that belies his usual plodding. When he catches me looking, he grunts and turns away, as if caught dancing in the moonlight. I ask Jacko to stay at my side, and he does, his nose madly sniffing the air.

"Can you smell the beast, Malric?" I ask.

The warg keeps walking. That could mean he doesn't understand my question. Or it could mean he does smell it . . . and he's not concerned. I'm hoping for the latter. Really hoping.

If I return to the castle and tell my mother I tangled with

another predator, she won't let me handle so much as a hoop snake by myself for years to come.

We start climbing the hill, and we're halfway to the summit when feet thump on the other side. I wave Dain and Kaylein into retreat. We have our weapons ready. Something crests the hill. I catch a flash of sunlight glinting off bright gold, and then there it is . . . a khrysomallos, in all its gleaming glory.

I exhale in relief. Then the beast throws back its head, gives that thundering cry . . . and charges.

Kaylein and I dive out of the way. In a flash, Dain switches from his bow to his slingshot and launches a stone straight at the charging ram. The pellet pings off the beast's magnificent curved horns. The khrysomallos doesn't even flinch. It just trumpets again. Dain wheels . . . and the khrysomallos butts him in the rear, sending him flying.

"Dain!"

I scramble to help him up, but he's already on his feet, one hand raised to ward me off. He turns to the khrysomallos, which is pawing the ground and snorting. Dain does the same. Well, not exactly, but I swear I heard him snort, and he certainly looks ready to paw the ground.

Dain faces off against the khrysomallos, fury darkening his face.

"Dain . . ." I say carefully.

"It's a sheep," he says between clenched teeth.

"No, it's a khrysomallos. A monster."

"Monster *sheep*."

He spits the last word with contempt. The hairs on my neck rise. This is a mistake that a monster hunter cannot make. Never underestimate your opponent. Never allow emotion to cloud your judgment. Even a sheep can be a threat, if it's big and it's angry.

This khrysomallos is Malric's size, and those thick curling horns suggest it's no yearling. Scars crisscross its face. Its left ear is in tatters, an old wound long healed. The right eye is milky. This is a battle-hardened old ram. Its wing is injured, tucked awkwardly at its side, and it is angry. Very angry.

I inch to the left. The khrysomallos doesn't notice—its full attention is on Dain. As they face off, I squint to get a better look at the injured wing.

"Uh, Dain?" I say.

He doesn't answer. Just keeps glaring at the khrysomallos.

"Part of an arrow is caught in its wing," I say.

He grunts. Or at least, I think it's him. It might be the khrysomallos.

"It was shot," I say.

Another grunt.

"I'm going to wildly speculate here . . ."

Dain definitely makes a noise at that.

I continue. "Given our cool reception—and lack of assistance—from the family, I'm guessing *they* shot the khrysomallos. It swooped down to feed, and they spotted a golden ram in their flock and saw a golden opportunity. When it tried to take off, they shot it. Which grounded it, but now it's really angry. That's why we were called in. Not to help a wounded monster. To take away a furious one that's scaring their livestock, which are all hiding in the barn." I pause. "I don't blame them." Another pause. "The livestock, that is. I totally blame the farmer."

"Excellent," Dain mutters. "I'm so glad you've worked out the khrysomallos's history, princess. Do you think, if you're done theorizing, you might actually sedate the blasted thing before it gores me?"

"Oh, right." I scramble for my pack. "I can do that."

He mumbles something under his breath.

"As for being gored," I continue. "Those are the wrong sort of horns for that."

"Princess . . ."

"I'm getting the sedative. I can do that while talking."

"Or you can do it *without* talking."

"I'm calming your nerves."

A growl sounds, one that I'm 99 percent sure doesn't come from Malric.

"You're happier when you're complaining," I say as I fill the syringe. "I'm giving you something to complain about."

Off to Dain's other side, Kaylein chuckles. She's been quiet so far. She's armed and watching, but she's been told not to interfere unless we're in serious danger.

"If you need my help," she says, "I am here."

"We've got this," I say. "I'll sedate the beast while Dain holds its attention. He's doing a very good job of that."

Another growl.

"Just keep that up," I call to Dain. "Growl, scowl, bare your teeth. Keep it occupied."

Still out of the beast's line of sight, I ready the syringe and take a deep breath. Then I start forward, rolling my footfalls.

Dain picks that moment to shift his stance. The ram pulls back, as if to charge . . . and it sees me.

As the beast wheels my way, I calculate two options and I pick the less advisable one, as always. I let out a roar and rush at the beast, which startles it enough that it stiffens in surprise. With that, I see my path. Jab the khrysomallos, throw the syringe aside, and roll out of the way before it charges.

A perfect sequence. Jannah would have been so proud of me.

Dain, on the other hand, sees me charge and decides I've lost my mind.

"Rowan!"

The wind catches the word as he lunges onto the khrysomallos, just as I'm jabbing in the needle. I hit the plunger, only to see it's embedded in Dain's sleeve. I yank it out, sedative squirting, and I manage to slam it into the khrysomallos instead, emptying the rest as the beast smacks me with its horns.

I told Dain that these were not goring horns. True. They're battering horns, and when they slam into my stomach, pain explodes. The next thing I know, I'm on the ground and I cannot breathe, and Dain has me by the arm and he's dragging me, which does *not* tickle.

I catch sight of Kaylein and Malric facing off against the khrysomallos, and I manage to find enough breath to call, "No! I've sedated it! Just take cover!"

They disappear from sight as Dain hauls me behind a feeding trough. He drops me so abruptly that my head slams against the wood. Jacko leaps onto my chest, long ears flattened as he chatters at Dain. Dain gives Jacko such a glare that I grab the jackalope, cradling him to my chest.

"I wouldn't hurt your blasted rabbit," Dain snaps. "Stop giving me that look and tell him I just saved you. *Twice.* First, you charged the beast, and then you almost got trampled."

"I don't *need* to be saved, Dain. What I need is a partner who trusts my judgment, which you do not."

"Then why'd you bring me along?"

"Because we haven't had much time alone together."

"You wanted to be *alone* with me?" He backs up, hands rising. "If you're smitten—"

"No!" I choke on a laugh. "Eww."

"Eww?"

I glance at the khrysomallos, wobbly from the sedative.

I turn back to Dain. "What I meant is that I'm not interested in anyone *that* way." I touch his arm. When he yanks back, scowling, I say, "You're swaying."

I take his arm again and push up the sleeve, ignoring his protests. There's a red dot on his dark skin.

"The sedative," I whisper. "I thought the needle only caught your sleeve."

"I'm fine," he says brusquely. "I can look after myself. Just stay out of my way and—"

We both stop as the air cracks with the beating of wings. We look at each other.

"The khrysomallos trying to take off?" I whisper. "Oh no."

I scramble up just as a shriek rends the air. A shriek that sets the hairs on my neck prickling.

Gryphon. There's a . . .

I lift my gaze to see exactly what I expect. A gryphon. Only it looks much smaller than . . .

"Tiera," I whisper.

She spots me and lets out a happy shriek of welcome. Another sound answers. A garbled trumpeting. I glance to see the khrysomallos stagger as it turns and sees me. It lets out another trumpet and charges, and Tiera shrieks again, this one a cry of pure rage as she dives at the khrysomallos.

CHAPTER ELEVEN

"Tiera, no!" I shout as I run from behind the feed trough, waving my arms. "Tiera. I'm fine. See? Dain! Drive the khrysomallos off!"

Even as I say it, I remember him snapping at me to stay out of his way. He won't help. He's angry and—

"Hey!" Dain shouts. "Baaa! Over here! Yeah, you, monster sheep."

The khrysomallos diverts course to charge Dain. Tiera swoops up mid-dive and circles instead, shrieking, as if not certain whether she should protect Dain or cheer the khrysomallos on.

"Tiera!" I yell. "Come on, girl. I'm right here. Everything's fine. Kaylein? Can you help Dain?"

"I'm on it," Kaylein calls back. "You just keep the gryphon away."

Jacko runs out, chittering at Tiera, who swoops playfully

at him. Jacko takes off running, and she follows, her protect-my-human agenda forgotten. She really is a baby still, easily distracted.

I glance over to see Kaylein, Malric and Dain surrounding the khrysomallos as it paws the ground, snorting. It's swaying, too, but it isn't the only unsteady one.

"Dain?" I call.

"I'm fine," he says, his words slurring.

"Kay—?" I begin, but before I can get her attention, Dain collapses.

I run for him. The khrysomallos sees him fall and mistakes the sudden movement for attack. It charges. Its horns smash into Dain, who's collapsed on the ground, still conscious enough to flail. One hand smacks the khrysomallos, and it makes that gurgling trumpet sound and bashes him again, only to tangle in its own legs.

A cry rings out behind me. Tiera's battle shriek. I grab Dain and flip backward as he flails. Then I realize Tiera is flying straight at the poor khrysomallos as it staggers to stay upright.

"Tiera! No!"

I drop Dain. I manage to knock the khrysomallos out of Tiera's path as Malric lunges between me and the young gryphon. Tiera pulls up, shrieking and clacking at Malric.

Jacko bounds from the pasture, trying to divert Tiera's attention while she surveys the scene below.

Does she think I'm in danger? Or does she think she's stumbled onto a grand game? I have no idea. I just need to get her away from the half-sedated khrysomallos.

The ram stumbles, and I grab it, which isn't easy when it's three times the size of a sheep. He falls onto me, and I laugh. It's a strained laugh, but it's all I can think of to convince Tiera I'm fine. It works. She flaps upward and then turns toward Jacko prancing in the grass.

Then, just as she's about to go play with her jackalope friend, something catches her attention. I glance over to see a flash of white. My brain whirls, Jannah and Berinon's commands sounding in my ears.

Don't lose track of your troop.

Do you know where everyone is?

Is everyone okay?

I'm struggling to do all that amidst the chaos, and when I see that white blob trot across the pasture, my brain blanks. That's not one of my companions, human or monster, so what . . .

It's a young sheep, venturing out from the barn, as if called to adventure. From the barn, an older sheep bleats as if to say, "Get back here!"

This is what Tiera sees. A young sheep, trotting our way. The perfect prey for a baby gryphon.

She shrieks, a cry of victory, a cry of the hunt.

I barely manage a syllable of her name before she strikes. She seizes the young sheep in her talons, and her beak chomps on the back of its neck. Then she hovers there, still holding the sheep, looking down at its limp body in confusion. Another shriek, this one the glee of a baby who has taken its first prey. She drops the sheep, pounces on it and begins to tear.

I glance away as Kaylein hurries over to me.

— 95 —

"It's all right, princess," she murmurs. "We'll repay the farmer for the sheep, and at least Tiera will have eaten. You couldn't have stopped her. She's so fast."

There's awe in Kaylein's voice . . . and a touch of fear, too. *She's so fast.*

You couldn't have stopped her.

As the gryphon rips into her meal, I turn to the others. Dain sits with his head down as if struggling to stay awake. The khrysomallos lies on its side, finally sleeping. Jacko hops around me, chattering. Malric watches Tiera, and I swear he shakes his shaggy head, as if to say, "What are we going to do with you?"

What are we going to do with her, indeed.

I swallow and turn to Kaylein. "We'll need to borrow a cart to transport the khrysomallos. I don't know how Tiera escaped, but I can lead her. She listens to me."

Unless she spots prey. Unless she moves so fast I don't have time to order her back.

Another swallow. Then I straighten and head for Dain. His head lifts, dark eyes struggling to focus. He goes still. Blinks.

"Rowan!" he says, and pushes up as if to rise.

I follow his gaze. Behind me, another figure has appeared. It's a boy, no more than five, walking from the farmhouse, his gaze fixed on Tiera bent over her prey.

"Is that . . . is that a gryphon?" the boy breathes, and he doesn't even look our way. He cannot take his eyes from her.

The moment seems to freeze. A boy, no bigger than that dead sheep, walking fearlessly toward Tiera. She lifts her head, her gaze meeting the boy's, her crimson-stained beak opening in a cry.

Every muscle in my body spasms, my blood running cold, a scream bubbling up as I leap forward.

I see what is going to happen. I see it as if it happens in the blink of an eye.

She's so fast.

You couldn't have stopped her.

I'm still opening my mouth to scream, still stumbling toward them, when Tiera looks up, her feathers bristling, her tail whipping in warning as she spots the boy. She meets the boy's gaze, opens her beak . . . and gives the smallest chirp of greeting before returning to her meal.

That's all she does. She glances up sharply, as if expecting a predator come to steal her dinner, but then she sees it's a human boy and greets him and goes back to eating.

The boy lets out such a squeal of terror that Tiera rises onto her hind legs, wings extending, bloody talons out. It's the equivalent of jumping back in alarm, but the sight—the monstrous sight of this bloodied and terrible beast—only makes the child scream louder.

Kaylein runs for the boy, calling that he's fine, he's just fine. He is. Tiera makes no move to attack. But she does shriek, matching his scream with her own.

Someone races from the house, brandishing a pike. It's the farmer, snarling at the gryphon, his weapon raised.

Kaylein already has the boy. She's scooped him up and he's safe, was never in danger. His father doesn't know that. He sees only this bloodstained monster rearing, its shadow falling over his screaming son.

I race between them, my arms raised.

"It's fine," I say. "Everything is—"

Hooves thunder. A gray stallion charges over the hill. I catch only a blurry glimpse of the rider, and I don't see him—I see his sword, the flash of it in the midday sun. I throw myself into his path, arms up, and I'm sure he sees me. He *must* see me. But he keeps coming.

A snarl of rage sounds beside me. Then Malric hits me and Tiera at the same time, bowling us over.

The rider thunders past . . . right where we'd been standing a heartbeat before. Malric snarls, his fur on end, and the rider shouts, "Call your hound to heel, girl!"

"Girl?" Dain calls, at the same time as I say, "Hound?"

Then I see who it is. Branwyne.

She points her sword at Tiera. "Step away from that beast, girl."

"She's the *princess*," Dain says, tottering toward us.

"Are you drunk, boy? Get back before I run you through." Her gaze flicks my way. "If the princess wishes to claim the title of royal monster hunter, she needs to earn it. Until then, she's a girl playing with her pets. You said so yourself."

Dain stiffens. "I—"

"You told me she wasn't fit to be anything but royal zookeeper."

"I didn't mean—"

Branwyne looks my way. "He's right. You're too busy playing with beasts to hunt them. You can't even latch your gryphon's leg band properly. I saw her flying off, and I rode in pursuit, and what do I find? The beast about to kill a small child."

Dain scoffs. "Tiera *looked* at the boy. That's all."

"That isn't what I saw."

"It's not what we saw either," the farmer says, taking his child from Kaylein. His wife comes up behind him, nodding.

"You saw me rescue your son, did you not?" Branwyne says.

The couple bob their heads even as Kaylein and Dain both sputter that the boy was in no danger, and if anyone nearly died, it was me . . . under the hooves of Branwyne's stallion. I say nothing. I can't. I keep seeing that child in front of Tiera.

I feel as if someone has pushed me into an icy lake. I need to fight and get my head above water, but all I can do is shiver. When a nose nudges me, I reach an absent hand, expecting to pat Jacko's antlered head. Instead, my fingers touch long, thick fur, and I give a start as I glance up into Malric's eyes. He nudges me again, less gently this time.

I wobble to my feet. Tiera is busy eating the dead sheep. Kaylein argues with Branwyne and the farmer, while the boy huddles behind his mother's skirts.

I hear again what Branwyne said. That Dain told her I wasn't fit to be anything but royal zookeeper.

It's the sort of thing he's said to me, in private. I ignore it. Just Dain being cranky. But to say it to Branwyne?

Why was he even speaking to her? He knows how she feels about me, and he told her I wasn't fit to be the royal monster hunter?

He didn't deny it either. He made no more than a weak protest.

I shake it off and straighten. "Branwyne."

I have to repeat her name, louder, before she turns.

"I thank you for following the gryphon. I will investigate how she got free."

"It's obvious how she got free, Rowan. Her leg shackle wasn't clasped . . . and you were playing with her this morning."

"I *fed* her this morning," I say, as calmly as I can. "And walked her but—"

"Fed and *walked* her?" the farmer says. "It's a *pet?*"

"She is a research subject."

"You keep a gryphon at the castle? A live gryphon?"

"Not anymore," Branwyne says. "This beast attempted to take the life of a royal subject. It's clear what must be done, and if our so-called monster hunter won't do it . . ."

She swings off her horse and raises her sword, and it isn't until she steps toward Tiera that I even understand what she means. Yes, like all of Clan Dacre, Branwyne is a trained monster hunter, but I've never thought of her that way. I've never even seen her with a sword in hand.

I'm leaping forward to stop her when Dain lunges between Branwyne and Tiera.

Branwyne laughs, a high tinkling sound that grates down my spine. "Move, boy. If you still hope for a job when I claim my throne, you'll get out of my way now."

"It's not your throne," Dain says. "It will never be. Put that sword down."

"Lady Branwyne," Kaylein says, her voice low. "Listen to Dain, please. I don't know what you think you're doing—"

"I'm doing the job this child cannot. My brother couldn't

be here, and so I will personally rid my land of a beast that threatens my people."

"I'll handle this, Branwyne," I say.

She glances at me. "You'll kill the beast?"

I try not to flinch. "No, I will return to the castle and put the matter to the queen."

"Who is your mother," the farmer sneers as he walks forward. "She'll believe you over us."

Kaylein shakes her head. "The council will handle this. They'll weigh the evidence and our testimonies and—"

"And who will die in the meantime?" Branwyne says. "This country has spent too long under the rule of a nervous queen."

"Nervous?" I snort. "You *have* met my mother, haven't you?"

She continues as if she hasn't heard me. She isn't making an argument here—she's making a speech, one I suspect she's been practicing ever since my aunt died.

"Tamarel needs a decisive leader," she continues. "One who is not mother and father both to her wayward children. I can be the queen Tamarel needs. I see a threat to my people, and I annihilate it."

With that, she charges at Tiera, her weapon raised. I'm only caught off guard for a heartbeat. Then I rush at her, my sword drawn.

Malric gets there first. He knocks Branwyne aside. She swings on him. Blood flies up. Malric's blood. I scream in rage. She swings again, but I'm there, and our swords clang.

Branwyne is a half-head taller than me. A grown woman. An adult fighter. As I parry her sword, sweat trickles down my forehead, threatening to drip into my eye. If I blink, she'll see her opening and take it.

Behind me, I hear Kaylein. I don't know what she's saying. Blood pounds in my ears. The farmer snaps something. I don't hear that either. I'm looking into Branwyne's eyes. There's no hate there. I almost wish there was. Instead, she barely seems to see me. I am a child, a small obstacle standing between her and the throne.

I bow my head. I let the sweat droplets fall as I step back, sword lowering. Branwyne sniffs and begins to lower her weapon. Then I attack. I fly at her, ebony sword flashing so fast she can only parry. Rage fills her eyes, and that rage makes her clumsy. Every time I strike, she gets angrier, and she fumbles.

She's a decent fighter. In a tournament, she would do very well. This isn't a tournament. It's her against a smaller, faster opponent wielding a legendary blade.

Then she does the last thing I expect.

She swings her sword at Jacko.

The jackalope hasn't run into the fray. He knows better. He's racing back and forth, chirping in excitement and worry, when Branwyne turns on him and swings.

I scream and throw myself at her, and at the last second, she wheels, and I see my mistake. She doesn't smile. Her face is set in grim determination, eyes blazing with the thrill of victory as her sword swings on me.

There's a shriek. More than a shriek. So many sounds at once—Kaylein's shout and Dain's snarl and Malric's roar, but above it all, I hear Tiera shriek. Branwyne's sword arcs toward me . . . and Tiera's beak clamps down on her forearm.

Branwyne tries to spin on the gryphon, but Tiera holds her fast. Branwyne doesn't so much as flinch, seeing a gryphon gripping her arm. She is brave, and I will grant her that. A gryphon has her by the sword arm, and she only turns to me and says, "Tell your pet to release me, Rowan."

I sheathe my sword and walk over. "Allow me to take your weapon."

"What?"

"Allow me to take it from you and return it at the castle."

Her eyes flash. "I will not release my sword to you or anyone else."

"And I will not tell her to release *you* until I am certain you will not be able to retaliate against us."

Her lips curls. "I would not have hurt you. I had you dead to rights, and that was enough."

"Release your sword."

"No. This beast is a menace—"

"Release—"

She swings her sword. It's an awkward move, but she tries, her arm wrenching in Tiera's grip, the sword rising my way. Tiera's beak clamps with a snap. Branwyne gasps. Her sword falls, hitting the ground with a thunk. Branwyne spins, her other fist lashing out, boots kicking.

"Tiera!" I shout. "*Release!*"

Branwyne's fist hits Tiera in the eye just as the gryphon begins to let go. Tiera shrieks and snaps, beak tearing into Branwyne's arm as the young woman screams.

I grab Tiera in both hands and pull her away as the others rush in. I don't need to drag Tiera off. She bit down in pain and fear, and that is not her fault. None of this is her fault. But as I take her aside, I see Branwyne's bloodied arm, and I know that what Tiera *meant* to do isn't important.

My gryphon has hurt someone. Badly hurt someone.

Nothing else matters.

CHAPTER TWELVE

I'm home in my room, huddled in front of the fire with Jacko on my lap. Malric lies close enough for me to feel the heat of him. His wound needed a few stitches, and he's been quiet since our trip. Malric is never noisy, but this is a different kind of quiet, almost thoughtful. I catch him watching me a lot, as if he's weighing the actions of today, deciding whether I've messed up badly enough that he can justifiably abandon me.

Rhydd's here too, sitting on the floor. He's holding Chikako, who keeps making moves my way, only to be warned off by Jacko's growls. I clutch Jacko tight. Maybe too tight. He doesn't complain, just snuggles in, making that purring sound of his, and if it's a little jagged, a little forced, I pretend not to notice.

"Someone released Tiera," Rhydd says. "I walked past her pen after you left, and she was definitely bound. If it wasn't Branwyne, it was Kethan."

I shake my head. "I don't think Kethan would do that."

"Then it was either Branwyne or someone who supports her for queen. They released the gryphon knowing she'd fly after you, and Branwyne followed. If the little boy hadn't come out just then, she'd have antagonized Tiera herself and forced her to attack."

"I don't think Branwyne intended to be attacked."

"No, I just don't think she intended to get *hurt*. She wanted Tiera to go after her so she'd have an excuse to slay her. Prove herself worthy of the throne. The boy only makes things worse. I'm sure the farmer lamed that khrysomallos. He thought he'd make his fortune with it, but a beast is smart enough to know who's responsible for its injury. The farmer is a horrible person . . . one who'll take Branwyne's side, knowing Heward will reward him."

"None of that matters," I say.

Rhydd goes quiet. Then he murmurs, "It should."

"But it doesn't, does it?"

He moves beside me, puts an arm around my shoulders, and pulls me against him. "I'm so sorry, Ro. This isn't your fault. It's not Tiera's either."

"She only killed that sheep because she was hungry. She only bit Branwyne to protect me. She's too young to know better, too young to be taught better. And none of that changes the fact that she is a gryphon, one who's getting bigger—and more dangerous—every day, and soon Branwyne *will* be right. Tiera will be a danger to everyone around her."

"I'm sorry."

"I know." I lean against his shoulder. "I also know what I need to do."

As I tell him my plan, sadness shadows his eyes, but he doesn't argue. He just puts both arms around me and pulls me into a hug and says, "You really would have made an excellent queen, Ro."

"But I'm the royal monster hunter. And now I need to act like it."

My mother is in a council meeting to discuss Tiera's fate. She needs to hear everyone else's story before mine, or Heward will claim she favors her children.

As for Branwyne, her arm is badly gashed. We had wrapped it at the scene and then Dain rode ahead to bring Dr. Fendrel from the castle. The doctor met us partway and stitched Branwyne's arm. He says it will be fine, but that's another of those things that don't matter. My gryphon attacked the next person in line for the throne. Even if it heals well, Branwyne may never wield a sword properly.

Branwyne has given her account. So has Kaylein and the farmer, who had been very eager to tell his tale. Dain has just finished his when I slip in. My mother dismisses him, and as he passes, he sneaks a look my way, but I pretend not to see it.

After Dain brought Dr. Fendrel, he tried to speak to me. I found reasons to avoid him for the rest of the trip, and I have continued doing so. When he tries again to catch my attention, I walk right past him, and he takes a seat next to Kaylein at the witness table.

Until then, she's a girl playing with her pets. You said so yourself.

You told me she wasn't fit to be anything but royal zookeeper.

Dain still hasn't denied he said those words, and that cuts deep as a warakin's tusks. Worse, I can't even pretend I never saw this coming. Dain has said things like that right to my face, and I'd made the mistake of thinking he was just challenging me to do better. Like Wilmot, who will snap at me in private lessons yet praises my skill to others. Pointing out my flaws is a training tool, and Wilmot never even does it in front of Dain. So I thought that's what Dain was doing.

Now I realize the truth. Dain doesn't respect me as a hunter . . . and he's been saying so to my worst enemies.

"I don't think we summoned you yet, Princess Rowan," Heward says as I walk toward the dais. "Your mother is in a council meeting. You can't just sneak in and ask whether you may have a honey cake."

"If I wanted a honey cake, I would take one," I say, fixing him with my best queen-in-training look. "This meeting is to decide the fate of my gryphon, yes?"

"Yes," Mom says carefully, "and you will have the opportunity to defend the beast soon, Rowan."

"I'm not here to defend her," I say. "I appreciate any testimony that has attempted to absolve my gryphon of blame, but I am here to say that it isn't necessary. What the gryphon intended doesn't matter. She was loose in our kingdom and could have wreaked serious havoc. She can no longer be contained. The fact she only killed one sheep is a blessing. She frightened a child. She could have killed him if she'd become confused, and as a young monster, she is easily confused, which led to Branwyne's injury. That, too, could have been far worse."

I straighten, feeling the weight of the ebony sword on my back. "I am the royal monster hunter. Not the royal monster keeper. Nor even the royal monster scientist. I believe that my studies and my bond with beasts will help our understanding of them, but my first duty is to protect my people from the immediate danger posed by monsters. My gryphon has become a danger, and she is my responsibility. I acknowledge that she has grown much faster than I imagined, and so she must be returned to the mountains. Immediately."

I unsheathe my sword and hold it out as I bend on one knee, my head dropping. "I hereby renounce any claim on the gryphon and pledge my sword to ensuring she is returned to her proper habitat and, if that cannot be done, I will . . ." I force the words. "I will end her life swiftly and humanely."

Mom tells me to rise, her voice thick with emotion. There's pain in her eyes. But there is pride, too, her face glowing with it. That same look shines from Berinon's eyes as he stands, expressionless and ramrod-straight.

Before anyone can speak, my great-aunt and council member, Liliath, walks over and embraces me, whispering, "Your mother cannot do this, so I will. Jannah would be so proud of you."

My gaze shifts to Wilmot, who stands at the edge of the council. He meets my gaze and nods, and relief floods through me.

I've made the right choice. As hard as it was, I've done it.

"A lovely sentiment, Princess Rowan," Heward says as Liliath returns to her seat. "However, I believe I speak for the council when I say that you are proposing an expensive and dangerous expedition, when a quick and painless execution seems the obvious answer."

Liliath opens her mouth to argue, but I beat her to it.

"I understand that," I say. "And so I will complete my proposal now. As part of my trials, I need to survive in the mountains alone. However, I have never even been *in* the mountains with others. I suggest that we combine this task with my training. I will personally return the gryphon, along with Wilmot and any of my companions who wish to accompany me."

Mom's cheek ticks, and I know she's biting back an argument. Our eyes meet, and she nods. I must complete the trials. To do that, I must first have experience in the mountains. She cannot protect me from that.

"A sound plan," Liliath says. "Now, let's put it to a vote."

There's debate and discussion before the vote, as the council members work out the exact details. They quickly declare that Rhydd may not come along. He won't be happy, but he's the royal heir first and my brother second. Also, Heward will only allow one of my human companions to join the party because the kingdom can't afford to send, as he says, "extra babysitters" on this mission. I can have Wilmot, one human companion and one palace guard.

After some debate, the vote is unanimous in favor of the quest. Even Heward sees no advantage in disagreeing. Maybe he hopes I'll perish along the route, and the throne and sword will pass to his children that way.

"Princess Rowan may select her companion," Liliath says. "I'm presuming you'll want Dain, your highness?"

Before today, Dain *would* have been my choice. He's the hunter in training. But now all I hear is his mockery, all I see are his scowls, all I envision is endless days of him grumbling and snapping about being "forced" on this trip.

I'd like to travel with someone who actually wants to be there, someone who'll make it a fun adventure. Rhydd would do that, but we both understand that our future will not hold many joint adventures. Our mother—and our kingdom—cannot afford to send us both into danger.

I choose my words with care. However hurt I am at the moment, I still would never embarrass Dain.

"Dain would be the obvious choice, and I would love to have him along. He is an excellent hunter and woodsman. We are heading into the mountains, though, and we are taking the gryphon. I have a companion with mountain experience, one the gryphon knows better. I choose Alianor."

I watch Dain out of the corner of my eye. When I start speaking, his expression is blank, as he waits to hear me confirm that he'll be my choice, so he can roll his eyes and grumble in response. When I finish, he stares, just stares, and I catch a flash of hurt and confusion on his face before he looks away and squares his shoulders.

"I understand," he says gruffly. "Princess Rowan is correct. Lady Alianor is the better choice for this journey."

"Your highness?"

I turn to see Alianor. I hadn't noticed her earlier, tucked into the shadows of the audience chamber. She steps forward, her head bowed. "I am very flattered by Princess Rowan's request. I consider her a great friend, and I would dearly love to join her on this adventure, but I fear my studies occupy too much of my attention. Perhaps another time."

"Then it is settled," Liliath says. "While the princess's reasoning was sound, it appears Dain will be accompanying her after all."

I glance Dain's way. Cold eyes meet mine for one heartbeat. As he stalks from the room, I realize there's one thing worse than putting up with Dain's moods for a week in the mountains: putting up with his moods when he knows I didn't want him along.

CHAPTER THIRTEEN

That evening I'm in Courtois's private pasture, each of us keeping one wary eye on the other. I'm only here for Sunniva, because my pegasus has no concept of "private" property. Or maybe she understands the concept perfectly well. She knows this is Courtois's territory, and that the unicorn, lacking wings, can do little about her intrusion. At worst, he'll charge her, and that is a merry game indeed. After failing to impale the young pegasus with his horn—despite multiple attempts that nearly stopped my heart—he has decided to pretend he doesn't see her.

Rhydd jokes that Sunniva sticks around for the free food. She's on the same diet as Courtois, which is the best the castle has to offer. It's the grooms who spoil her. She is a pegasus, after all—a beast so rare most of our staff never expected to see one in their lifetime.

I convince myself, though, that I'm the reason she stays.

I'd like to think it's because she recognizes me as a worthy companion who will protect and love her forever. However, I'm pretty sure it's the grooming.

As a princess, I get my share of pampering. Maids wash and braid my hair. Manicures and pedicures keep my nails ballroom-ready. Weekly massages work out my training-sore muscles. I would be lying if I said I didn't love all that, so I cannot begrudge Sunniva her own princess moments.

There are few things Sunniva likes more than her daily grooming, and if I'm late, she'll come find me. Once, when I was preoccupied with an archery lesson, she snatched my arrow in midair and brought me her currycomb instead, which didn't make nearly as good a projectile.

I'm late that day, having had to attend the council meeting. As I brush her, the sun drops and my mood drops with it.

I fear my studies occupy too much of my attention. Perhaps another time.

Those words sting. Really sting. I invited a new friend on an adventure . . . and she'd rather stay home and study. Worse, Alianor is far from a conscientious student. How many times has she tried to entice *me* out for a bit of fun while I was buried in my own lessons?

Have I misinterpreted our friendship? Maybe it truly is more about getting close to "Princess Rowan" rather than "Person Rowan." Maybe I'm so desperate for a friend that I've made a fool of myself, thinking Alianor actually liked me.

And if that hurts, well, I just did the same thing to Dain, didn't I? I rejected him. Except I have reason for that. After what he said to Branwyne, I can't trust him.

Like Alianor, Dain isn't here by choice. I need Wilmot's training, and Wilmot needs the castle's medical care, and so Dain, who is Wilmot's charge, is stuck with me. Maybe that's why he's become increasingly ill-tempered. He's been forced into false friendship with a girl he doesn't actually like very much.

The more I think about it, the more I'm convinced that the only person who actually wants to spend time with me is Rhydd, who doesn't have much choice either, being my twin brother. Of course, as soon as I've decided that, Jacko climbs onto my back and purrs. Even Sunniva turns and rubs her cheek against my shoulder. I have to smile, if weakly, at that.

I reach for the mane comb and a voice says, "That is one spoiled pegasus."

My smile widens as I turn to Rhydd. "She's more of a princess than I am."

"She is indeed." He takes an apple from his pocket and feeds it to her. "So what's up with you and Dain?"

"Me and Dain? Or me and Alianor?"

He scrunches his nose. "Yeah, Alianor not wanting to join you is weird. But Clan Hadleigh is coming this week, and I wonder if her father wants her to spy on them. You know they're old enemies."

"No, they're old allies who *became* enemies, which is always worse."

"True."

Our father was Clan Hadleigh. They're river people, who know how to navigate the waterways, including those in the mountains. That brings them into conflict with Clan Bellamy, who want to be the only option for mountain guides . . .

because if you have to pick between being guided by bandits or not-bandits, the choice is clear. The only reason anyone hires Clan Bellamy is because the main river through the mountains mysteriously dried up years ago.

Rhydd bites into a second apple. Sunniva whinnies and tosses her mane . . . as I'm combing it.

"Hey!" I say. "Do you want your grooming or not?"

"She wants the apple more, and I'm teasing her." He feeds her the rest of it. "About you and Dain . . . I know things have been strained between you, but he really was the obvious companion choice for this trip."

I make a face. "I know."

"So why didn't you pick him first?"

I shrug.

"Rowan . . ." He lowers his voice. "It's just you and me here."

Yes, but the truth sounds like whining. Like running to your parents saying that someone was mean to you. Sometimes you should tell a grown-up. Other times, you should work it out yourself. I don't know which this is. When Dain complains about me to others, is he disrespecting the royal monster hunter? Or is he just complaining about another person?

Either way, if I tell Rhydd, then he's honor bound to assure me that I'm fit for my position, and that's just awkward and embarrassing.

So I don't lie—I just . . . shift the focus of the truth.

"We got into an argument about why I invited him on the khrysomallos mission. I said it was because we haven't had much time alone together lately, and he thought that meant I liked him as a *boy*. I said 'Eww.'"

Rhydd chokes on a laugh. "*Eww?* Well, now I know why he's annoyed with you." Another laugh, louder, as he shakes his head.

"I meant 'eww' to liking anyone *that* way. I explained, but he still seemed offended."

"I can't imagine why," Rhydd murmurs.

I finish Sunniva's mane and put the comb into the box. "Yes, under the circumstances, 'eww' is never the right response. Now he's offended, and I didn't need a week of him scowling and complaining."

"Fair enough."

I glance sidelong at my brother as I rearrange the grooming box.

Rhydd shrugs again. "I mean that. If he's not going to enjoy the adventure, why take him along? Others would love to go. I would."

He settles on the ground, his bad leg extended. I sit cross-legged, with the brush in hand and Jacko on my lap, wriggling with anticipation at a little grooming of his own.

"In Dain's defense," Rhydd says, "he might be getting teased about you. He's your age, and he's a boy, and people are always quick to see a potential romance there. If someone teased him, he might be uncomfortable with you. He needs to deal with it, because the teasing is going to happen. Same as I get for hanging around girls my age."

I eye him. "Like Alianor?"

His lips twitch in a smile. "Oh, it's worse with Alianor. Her father is already planning our wedding."

"Wh-what?" I sputter.

"Not exactly, but let's just say that's another reason Everard was so quick to leave his daughter here. In case she catches the eye of a future king."

His grin turns to a laugh. "You should see your face, Ro. Don't worry—I'm not in the market for a queen, and Alianor isn't in the market for a husband. But I've overheard enough to suspect her father has matchmaking in mind."

Is *that* why Alianor is staying behind? To spend more time with my brother? She obviously isn't in the market for a husband, but she *is* interested in boys already. Even if she doesn't know her father's hopes, she might still look at Rhydd and see . . .

The thought makes my head hurt. It makes me feel like a child, everyone else growing up and me staying the same.

"Don't tell her I said that," Rhydd says. "I like her as a friend, the way you like Dain. I hope she doesn't find out what her dad wants. That would make things awkward."

"I won't tell her."

"Thank you. As for Dain, maybe this trip will be good for both of you. Work out your problems. If not, well, you can always abandon him in the forest somewhere. Jacko wouldn't mind, would you, boy?"

Jacko chitters and preens under my brush, and Rhydd and I switch to the more interesting subject of my impending journey.

CHAPTER FOURTEEN

The expedition party leaves at dawn the next day. Rhydd has been given permission to accompany us to the foothills, and I wonder whether that means Alianor will join, but she only says a breezy farewell and then returns to her studies.

The first leg of this journey is a full procession. That was my idea. We will take the main roads, with Tiera on a long, lightweight chain, which allows her to be seen by villagers. This is their opportunity to view a young gryphon . . . while also seeing their royal monster hunter doing the right thing and returning her to the mountains.

Mom was very pleased with my plan. Wilmot, on the other hand, was as thrilled as Dain at the idea of parading through the villages. When he grumbled, Mom gave him leave to avoid the towns and join up with us later, and he and Dain both chose to do that.

Malric is still limping slightly, but there's no way he'll stay behind. Jacko is also with me. Sunniva is not. I took her for a pre-dawn run and then left her sleeping beside a quarter-bushel of apples, so hopefully by the time she realizes I'm gone, we'll be past the villages. We already have a gryphon, a unicorn, a warg, a jackalope, a princess and a prince. I want to put on a parade, not a theatrical performance.

When I first went to find Wilmot in the forest, it'd taken three days to get there. We're entering at a closer point this time, so it is the end of the second day before we reach the Dunnian Woods. Tamarel is shaped like a capital *D*. Along the curved edge is ocean, thick with both fog and sea monsters. There are coves where fishers ply their trade, but no one ventures far. The straight part of the *D* is the mountain range that separates us from other countries. Those mountains are also filled with fog and monsters. That explains why monster hunting is so important to Tamarel. We're literally surrounded by the beasts.

Before reaching the mountains, we need to pass through the Dunnian Woods, which thankfully are not foggy. Monsters, though? Oh yeah. The woods are full of them. Monsters, monsters, more monsters and very few people, which is why Wilmot chose to live there.

When Clan Dacre united the clans and created a monarchy, they built their castle in the middle of Tamarel. A path directly west takes a day and a half. Two days if you're slowing in every village and stopping in every town. Dain and Wilmot rejoin us after that part.

Rhydd stays with us until the third morning. Then he's homeward bound with his guards, along the quicker and quieter route. He still has Courtois, and that's enough to draw people from their homes, especially when they know the only unicorn in Tamarel is also the new mount of their future king.

Speaking of mounts, we can't ride ours into the forest. It's too thick, and the monsters make them nervous. Two guards set up camp by a stream with our horses, which they'll keep ready for our return.

Once we head into the forest, I'm alone with Dain, Wilmot and Kaylein, and I will forever be grateful for Kaylein's presence. While Rhydd was with us, she'd stayed back with her fellow guards, but since then, she's been walking with me, and we chatter away, saving me from the abyss of silence I'd fall into otherwise.

Wilmot is never exactly talkative. That'd been different when we first met and, in his mental confusion, he'd mistaken me for Jannah and been thrown back to their childhood together. Then, he'd been all easy conversation and easier smiles. Now that his head is clear, he is what I'd been warned to expect. Gruff but fair. Quiet and reserved and stingy with praise. I don't mind that in a teacher, but it would make a weeklong walk endless.

Wilmot is still more companionable than my actual companion. Now that it's the four of us, it's very obvious Dain and I are avoiding each other. So I value Kaylein's company—and Jacko's and Tiera's antics—all the more. Even Malric's plodding silence is better than Dain's active avoidance.

This is Kaylein's first time in the Dunnian Woods. Her family lives along the coast and fishes the ocean. They're Clan Montag, same as Berinon. She's the daughter of his cousin, which is how she ended up in the guard service.

As a child, Berinon had been apprenticed to a black-smith in the castle village. He saved my father's life and became Dad's bodyguard. That's unusual—royal positions are usually inherited, like most jobs. If your family farms, you become a farmer. If your family fishes, you become a fisher. If they're monster hunters or royal guards, you become that.

Berinon had been apprenticed to a blacksmith because he was big and strong, and his clan wanted him to train and bring those smithing skills home. They gladly surrendered that dream when he became a young lord's personal bodyguard. Especially when that lord grew up to marry the queen.

Kaylein tells me that Berinon is a legend in his village: the boy who went away to become a blacksmith and wound up the queen's personal bodyguard. When Kaylein was five, Berinon returned for a visit, and Kaylein declared she, too, would be a royal guard. So he made her a tin sword and taught her a few moves, all in good fun. He came back five years later to find Kaylein fully trained in sword fighting and pugilism, having sought out everyone who could teach her. He'd said if she was still interested at sixteen, he'd take her to the castle. And so she began her service.

When we stop for lunch, I regale everyone with a Jannah story. That's a guaranteed way to get Wilmot's attention. I'll tell him one, and then he'll tell me one. We do that now, as we eat and I feed Tiera. Then I stretch out against the gryphon as she naps, her belly full. Wilmot is in the midst of a chick-charney story when a distant cry has me looking up. I glance Wilmot's way and whisper, "Firebird?"

At Wilmot's nod, I scramble to my feet, unceremoniously dumping Jacko from my lap. I scan the sky and the surrounding trees. When I look at Wilmot again, a second nod grants me permission to scale one.

I take off, Jacko following. Halfway to my chosen tree, I turn to see Dain still eating his cheese and bread, gaze fixed on his meal.

"Dain?" I call.

He glances over, but in that way he's been doing, where he turns his face to me while his eyes stay elsewhere.

"Aren't you coming?" I say.

He shakes his head and returns to his lunch.

"You wanted to see one," I say. "You said that when we found the feathers last time."

Another shake of his head, and annoyance darts through me.

He really had wanted to see a firebird. He'd told me that Wilmot knew where to find them, and he'd been bugging him to go, but it was too long and dangerous a journey just to see a monster. Now there's one about to fly overhead . . . and he can't be bothered climbing a tree for a look?

When I hesitate, Wilmot says, "Go on, Rowan, or you'll miss it."

"I'll join you," Kaylein says.

We jog off. Jacko hops along at my side as Malric watches from the campfire, lying beside the sleeping Tiera.

I climb as fast as I can. Below, Kaylein tells me not to go so high, but I pretend not to hear her. I finally reach the right spot and stand on the branch, clutching the trunk as I peer

— 123 —

through a hole in the foliage. Kaylein sits on the branch below mine.

Overhead, the firebird croaks again, the call harsher than a crow's caw. Legend says that firebirds used to have a beautiful song but, when combined with their beauty, it meant people would risk their lives to steal eggs and capture live chicks. So firebirds started using this harsh croak instead.

Jannah always said that with many legends, if you dig deeply enough, you'll find a scrap of truth. With this one, she theorized that the firebirds with the worst voices were the ones who had survived to breed, and so eventually, they evolved to have that croak.

I don't care what they sound like. I only want to see one. This spring, I found three firebird feathers, now among my greatest treasures. I didn't get to see any birds, though.

I hold the tree tight as Jacko scrabbles up beside me, his semi-retractable claws digging into the bark. Jackalopes aren't climbing rodents, but he's learned because I love climbing.

Jacko hops excitedly at my feet . . . too excitedly, considering we're fifty feet above the ground. I heft him onto the branch near my shoulder. Then I grip it for extra safety, while he digs in his claws and presses against me, his gaze tracking mine.

We've barely settled when flame streaks across the midday sky. My breath catches, and I blink against tears of wonder as the firebird soars past, low enough for me to make out the flame patterns on its tail feathers. I sigh, and Jacko squeaks, and below us, Kaylein echoes my sigh.

I watch the bird disappear from view. Then I'm glancing down at Kaylein when I spot another figure, lower in the tree, and my heart leaps when I think Dain came along after all. But this figure has light hair and light skin. Wilmot. I open my mouth to call down, but he puts a finger to his lips and points up.

I squint into the sky. The firebird is gone, so I'm not sure why he's . . .

A second firebird appears, and then a third, and I stifle a gasp. A fourth. Then a fifth. A flock of firebirds? Do they always fly in flocks? I'm embarrassed to admit that I don't know. I've studied them—where they live, what they eat, their size and lifespan—but I'm not sure I've ever seen anything saying whether they flock or—

A fluttering sounds above me. I squint into the sun, suddenly bright orange as if it's setting already. Then I blink and realize it's a firebird settling into the tree. Into *this* tree, twenty feet over my head.

I presume it didn't realize I'm here. Then it hops along the branch to peer down at me. It's a young bird, as curious as I am.

It's careful, having landed well above us. For a young bird that has probably never left the forest and mountains, seeing a human would be a very rare event, so it doesn't fear a poacher's arrows or darts.

The beast cranes its long neck down . . . and Jacko and I crane our much shorter ones up. Below, Kaylein giggles. I'm sure we look giggle-worthy. At least she can't see my mouth gaping. I stare at the firebird, taking in its flame-colored feathers and brilliant head comb, and it stares back at me. Then it cocks its head and croaks.

"Hello," I say.

It pulls back sharply, looking so surprised that I chuckle, and it shakes its head at the sound. Then it bends again.

I talk to it, half speech and half croon. Jacko chatters, and the firebird peers at him and makes a noise that sounds like an imitation of his chatter.

The firebird sidesteps and shakes. Two feathers fall, and I watch them drop like flames, spinning to the dark earth below. "Thank you," I say. "We'll make good use of those. I only wish I had something to give you in return."

The firebird lowers its head and croaks, beady eyes studying me. Then a larger firebird circles over the treetop, clearly a parent telling this half-grown bird to stop dawdling. I can't tell whether the newcomer is male or female—both sexes have the same plumage. This one has a truly glorious train, and as it waggles its glowing tail feathers, I stare, transfixed.

The young firebird is not nearly as impressed by the display. Even when the older bird half-fans its tail mid-flight and my breath catches, the young one ignores it. The older bird flies down and gives it a poke, and the younger one squawks its indignation.

A harder poke. The young firebird bristles and fans its own tail, and they face off on the branch, the parent squawking and shaking its tail while the juvenile does the same. As they bicker and fluff their plumage, feathers fall, as if the younger one is molting, and with each one that drops, I salivate. I'm almost tempted to let them keep arguing . . . and keep dropping those glorious feathers. But finally, I call up, "You really should go. The others won't wait."

The parent gives one final hard poke at the child, and with a last indignant squawk, the younger one lifts off. I watch them go, streaks of fire against the sky. Then Kaylein taps my boot.

"You don't want to collect those feathers, do you, your highness?" she asks, her dark eyes dancing with a grin. "Just checking before I climb down and gather them all."

I race her, grabbing feathers as we descend. At the bottom, we both spot a tail feather and charge toward it, only to have Wilmot scoop it up and stick it into his hair band. Jacko leaps onto Wilmot's leg, climbs up, and is reaching to snatch the tail feather when the hunter pulls him away.

"Don't you dare, bunny," he says. "Get your own." He sets Jacko down with a tap on his rump, and the jackalope gives one affronted snort before dashing off and grabbing a smaller feather for himself. As he prances with it, head held high, Kaylein and I dart about, gathering the rest.

"Six!" I say when I'm done.

"Four," Kaylein says, holding up her prizes. "Unless the royal princess demands her loyal subject turn over the bounty."

I roll my eyes, and she grins and pokes a couple into her tight curls. When we get back to camp, Dain is still there, whittling an arrow. I walk over and hand him two feathers.

"For the fletching on those," I say. "Now we'll both have night arrows."

Dain holds them, his hand frozen there as if he's struggling for a response. Wilmot walks over, plucks them from Dain's hand and gives them back to me.

"No, Rowan," he says. "Dain chose to stay behind. If he doesn't take the risks, he can't collect the bounty."

I want to say there was no risk. Wilmot knows that—what he really means is that I shouldn't reward Dain for his sulk. Dain mutters something and pushes to his feet.

"Can we go now?" he says. "If the princess is going to stop for every pretty monster—"

"No," Wilmot says, his voice even but firm.

Dain flushes and scuffs his boot against the dirt.

"Tiera needed her nap," Wilmot says, nodding to the sleeping gryphon. "She's still a baby, and we cannot push her. We'll break camp, and once she stirs, we can set out."

CHAPTER FIFTEEN

It's a quiet afternoon walk. Tiera's initial excitement over entering the forest faded as she realized there was no cart to ride nor any villagers to throw her dried meat. When Wilmot decides she's had enough walking, it's not yet dark. I expect Dain to complain. He only mumbles something about it being a good time to hunt and stalks off to do just that. I'd have loved to go along, but I certainly wasn't invited.

As I watch Dain go, Wilmot clears his throat. I brace for him to say something about Dain. Instead, he says, "Twilight is indeed the best time for hunting. Dain can catch tomorrow's breakfast, and I'll teach Tiera some tricks for catching her dinner. You, too, Rowan. You might be excellent with a sword, but you will starve if left in the forest too long." He glances at Kaylein. "I presume you wouldn't have that problem."

"It depends on whether there's water nearby," she says. "I can fish for my supper. Otherwise, I'm with Rowan." Kaylein hefts her sword. "I can only take down a deer if it runs straight at me."

"Then it's hunting lessons for all. Good thing we stopped early."

That's how we spend our evening. I appreciate the lessons for myself, of course, but I appreciate them for Tiera even more. When I fret about her, Wilmot reminds me of how easily she killed that sheep. We both know, though, that there's a big difference between a domestic sheep and a wild one. Food isn't just going to walk up to Tiera in the wild.

One reason we stopped here is that there's a nearby stream. That also means fish, and Kaylein spends part of the evening showing Tiera how to fish—and even imparting some new tips to Wilmot.

Being half bird, Tiera is well equipped for fishing. Kaylein only needs to catch and feed her a couple before she starts grabbing her own. Well, after some time spent splashing in the water, shrieking because, weirdly, when a gryphon splashes and beats the water with her wings, the fish swim *away* from her.

Kaylein demonstrates better techniques. In the end, though, it's Malric who deserves the credit. He sits on the bank, watching the fish pass and then scooping them up on one giant paw. Tiera tries that with her talons, and soon she's poised like a raptor, snatching out fish with beak and claws, eating until she can barely toddle back to camp.

Dain's there when we return. He's caught a few grouse, and we add that to our fish. I suggest drying the meat overnight, so it lasts past breakfast. Dain grumbles that means someone will need to keep the fire going, but Wilmot agrees it's an excellent idea. He shows me how to set up a drying rack while Dain stalks off to his sleeping spot.

I wake to the nudges of a small fuzzy nose, whiskers tickling my cheek. Jacko chitters softly as my eyes open. I glance around. Kaylein lies at my left side, Malric on my right. Both are deeply asleep. So is Tiera, beyond Malric, curled into a ball and peeping in slumber.

Jacko bops me with his antlers. I rub my eyes and stifle a yawn.

"What's up?" I whisper.

He bounds over to Malric, and he clears the warg by a good handsbreadth, but Malric's yellow eyes still open, and his jaws snap at the jackalope's tail. Jacko ignores him and looks back, chittering softly, telling me to follow.

I groan. I presume he needs to answer the call of nature, but he isn't a baby and can do that perfectly fine without an escort. Even as annoyance ripples through me, though, I see the dark and unfamiliar Dunnian Woods, and I must admit that even I wouldn't be eager to wander in there alone at night.

Malric lumbers to his feet and starts after the jackalope, with a growl tossed over his shoulder as if to say, "I'll take him. You stay."

Malric nudges Jacko, and the jackalope squeaks a protest, glancing at me. I look toward the fire, burning low. There's a figure seated beside it with his back to me, and I only need to squint a little to see that it's Dain. He sits with his knees up, poking at the fire. The crackle and pop of it must drown out any noise we're making, and he doesn't turn even as I push to my feet.

I start toward him. That's what I would have done before this trip. I'd go over and tell him Jacko needs a short trip into the woods so he knows where I've gone. Now I stare at his back while he pokes the fire and all I imagine is him grumbling about me "playing" with animals.

I consider waking Wilmot and Kaylein, but when my mother first sent me to find Wilmot, she'd let me go into these woods accompanied only by Malric and Jacko, as I'm doing now. No reason to disturb anyone else for a call of nature.

Still, I set out with my sword in hand. This is the Dunnian Woods. We may not have spotted many animals or monsters—they smell Malric and Tiera and steer clear—but we've seen plenty of scat and prints. Wargs, warakins, even a set of feline prints that may belong to a cath palug. Then there are the regular animal predators—wolves, bears and big cats.

We walk about fifty paces into the forest, Jacko in the lead. I'm opening my mouth to tell him we've gone quite far enough when a soft cry stops me in my tracks. It's the cry of a wounded creature, faint, as if it barely has the energy to make any sound at all. Jacko's ears swivel, tracking the noise as he chitters.

The cry is close by, so I continue forward, following Jacko through a forest that otherwise stays silent. I glance at Malric, ready for him to growl at me to head back, but he keeps going, his ears perked as he peers into the woods. A couple of times, he cocks his head to listen. Jacko does the same, his ears swiveling with each whimper, his nose working, telling me that whatever lies ahead, he doesn't recognize it. Neither creature seems alarmed, though. Just curious.

The cry grows louder. Jacko's nose twitches madly. Malric lifts his muzzle to sample the air, and he grunts in frustration. And then, just as I'm slowing to consider our next move, the sound stops.

I stop, too, a mere heartbeat before Malric snags my sleeve in his teeth. Jacko sits on my boots, and whether that's to stop me or protect me, he's obviously not eager to go on. Neither beast, however, urges retreat.

They don't recognize the scent or the cry of whatever lies ahead. Malric has spent enough time out here with Jannah to know any normal forest dweller. Could it be a monster? A *rare* monster?

The thought sets my heart tripping with excitement. Last spring, I saw a jba-fofi—saw it far more closely than anyone wants to see a giant spider. According to our books, jba-fofi are either completely made up or long extinct. Yet Wilmot and Dain knew they were in the forest, so it wasn't as if I was the first person to *ever* see one. What if this is a monster *no one* has ever seen? My heart trips as my mind races through all the possibilities, mysterious beasts relegated to the realm of lore and legend.

I shiver with anticipation and reach down to lift Jacko off my feet. He growls. That startles me so much I stumble back, and he chitters in apology. Then he peers into the forest, ears back, growling louder, as if demonstrating that it wasn't *me* he'd growled at.

I look at Malric, who only chuffs and lies down, head on his paws. Okay, so whatever's out there no longer worries *him*. And Jacko doesn't seem truly worried. He seems annoyed. Huh.

Jacko continues to growl, his gaze fixed to my left. As I tighten my grip on my sword, two round balls of yellow appear, tripping through the forest. I glance down at Malric. His yellow eyes will reflect light, but they don't glow. Even a cat's only reflect existing light, and there's little of that with the moon sliding behind cloud.

The eyes continue my way, bobbing oddly, like Chikako when she walks. They're set close together, suggesting a small animal or beast. My ears pick up only the soft rustle of late summer foliage underfoot.

Jacko has settled back, cleaning his paw, studiously ignoring the approaching creature. Malric has his eyes shut. What could—?

"Haven't you caused enough trouble already, princess?" The voice says *princess* with a familiar edge that twists honorific into insult.

"Dain?" I say.

The yellow eyes rise . . . and turn into a lantern's glow, the flame duplicated in its reflection off the glass. Dain lifts the lantern beside his head, letting me see it's him. I sheathe my sword.

"I thought that warg was supposed to keep you from wandering off," he says as he glares at Malric.

"He's a bodyguard, not a nanny," I say.

"Well, then, you need a nanny."

"No." I keep my tone even. "Malric's job is to protect me and to warn me of danger. I thought Jacko needed to relieve himself and was afraid to go into the forest alone, but it seems he's concerned about a wounded creature."

Dain peers into the forest. "What wounded creature?"

"The noises stopped. Malric and Jacko can smell it, but they don't seem to recognize the scent."

"Which means you should turn back. We don't need you running off. We're all taking a risk out here to return that gryphon you just had to have."

I bristle. "Yes, of course. I *had* to have it. As a pet, right? That's my true calling. Royal zookeeper."

He doesn't seem to hear, barreling on with, "My point is that we're here for you, and you can't sneak off into the forest following every strange sound."

"I didn't sneak—"

"I was awake. You could not have missed me when you left."

"I didn't miss you. I chose not to speak to you."

He stiffens, something unreadable flitting over his face before he finds his scowl. "Yes, princess, I am very aware that I am here uninvited. I'm terribly sorry to inconvenience you with my presence, but I had no say in the matter. Believe me, I asked—begged—Wilmot to leave me behind. The council spoke, and we're stuck with each other."

"On this journey, yes. At this moment, no." I turn to walk away.

Dain strides into my path. "Back to camp, princess."

"That's where I'm going. I'm circling around you to return to camp and get Wilmot. I know what I'm doing, Dain. I *am* the royal monster hunter, whether you think I deserve that title or not."

His brows knit in a split-second of confusion before he smooths them out and says, "As your hunter, I'm responsible for you."

"No, you aren't, and really, I don't see why you'd bother. Doesn't it make a better story if I traipse off into the forest and befriend some woodland creature? Proof that I'm only fit to cuddle beasts? That would help Branwyne's cause."

This time, he doesn't bother to undo that brow knot of annoyed confusion. "And why would I want that?"

"Why indeed." I step forward, my face a handsbreadth from his. "No, I didn't choose you for this adventure, Dain. Do you know why? Because I spent twelve years of my life training to be queen, and the biggest lesson I learned was to surround myself with people I can trust. I cannot trust you."

He blanches. "What?"

"I understand that you don't think I'm a proper monster hunter yet. That's fine. I need to earn your respect. But whether you plan to become one of my monster hunters or not, you are acting as one now, and if you have a problem with me, it stays in the troop. You can tell *me* that I'm only fit to be a royal zookeeper. You can decide not to follow me because of that. What you *can't* do is remain in my troop while telling others what you think of me, giving my enemies ammunition against my family. If that's the side you're on, then get on it and stay on it. You cannot do that and expect to be my companion. You certainly can't expect to be my friend."

He stares at me. Just stares. Then his eyes widen as he breathes, "Branwyne."

"You were *there*, Dain. You heard what she said."

"I didn't . . ." He swallows and tries again, only getting as far as "I . . ."

"Did you say those words? That I was a girl playing with her pets? Unfit to be anything but royal zookeeper?"

"It . . . it wasn't exactly . . ." His cheeks flush dark, and he swallows again before straightening. "I made a mistake, princess, but it wasn't like that. I . . . I wouldn't—I'd never . . ."

As he stammers, leaves rustle overhead. The hairs on my neck rise, and I squint up into the darkness, seeing nothing but the trees, still in the quiet night.

"Rowan?" Dain says.

I lift a finger to my lips, my gaze still on the trees as my hand brushes the hilt of my sword.

"I know you're angry," he says, his voice softer. "But I want to explain. Or try to explain . . ."

Something moves in the trees. Red eyes peer down as Dain keeps talking, oblivious. I leap forward, my hand covering his mouth. He jumps back . . . and something drops, gray-brown fur falling onto him with an unearthly screech as needle-like fangs slash at his throat.

CHAPTER SIXTEEN

I swing at the beast. It's too close quarters to draw my sword, so my fist responds, on a collision course with that saucer-sized head. Jacko gives his battle scream, cut off mid-note as he springs, his body flying through the air, teeth sinking into the beast's haunch. As the creature falls, my fist grazes its head . . . and slams into Dain's jaw.

Dain staggers back as another gray-brown beast drops. This one lands on me, but I manage to elbow it away from my neck. Dain grabs it as flailing claws scrape my cheek. I swing to look for the first creature, only to see Malric holding it under one giant paw, Jacko beside the beast, crowing in victory.

Dain holds the other beast out at arm's length. It looks like a children's toy. A stuffed bear, all fluffy brown fur frosted with gray. Its ears are perfect rounded half-circles on each side of its face. It has an oversized black nose and a fuzzy white belly. It should be adorable, which makes it even more horrifying. It's like falling asleep cuddling a toy bear and tumbling into a nightmare where it attacks you, all beady red eyes, curved black claws and razor-sharp teeth.

"Dropbear," Dain and I say in unison.

It's not actually a bear. It's a marsupial, like an opossum. It's called a dropbear because it looks like a toy bear. And it drops. From trees. Onto unsuspecting prey.

"Have you ever seen one before?" I ask.

He shakes his head, still holding out the gnashing, flailing beast. His gaze moves to those inch-long claws, and he shudders. "Wilmot says he and Jannah ran into some once and . . ." He closes his eyes, wincing. "And they were lured in by the sound of crying. Wilmot thought it was a wounded beast." He opens his eyes. "I'm sorry, Rowan. You said that's what you heard, and it never registered."

"Because dropbears are, thankfully, very rare, and they don't come this far from the mountains. Jannah probably mentioned the crying in our lessons, and I forgot it, which is unforgivable. I do remember her saying . . ."

I trail off as my gaze lifts to the trees.

"Saying what?" Dain prompts.

"That they travel in packs," I whisper . . . as I stare up at a half-dozen pairs of red eyes.

As Dain looks, his dropbear twists, taking advantage of his momentary distraction. I yell a warning, swinging at the beast, but it already has its fangs embedded in his hand.

I grab the dropbear and pry open its jaws as it screeches. When it suddenly lets go of Dain, I stumble back. I trip over

Jacko, who's leaping to my rescue, and I fall flat on my back, the dropbear rising over me, jaws opening impossibly wide. It screams, and I'm swinging at it when Dain grabs the beast by the scruff of the neck and hurls it into the forest . . . just as another one drops onto his back.

I snatch that dropbear and yank it off Dain. Another falls, and I stagger out of the way just in time. I throw the one I have and yank out my sword, but they're dropping all around us.

"Run!" I shout. "Just run!"

Dain has his dagger out, slashing at the beasts as he wheels toward camp. I shout, "No!" but the screams of the monsters drown me out. I grab the back of Dain's shirt and dig in my heels, shouting, "We can't lead them to camp!"

Dain only hesitates a second before changing course. He tries to take the lead, but I'm the one with the sword. I shoulder him behind me and swing my weapon, which clears a path better than his dagger ever could.

Malric stays in the rear, grabbing dropbears and pitching them headlong into the forest. Jacko races beside him. When the jackalope tries to dart ahead to me, Malric grabs *him*, keeping Jacko safely at his side, which I appreciate. As good a fighter as the jackalope is becoming, we haven't gotten far in our "how to protect Rowan without tripping her" training. Fortunately, the dropbears are ignoring the jackalope in favor of the larger threats.

I don't know how many dropbears there are. They all look the same—gray-brown fur, coal-red eyes and razor-sharp teeth flashing in and out of the darkness as they charge us, only to be driven back by my sword or Malric's fangs or Dain's boot.

There's blood. Some of ours. More of theirs. I'm not trying to kill the dropbears, but I can't actively try to *avoid* killing them either. While they may be tiny compared to a warg or wyvern or warakin, they are deadlier than all of those, a frenzied swarm that will not quit until they have their prey.

As I keep moving forward, keep fighting, Jannah's story comes back to me. She did say they'd been lured into a trap—she just hadn't specified how. That was the only dropbear swarm Jannah had ever encountered, and she didn't like to talk about it. They'd lost two hunters that day. Experienced monster hunters.

Recalling that story, I do not hesitate with my sword. I slash and I move, as fast as I can. With each step, we're heading deeper into the woods, and I'm aware of that, too—the danger of it, those we're leaving ever farther behind. We cannot risk leading the dropbears to camp, though. We must keep going until we've driven them off.

I'm fighting and moving, my gaze on my path, when something drops into it, hitting the ground with a thud that reverberates through me. It's a dropbear ... only it's *huge*. It is twice the size of the others, standing four feet tall, a grizzled and scarred old beast with one milky eye.

The alpha dropbear doesn't charge. It doesn't need to. It stands on its hind legs and brandishes claws as long as my fingers. That huge jaw opens, and all I see are teeth. Jagged, horrible teeth in a jaw that stretches wider and wider as the creature screeches a guttural keening.

Malric snarls, and the beast rocks forward, as if to attack. I can't see the warg, but I know he checks himself. He cannot charge without the dropbear doing the same, and the dropbear will reach me before Malric does.

The dropbear swipes its claws against the air. That is a challenge. I know it is.

Come here, little monster hunter. See if you can slice me before I slice you.

I test my grip on my sword.

"Rowan?" Dain murmurs behind me. "Let me help you."

"I've got this." I adjust my grip, sword raised.

"You don't need to prove anything to me."

"I'm not. I'm getting us out of here. Which means getting us past this beast."

"Let me help. Please."

I heft my sword.

"Rowan," he says, voice low. "You can trust me. I swear you can. I would never—" He swallows. "Whatever I've done, I didn't mean to betray you. I wouldn't do that."

I wriggle my right foot, checking my footing.

"Please," he says. "May I help you?"

I hesitate. Pride demands that I prove I deserve to hold the ebony sword. If there had been anyone else with us, I might have let pride win. But I've already lost Dain's confidence. My duty now is to protect my companions, both human and beast.

I dip my chin in agreement.

He exhales audibly. "Thank you. All right. On the count of three, drop to one knee. Your right knee. Okay?"

I tense, my shoulders stiffening. He's not just asking me to accept help. He's putting me in a weakened position.

"Rowan, please. Do you trust me?"

I don't answer. I can't.

"Will you trust me right now?" he says. "In this one thing? Trust that I will do nothing to hurt you. Please."

"Count," I say, more grunt than word.

"Keep hold of your sword. Just drop to your right knee. Do it on one." He inhales. "Three. Two. One."

I drop and something flies over my shoulder. Silver winks in the moonlight. Dain's dagger hits the dropbear in the chest, and the beast staggers back, shrieking. Then the forest erupts. Every dropbear that had fallen silent watching its alpha now sees him fall, and the forest bursts into a cacophony of crashing branches and screaming dropbears as they all rush at us.

"Run!" I say.

I run straight at the fallen dropbear blocking our path. I manage to wrench out the dagger before Dain shoves me, and then I keep going, running full out. A yipping sounds above the screams. The dropbears shriek louder, as if the sound drives them to a frenzy. Several break off and run that way, crashing through the forest.

"Left!" a human voice shouts. "Go left!"

I do, mostly because that yipping—and the voice—come from the right, which is where half the surviving dropbear pack is running to. The opposite direction seems like a very fine idea.

"House!" Dain shouts.

I think I've misheard. I must have. But then he pokes my shoulder, turning my attention to a structure of some kind. I veer toward it. The forest opens up, and ahead there is indeed a building. I can't quite tell *what* it is—I'm running through a moonlit forest, pursued by dropbears, the world rushing by too fast for me to get a good look at anything. It's a structure with walls and a roof, and that is enough.

I check that Jacko is still with us. I know Malric is—I can't miss the pound of his paws. When I look back, the warg glowers, as if knowing very well I'm checking for my jackalope and taking offense that I might presume he'd leave Jacko behind. The jackalope is right there, running at Malric's side.

The building is in a clearing, and as soon as we enter that open space, the dropbears fall back, yipping and shrieking, uneasy about leaving the forest. I race to the house and lift my hand to knock, but Dain catches it.

"This is one case where a princess may intrude on her subjects without knocking," he says, casting a pointed look toward the dropbears cautiously emerging from the safety of the forest.

Dain grabs the knob and twists. Nothing happens. He throws his shoulder against the door, and I rap on the frame as loud as I can, calling, "Hello!"

Please help, as we are currently under attack by dropbears.

Somehow, I don't think that would encourage anyone to open a door.

I bang louder and shout louder. The dropbears may have hesitated at the tree line, like warriors reaching the end of their defensive wall, but they're venturing out, a silent wave of fur and fang rolling over the night-dark grass.

Malric growls, as if to say, "Hurry it up, humans."

I spot a window, shuttered tight. I'm about to run and try it when I notice a latch high atop the door.

A dropbear yowls, and they all answer, a trumpet blast before they charge.

CHAPTER SEVENTEEN

I leap to grab the latch and flick it open, and I'm about to warn Dain when he slams his shoulder into the door. It smacks open, he falls in and we tumble after him. Well, I tumble, and then Malric barrels into me, and I twist out of the way, and Malric falls onto Dain as I slap the door shut and lean against it.

A dropbear hits the door hard, and the wood smacks against me.

"Dain!" I shout.

Jacko races over and braces himself against the door, which I appreciate but . . .

Another dropbear hits it, and then another, the door banging open an inch with each hit, my boots sliding across the rough wood floor as I scramble to get my footing. I squint beyond us. The building is pitch-black.

"Dain! Need some help here!"

"Under . . . a . . . warg," Dain grunts from the darkness. "Malric . . . get . . . your . . ."

A scrabble of nails on wood, and then Malric is pushing against me, nudging me aside, telling me he has it. Still holding the door shut, I squint along the frame. I see a door latch just as Dain strikes a fire stick. As I slap the latch shut, I spot another near the base and fix it into place.

"Princess . . ." Dain says, his voice low.

"I think this will hold," I say as I test the latches. "The fact that they weren't locked—and the fact that no one has come screaming from bed—suggests nobody's in here."

"Turn around slowly, please."

I do . . . and there is a dropbear right behind me. I blink at the beast. It must have tumbled in before I got the door shut. Now it rises on its hind legs, gnashing its teeth with glee as it realizes it is the sole member of its pack to make it through the door.

Jacko hisses and shakes his antlers. Malric steps up beside the dropbear and pulls to his full height. Dain moves forward, and I ease my sword from its sheath. The dropbear casts one slow look around and realizes . . .

Well, it realizes that it's the sole member of its pack to make it through the door.

It is alone, trapped in here with us, and it's a young dropbear, barely bigger than Jacko.

The dropbear gives one shaky snarl and wheels, diving deep into the shadows. There's a skitter of claws, and when Dain lifts his fire stick, the dropbear freezes, poised on an exposed rafter. It takes one careful step along the beam, red eyes fixed on us.

"Uh-uh," I say. "You really think we're going to let you creep along that beam so you can drop on us? Think again, bear-beast."

I stride toward it, sword raised. It takes one look at the blood-flecked blade and scampers into the roof corner, chittering to itself.

"Stay there," I say. "When the coast is clear, Dain will help you down."

"What?" Dain says, his voice rising two octaves.

I sheathe my sword. Then I take the dagger from my side, the one I'd retrieved from the alpha dropbear. I return it to Dain.

"You'll need that," I say. "But please don't use it on the dropbear. You should be able to just carry the beast back to camp. It's small enough."

"What?" His voice cracks as he stares at me.

I wave at the beast. "It's a young dropbear. I'm taking it home, of course. Unless you want it." I peer at him thoughtfully. "Do you want it? You probably should have a bodyguard of your own, and a baby dropbear seems like a fine idea. It looks very cuddly. Except for the sharp parts."

"She's teasing you, Dain," a voice says.

We all give a start. Well, all except Malric, who only grunts, as if he'd known all along that we weren't alone.

Alianor walks in from a back room.

"What are you—" I begin.

"Rowan is joking about the dropbear," she says to Dain. "Though personally, I think she *should* make you carry it home. You owe her. A baby dropbear will do."

"Something tells me he wouldn't survive the transport," I say.

"The dropbear?"

"Dain."

Alianor shrugs. "Accidents happen. At least you'd have a dropbear."

Dain scowls at her. "What are you doing here?"

She jerks a thumb toward the back of the cabin. "There's a rear door. Don't worry. I latched it."

"I mean what are you doing in the Dunnian Woods. Instead of back at the castle."

"Studying," I say.

Her brows lift. "So you *did* believe that? Rhydd said you did, but I figured you were playing along."

She moves into the room and falls onto an overstuffed chair before continuing. "I guess Dain isn't the only one who needs to apologize, then."

"I need to apologize?" Dain says. "For what?"

"Uh, everything?" Alianor says.

I take the fire stick box from Dain and light a lantern in the corner. I move it under the dropbear, so we can keep an eye on it. As I draw near, Malric growls.

"I'm not going to walk beneath the beast," I say as I push the lantern into place. "You really think I'm a very stupid princess, don't you?" I glance at the warg. "Don't answer that."

He grunts and pads over, taking up position between me and the dropbear. As I return to Alianor and Dain, I glance around the half-lit shadows. It's a small cabin, with a fireplace, a sleeping cot and a few chairs. Dried vegetables and herbs hang from the ceiling. My gaze catches on a particular herb, oddly shaped, before I turn my attention back to Alianor.

"Sorry," I say. "Go on."

"I was apologizing for presuming you'd understood my ploy. You asked me to join you, and I said no because I knew Dain should come along, as a monster hunter. I knew Dain *wanted* to come."

She shoots a hard look Dain's way as his mouth opens to protest. He shuts it, and she continues, "You picked me because he's been a jerk."

"Jerk?" Dain says.

"Sorry," Alianor says. "He's been a *boy*. Boys are sometimes jerks, and if they're Dain, *sometimes* means 'almost always.'" She ignores his squawk of protest. "If you went without him, he'd sulk for the next decade. No one needs that. So I bowed out, knowing I could follow later. Which I did."

"Rowan's only supposed to have one companion," Dain says. "That was Heward's rule."

"That was Heward also being a jerk. His argument was that more companions would mean more guards, which the castle couldn't afford to spare. Since I don't require a guard, it's fine. Also, this is training for her trials—not an actual trial."

"Does anyone know you're here?" I ask.

"Rhydd does. He'll tell your mother that he warned me it was a dangerous idea—which he did—but that I insisted—which I did." She leans back in the chair. "I'm Clan Bellamy. No one expects me to do as I'm told. I asked

Rhydd to come along, but he was being responsible." She rolls her eyes at the word.

"He has to be," I say. "He's the future king."

"Oh, I know. I understand, and I even approve. Just don't tell him I said that. I admire his sense of responsibility, even when it's inconvenient. It'd have been fun to have him along, though."

"It would have," I say. "But I'm glad I have you." I glance at Dain and quickly add, "Both of you."

Dain retreats into the shadows, mumbling under his breath.

"That's Dain-speak for 'I'm glad to be here too, princess,'" Alianor says.

"No," I say with an awkward smile. "He's definitely not glad to be *here*, trapped in an abandoned cabin, surrounded by dropbears."

Dain grunts at that and relaxes onto a stool. "Any idea what we're going to do about that, your highness?"

"Ransom that one." I point at the young dropbear. I walk to the window and push against the shutter, which opens a crack, before I yell, "We have one of your own! We will trade him for safe passage. Please appoint a representative to discuss this on your behalf."

Alianor snickers. Dain blinks, frowning, before catching Alianor's laugh and shaking his head.

"Joke," I say. "Apparently Malric isn't the only one with a low regard for my intelligence."

"Or perhaps your jokes just aren't that funny, especially when we're surrounded by killer bears."

"They aren't bears. They're marsupials. You can tell by the pouch. Just grab that one up there, look at its belly, and you'll see—"

"If you're considering switching your job to royal jester, princess, may I suggest you stick with monster hunting? At least you show some aptitude for that."

"*Some* aptitude? I'll take that as a compliment."

"If I didn't think you made a good royal monster hunter, I wouldn't be sitting here waiting for you to come up with a plan, would I?"

"Unless you're just waiting for me to come up with a plan so you can say it's horrible and proves I don't deserve the job."

I meant to say that lightly, teasing. Instead, it comes out with an edge that has Alianor straightening, her gaze shifting between us. Tense silence stretches, and I tense with it, ready for the insult that is sure to follow. Dain sits there, completely still except for his jaw, working as he considers responses.

Finally, he murmurs, "I never said you don't deserve the job, Rowan." His gaze lifts to mine. "*Ever*. I have made mistakes, but I would not say that."

Now I'm the one fidgeting, feeling their gazes heavy on me. I clear my throat. "All right. Step one is to count the surviving dropbears. We can hear them out there, and it sounds as if we're surrounded by dozens, but the pack wasn't that big. So I need a firm count before we plan anything. The windows are latched on the inside. Open with care."

As we count, I keep getting distracted by the cabin itself. The way the herbs are tied bothers me. They're arranged in odd wreath-like shapes.

When I catch Dain eyeing one, I murmur, "Do you recognize that design?"

"No," he says. "But I don't like it. It reminds me . . ."

His shoulder rolls, as if throwing off the memory.

"Reminds you of what?"

He shakes his head and walks to another window to continue his count. I want to pursue it, but I know this isn't the time. What matters isn't what's in this cabin—it's what's outside.

Once we've completed our count—either six or seven, plus the alpha—I say, "I don't want to kill them." I avoid looking Dain's way—I don't need to see his reaction to that—and hurry on with, "They can't be left here, of course. I'm not sure why they're this far east, but we can't risk them continuing on to Tamarel. Once we get home, we'll need to launch an expedition to drive them back. The council may decide they all need to be killed, but we also need to know what drove them from the mountains, so I'd rather not eliminate the entire pack now."

"Too dangerous anyway," Dain says, which surprises me. I expected a sarcastic comment about my not wanting to kill the poor beasties. When he agrees, I falter before continuing.

"If we need to kill them to escape, then I'm okay with that," I say, "but I think it can be avoided. In fact, I think we can even make it easier for the monster hunters later. Right now, we're trapped in this cabin. But what if we flipped that? The young one came in easily enough. What if we . . ."

I trail off, feeling my cheeks heat as I realize that what I'm proposing may sound ridiculous.

"Lure the rest in?" Alianor says. "Preferably without trapping ourselves alongside them?"

I nod. "There's food, so they won't starve. They may break out again before I can return with the hunters, but at least it'd give us a chance to escape."

"They'll need water, too," Dain says. "And we'll need to post a warning."

"*Dropbears inside?*" Alianor says with a chuckle. "I'm not sure anyone would believe a sign like that, but at least they might pause long enough not to throw open the door." She looks at me. "How do you propose we get them in?"

"Well, first we need bait . . ."

CHAPTER EIGHTEEN

"I know you two love to compete," Alianor says. "But this is ridiculous."

"Do you have a better idea?" I ask as I lay a towel over the small stool.

"I do," Dain says, "but Alianor refuses to help."

"Yeah, sorry," Alianor says. "Clan Bellamy may not be Tamarel's most loyal subjects, but I draw the line at knocking the princess over the head and tying her up."

"Really?" Dain says. "Because I seem to recall you helped your clan put Rowan in a *cage*."

"I didn't help. It was just my idea." She turns to me. "I'm not going to tie you up to keep you from playing bait, but Dain's right—he should take the risk here."

"It is the job of the royal monster hunter to accept the most dangerous role in any mission," I say. "Clan Dacre made a pact with Tamarel, promising to risk our lives keeping them safe—"

"Ugh, stop. You're as bad as your brother. Fine. Fight it out."

I kneel in front of the stool with my elbow on it, hand raised. Dain grumbles but kneels on his side and grips my hand.

"You won't win, princess," he says. "A sword fight, yes, but arm wrestling? That's no contest."

"Then why are you trying to talk me out of it?"

"Because I don't want to embarrass you."

I snort and adjust my grip. "Referee?"

Alianor sighs. "Fine. Three, two, one. Go!"

We grapple, grunting. It's been two years since I've beaten Rhydd in arm wrestling, but Dain's smaller, more wiry, and I hope to stand a better chance. I might, too, if I can outlast him. That's the trick here. Stamina over brute strength. Just—

Jacko leaps onto Dain's back, digging in all his claws with an ear-splitting screech. I slam Dain's hand down as he yowls. Jacko scrambles over to me, climbing to perch on my shoulders and chitter at Dain.

"*That* does not count," Dain says, turning to Alianor. "I demand a ruling."

"A rematch," I say, flexing my arm.

"No, he's right," Alianor says. "Game forfeited to Dain, on account of jackalope interference."

I argue that Jacko was just confused, thinking I was under attack. It's no use. This gives them the excuse to do what they wanted—let Dain play bait.

We've set up the cabin as best we can. We pulled a half-full rain barrel in from the back and filled every bowl and basin with drinking water. We opened an underfloor pantry filled with dried meat. We'll obviously need to reimburse the owner for their losses, but the building should contain the dropbears until an expedition returns to deal with them. Hopefully, I'll be part of that expedition.

Once the cabin is prepared and secured, we take up our positions. Alianor and I flank the front door. I have Dain's bow ready—this is why it made sense for him to stand guard, and me to be the bait, but no one listened to that reasoning.

Alianor has her short sword, and Dain holds his dagger. Malric stands beside me, and Jacko's settled on my feet. Throughout it all, the young dropbear has watched with intense interest from the rafters, but it's made no move to leave its safe spot.

Now it's time for *us* to leave *our* safe spot. Dain opens the rear door and steps through, his boots tramping loudly on the tiny porch. Outside, the dropbears had gone silent, but hearing Dain, they yip and yowl and race toward the house. A few go overtop, their paws clattering against the wood. They're planning to drop on Dain from the roof. I open my mouth to shout a warning, but Alianor's hand claps over it.

"Don't *you* underestimate *him* either," she whispers. Then she's on her feet, pulling me along as I grab Jacko and we yank open the unlatched front door. We slip out, and I wheel just in time to see Dain racing through the house, pursued by dropbears.

Dain makes it through the front door, and I yank it shut and throw the latch as Alianor's footfalls thump around the side of the house. Dain takes off after Alianor.

The rear door smacks shut, and the latch clanks just as the dropbears inside hit the front door, their bodies slamming into it.

I lean against the door, but Malric pushes me aside and takes my spot, his glare warning me against trying to move him. Inside, the thud of bodies stops as the dropbears reverse course and run to the door they'd entered through, *thump-thump-thump*-ing against it.

I check the latch. It's sturdy. Both doors open inward, so the dropbears won't be able to force them open.

I step back and survey the cabin. Malric follows, padding alongside me as we circle the building, searching for signs that the dropbears have found an exit we missed.

"They're trapped," Alianor says as she joins us, Dain straggling, still eyeing the building. "Let's see how *they* like it."

"Hmm," I say.

"It was a good idea, princess," Dain says.

"As long as we can find our way back later, and they don't die horribly in there."

Alianor says, "As long as *we* don't die horribly, I'm okay with that."

Dain shakes his head. "Rowan's right to be concerned. Starvation would be crueler than killing them outright. But I think they'll be fine. We should get back to camp."

"I need to leave a note," I say. "So the owner doesn't return and open that door."

Dain doesn't answer. He stands there, his face shadowed in the moonlight. I might not be able to read his expression, but I feel the unease seeping from him.

"Dain?" I say.

He shrugs it off and lights a fire stick, then blows it out and passes me the smoldering splinter of wood. "You can write with this."

"Good idea. Thank you." I head to the front door. As the others follow, I say, as casually as I can, "You were thinking something, Dain."

I glance back. He shakes his head, eyes sliding across the clearing. It could seem as if he's only surveying our surroundings, but I know better. He's avoiding my gaze.

At the door, I use the burned end of the fire stick to write BEWARE! DROPBEARS INSIDE! Jacko jumps onto Malric's back to sniff the lettering and then chirps, as if pronouncing it fine work, very fine work indeed.

I head around back. As I write, I murmur to Dain, "Strange, isn't it? Finding a cabin so deep in the Dunnian Woods."

"People do live here," Dain says as he strikes another fire stick for me.

"Do they?"

"I did. Wilmot did."

"But otherwise?" I use the fresh stick to finish the back door sign. "I always got the impression from Jannah that people might pass through, and they might camp here—for trapping and hunting and fishing—but they don't stay. This looks like a permanent residence."

"No one's been here in days. There are buildings like this. Not permanent residences, but long-term hunting shacks, used for generations."

I glance at Alianor. She's just listening. When I look over and tap the sign, she takes the stick and adds one more exclamation mark and underlines *beware*.

We circle the cabin one last time, but there's still no sign of escaping dropbears. Time for us to head out.

When I start walking, Alianor calls, "Uh, Rowan? I see how you two got lost in the first place. The camp is that way."

"Yep," I say. "So is the trail of wounded and angry dropbears we left in our wake."

"Ah. Good point. This way it is."

As we walk into the forest, I pick up the conversation. "You said there are more permanent buildings out here, but that place was a house, not a hunting shack."

Dain mutters something incomprehensible.

"Those herbs," I continue. "The way they were tied. You said it reminded you of—"

"Witchcraft, all right? Is that what you want me to say, princess? Yes. I've heard stories of old women who live in the forest. When I worked for the mayor, someone brought herbs shaped like that. He said it was witchcraft and burned them, and then his hay barn caught on fire, and everyone said it was because he'd burned those herbs."

"Huh."

Dain glares at me. "Go on."

"She only said 'huh,' Dain," Alianor says.

"That's not all she *wants* to say. Believe me, I have already been treated to Princess Rowan's views on witchcraft and the stupid people who believe in it."

"I would never call my subjects stupid." I glance over my shoulder at him. "And I'd certainly never use that word for my friends."

His cheeks flush. "If you mean me, princess, I never claimed to believe in witchcraft."

I bite my tongue. Hard. When we first met, before he knew who I was, he'd accused me of bewitching Jacko and Malric. However, I will admit that I may have been a little quick to dismiss such things as superstitious nonsense, and therefore, understandably, he's not going to say he believes in them now. So I choose my words with care.

"My father believed in magic," I say as we walk. "He said proof of it was all around us. The sun rising every morning. The flowers blooming every spring. The snow falling in winter. Mom would say that was science, and he agreed, but he said it still made life magical. He'd also say there are things science couldn't explain. Like how Berinon just happened to be there when Dad needed him in that fight. Like how when Dad fell in love with Mom, she magically fell in love back. Or how Clan Dacre has a gift for monsters, Clan Hadleigh a gift for navigating waterways, Clan Bellamy a gift for . . ." I glance at Alianor. "Teaching travelers to pay better attention to their belongings."

Dain snorts. "That's not what you meant by magic, though, princess."

"Maybe not, but people can mistake science for magic, and that's okay, as long as you're not afraid of it. If you know that sometimes the moon passes over the sun, and you can calculate when the sun will disappear—and know it'll come back—then that's not scary. If you believe it's magic, though, you might mistake it for a curse and think the sun is gone forever."

"The mayor's barn really did burn down that night."

"I'm sure it did. What if someone who hated him knew he believed in hexes and realized they could get away with destroying his barn by blaming the witch?"

Dain walks a few minutes in silence. Then he says, grudgingly, "That's what Wilmot said, too. A lot of people did hate the mayor." He takes another couple of steps and then says, "Wilmot also says there are healers who live in the woods. They harvest herbs and plants only found here, and then they sell tinctures and salves in the villages. They're usually women—widows who don't have children or women who never married. He says people are happy to buy their medicine when it works, but if it doesn't, then they call them witches."

"People are stupid," Alianor says.

I give her a look. She throws up her hands. "I'm not a princess. I don't have to watch what I say. And you know I'm right."

"I know that people can be cruel, which isn't the same as stupid. They know exactly what they're doing."

"True." Alianor glances over her shoulder. "So do you think that's a healer's hut? Clan Bellamy tells the same stories of women living in the forest. Only they say if you find the huts, you're lost forever, because it means you've passed into another realm."

"And you accuse *me* of silly superstitions," Dain mutters.

"It's not a superstition. It's a story."

"It's kind of both," I say. "It's a story that keeps people from searching for the healer huts, which is a good thing. If these women want to be left alone, they should be."

"Well, that one won't be alone anymore," Alianor says. "She has a houseful of drop—"

Malric stops suddenly. We're walking single file on a narrow deer path, with the warg in the lead, and when he stops, we all do, stumbling and staggering in the dark as we knock into one another.

"Princess . . ." Dain growls between his teeth.

"It wasn't Rowan," Alianor says. "It's—"

My hand flies up, warning her to silence. Malric has gone still, his gaze swiveling left and then right. It fixes on something off to our right, and a low rumble sounds in his chest.

"Dropbear?" I whisper.

Malric takes a few steps off the deer trail. When I move toward him, he tosses a growl over his shoulder, telling me to stay where I am. Another step, and his muzzle rises to sample the air.

Something whistles overhead. I look up, hand going to my sword as I scan the treetops for a dropbear. Instead, Malric snarls, and I yank out my sword, plunging into the forest only to see the warg twisting on himself, snapping at something on his back. Jacko leaps and grabs what looks like a small arrow protruding from the warg's shoulder. He tosses it aside and glances back at me.

The warg collapses. One second he's looking over his shoulder at Jacko, and then his legs slide from under him, and he pitches muzzle-first into the undergrowth. Jacko tumbles off. I run for him, sword lifted.

"Rowan!" Dain shouts.

He pushes past Alianor and races toward me. There's another whistle. Something jabs my neck. I yank it out and see a dart.

A dart, like the ones Dain has been experimenting with, only this one is smaller and sleeker, made of a wood I don't recognize.

My brain stutters, sliding and stumbling like a chickcharney on a patch of ice. Dain grabs me as I stagger.

Darts.

The darts Dain has been experimenting with . . .

To sedate monsters.

Dain's saying something, his mouth working; Alianor pushing past, her hands going to my face as my feet slide from under me. Dain grapples to keep hold of me; Jacko screeches his alarm cry. Another whistle. Alianor gasps.

Something in the forest.

I see something in the forest.

The wrinkled face of a white-haired woman with a stick in her mouth. She blows. Another whistle.

Darkness.

CHAPTER NINETEEN

I wake still in darkness. Something covers my eyes. I reach up to yank it off, but my hands won't move. I twist and pull and feel something pull back—a binding around my wrists. I kick, but my feet are bound, too.

I cry out and hear only a grunt. There's a gag over my mouth. I can't see, move or speak. Panic nestles in the pit of my gut, blossoming as my heart begins to hammer.

I writhe and struggle and knock against something soft. Soft and warm, like a person. Teeth gritted, I slam my elbow into it. A sharp *oomph*. Then a groan. A familiar groan.

"Dain?" I say into my gag. It comes out as, "Aa-n?"

A swish, like fabric shifting against the earth, and then a muffled, "Ow-n?"

I don't try articulating an answer, just make an urgent noise that can be interpreted as "Yes!" I waggle my fingers and manage to snag the rope around my hands, but when I pull it, Dain grunts.

I keep hold of the rope and mentally struggle to orient myself. I'm lying on my side. Dain is behind me. I lift my bound feet and give an experimental kick. They thump into something, and Dain grunts and snarls.

I wriggle my feet and feel his boots. Okay, so we're lying on our sides, bound together, back to back.

"Alianor?" I ask. Or, in gag-speak, "A-a-a-na?"

Dain doesn't answer. I'm asking where she is, but he must think I'm calling for her. I try it again, louder, calling in earnest now. No answer.

Then, "Malric?" or, "Ah-ic?"

Panic grips me anew, my heart racing. If Dain and I are fine, Alianor will be, too, but Malric is a warg. A monster. Whoever captured us might have . . .

I don't finish the thought. I can't. It makes my fingers tremble so hard I lose my grip on the rope and have to fumble to retrieve it. I feel my way along it, and I just find the knot when the rope scrapes through my fingers, and there's a grunt behind me as Dain sits upright.

I mutter under my breath.

"Did you say something, princess?" he asks.

I'm about to mutter again when I realize I'm hearing Dain's actual voice, not the gag-muffled version.

"Rub your cheek against your shoulder," he says.

I do, and the gag isn't as tight as it seemed. I'm able to scrape it down over my cheek, and I'm working it off my jaw when something thumps beside me. I go still. Another thump.

Thump-thump-thump.

Before I can place the approaching sound, a familiar scent hits, and I smile behind the half-fastened gag. Jacko. Whiskers brush my cheek as he sniffs me. Then he keeps sniffing, hops over my hip, and begins gnawing at the rope binding my hands.

"Rowan?" Dain whispers. "I think something's in here with us."

I roll my eyes. For a monster hunter, it takes him a remarkably long time to detect a monster. The bindings on my hands slacken, and I pull free and then yank the gag the rest of the way down.

"It's Jacko," I whisper. "He's chewed through my bindings."

"Very funny."

I yank off the blindfold. Everything's still dark. I find a half-used fire stick in my pocket and strike it on my boot. It lights up Jacko, who is determinedly gnawing through the rope tying my feet. I pull off Dain's blindfold, and he stares at the jackalope.

"That is . . ." he begins.

"Awesome?"

"I was going with weird."

I help Jacko by pulling off the frayed rope. Then I give him a hug. "Who is the most awesome jackalope ever?"

Jacko chirps and nuzzles against my chin as his antlers bop my nose.

Dain shakes his head. "Definitely weird."

Jacko hops over to Dain's feet, picks up the end of the

binding rope, looks straight at Dain, drops the rope and hops back to me.

I sputter a laugh. "No jackalope rescue for you."

"Yeah, yeah. Untie me, princess."

"Mmmm, I don't know." I stretch my legs. "I was trying to earlier, but you pulled away. I think that means you don't need my help. Or Jacko's. You can get yourself free."

"Princess . . ."

When I only raise my brows, he growls under his breath, muttering, "This is not the time," but then breaks off with, "Fine. Rowan, will you please untie me?"

I do, because as much as I'd love to make him squirm some more, he's right that this really isn't the time. Before I untie him, I poke the fire stick into the dirt so I can see. We're in a tent. It's beautifully tanned, with what looks like a river-rafting scene embroidered on a wall, and any other time, I'd have lifted my fire stick for a closer look. Right now, though, all that matters is that this tent is very small and holds nothing except the two of us.

"Jacko?" I whisper as I untie Dain. "Have you seen Alianor? Or Malric?"

A grunt sounds behind the tent. Then a giant paw slides under it, and I exhale in relief, leaving Dain half untied as I crawl over. Before I can think better of it, I lay my hand on Malric's paw. He doesn't pull away. Just stays there and lets me grip his paw a moment before withdrawing it.

"They didn't take the beasts," I say. "Malric was knocked out by the dart, so they left him there. They must not have noticed Jacko. But Alianor . . . Did you see her fall?"

Dain shakes his head as he tugs off the ropes. "You went down, and then I did. I was unconscious before I saw what happened to Alianor. She must have gotten away."

I nod. "Okay, the old witch captured you and me and then—"

"Wait. Did you say *witch?*" He makes a face. "I must have heard wrong. I could have sworn you just said old—"

"Elderly healing woman."

His exaggerated frown deepens. "No, that doesn't sound the same at all. You said—"

"Just before we were captured, I saw an elderly woman with a tube in her mouth, which seemed to be shooting the darts that sedated us." I pause. "You didn't happen to get hold of one of those darts, did you? I'd like to study it."

"Why, yes, princess. As I was falling, I yanked out the dart and tucked it into my boot, where the witch—sorry, *elderly healing woman*—wouldn't find it."

"Excellent!"

He glowers at me. "I was being sarcastic."

"Oh. That's disappointing. Well, we're going to want to get one before we leave."

"Certainly. Why don't I just go out and find one while you and your monsters escape?"

"That's very kind. Thank you."

His glower deepens. "I was—"

"Being sarcastic. I know. Still, you did offer . . ."

"Might I suggest, princess, that we focus on the escaping part first, before this 'elderly healing woman' puts us into a giant pot and boils our bones for her dinner?"

"That's a story. You shouldn't believe everything you read."

"True. Once I saw a trader hawking pamphlets with a story about the royal princess and how terribly clever she was."

"I am clever. I befriended a jackalope who chewed through my ropes. You, on the other hand, were foolish enough to mock him for it. If not for me, you'd still be tied up."

"If not for you, I wouldn't be here at all."

I lean over, my face close to his as I whisper, "I know. And isn't it marvelous that you have such a friend to take you on grand adventures?"

His lips twitch, and then he laughs, a real laugh as he pushes me away, shaking his head. "You are as weird as that jackalope of yours, princess."

"Yes, and being odd, I naturally surround myself with odd beasts . . . and odd friends. Friends that I allow to join me in escaping a witch's tent, even when they refuse to risk their lives finding me a dart along the way."

"You said witch."

"Sardonically."

"Do you even know what that word means?"

"I know what all the words mean." I slip toward the tent flap. "Now hush. We're lucky we haven't brought our captor running already."

It's more than lucky. It's downright strange.

I tug the flap open the tiniest bit, and Dain tries to peer over my head while Jacko squeezes under me to look through. I wave them both back so I can get a better look at . . .

Nothing.

I see trees, trees and more trees. The smell of damp earth

wafts past. Gray dawn crests the forest, casting enough light for me to be certain there's no one in sight.

I creep through the tent, lift the bottom and see a warg tail. I move that aside, gingerly, and Malric spins, but only to fix me with a look that says, "If there was someone on this side of the tent, princess, do you really think I'd be lying here?" Good point. Again, there is no one in sight.

"Where's Alianor?" I whisper to Malric.

He grunts and looks to the left, but even when I stick my entire head out—ignoring Dain's squawks of protest—I see nothing except trees.

I pull back in. "There's no sign of the w—" I clear my throat. "Woman."

"You were going to say *witch*."

"Misunderstood natural healer."

He gives me a look. "She knocked us unconscious and left us bound and gagged in a tent. Not much to misunderstand there."

"To be fair, you did fill her cabin with dropbears."

"Me?" His voice rises to an indignant squeak. "It was *your*—"

"Shhh." I tilt my head. "Do you hear that?"

He glares, as if I'm faking it to keep him quiet. Then his head swivels, following the distant sound of a voice. At first, it's muffled, but then it comes clearer, as if a gag has been pulled away. I can't make out the words, but the voice is unmistakable.

"Alianor," Dain and I say in unison.

CHAPTER TWENTY

Dain and I are out of the tent, slipping through the dew-damp forest toward Alianor's voice, intertwining with an old woman's voice, bristling with anger.

I know this isn't a witch. At least, not in the sense of someone who can cast hexes and curses and spells. There is no such thing. But that doesn't mean she isn't dangerous. She lives alone in the forest. That means she probably doesn't like people very much. Plants and herbs can be used for more than healing, as she proved with those darts.

I don't have my sword. I remember it falling as I lost consciousness, but I have no idea where that happened. Dain's dagger and bow are gone, too. We have Malric, though, and I'd choose him over my sword any day.

As we creep through the woods, the warg follows at our heels. Jacko rests on my shoulders, his front paws across my head.

In the distance, Alianor argues with the old woman. I catch snippets of the conversation, Alianor saying, "I don't know what you're talking about," and the woman replying, "Don't lie to me, girl." They keep circling that—the old woman is obviously accusing Alianor of something that she's denying.

She's obviously accusing Alianor of filling her house with dropbears. The only solution to this problem doesn't involve wargs or swords. It requires another weapon entirely. The truth.

Finally, we're close enough for me to see Alianor on her knees, hands tied behind her back as the old woman snaps at her. I peer at the woman. Her skin is the same shade as mine and wrinkled like a walnut shell. She wears her dark-streaked gray hair in a simple plait down her back, and she's dressed in leather leggings and a tunic, with a dagger in her belt and boots laced to her knees.

Despite her age, she's no bent-back elder, toddling along on a walking stick, and seeing her, I quail at the thought of what I'm about to do. I don't reconsider, though. I take a deep breath, and then I step from the forest, ignoring Dain's intake of breath and Malric's jaws snapping at my shirttails to hold me back.

"It was me," I say as I walk from the forest. "I trapped the dropbears in your cabin."

The woman turns sharply. Then she sees me and stares. Just stares. Rendered speechless by the sight of the royal princess. Then a voice says, "Is that a . . . jackalope on your head, girl?"

I quickly pull Jacko down and cradle him in my arms. Then I realize the voice didn't come from the old woman. I turn to see another woman with a bow. Beside her stands another woman, this one holding a spear. Two more step out on my opposite side, both armed.

"Yes, that's a jackalope," Alianor says, her voice ringing out. "This is Rowan, princess of Tamarel, royal monster hunter, tamer of wild beasts . . . and my friend."

The women laugh. Throw back their heads and laugh.

"Nice try, child," one says. "She's a girl who's tamed a jackalope. Easy enough to do if you catch them young."

"Easy?" I sputter. "Jackalopes are untamable."

"Then what do you call that?" the woman says, pointing at Jacko. "Unless you've stuck antlers on a rabbit."

"Obviously she has," another woman says. "It's a Clan Bellamy trick to pass herself off as the princess by pretending she's tamed a jackalope."

"Excuse me?" I lift Jacko's paw. "Semi-retractable claws." I pull up his lip. "Sharp teeth. He's a jackalope, which makes me Rowan of Tamarel."

The women all laugh.

"What's so funny about that?" I say hotly.

"The princess of Tamarel . . . wandering the Dunnian Woods with no one to guard her but a Clan Bellamy brat."

"Hey!" Alianor says. "I'm the *warlord's* daughter."

"You're still a bandit brat come to spy on us, along with your little friend here. Where's your entourage, princess? Where's your royal sword?"

"Take me back to where your dart felled me, and I'll find my sword. As for an entourage, I don't need one. I have him." I jerk my thumb toward the forest. "Malric? Come out, please."

There's no response.

"Malric?" one of the women snorts. "Princess Jannah's warg? Yes, child, show us *him*, and we'll believe you."

"You've already seen him." I nod toward the old woman. "You knocked him out with your darts."

"A warg?" Her steel-gray eyebrows shoot up. "I think I'd have noticed that."

I sputter. Then I stop. It doesn't matter. I can fix this easily enough.

"Malric?" I call.

No answer.

I turn around and shout, "Malric!"

Still nothing. Of all the times to ignore me . . .

"Fine," I say. "Don't believe I'm the princess. I'm sorry about the dropbears, but together, we can get rid of them."

The old woman's blue eyes narrow. "You're responsible for the dropbears?"

"Of course," a younger woman mutters. "They're Clan Bellamy. If there's trouble, they're behind it."

I start to argue that I am not Clan Bellamy, but Alianor shakes her head, telling me not to bother.

"The dropbears were chasing us," I say, "and we ran into your house to escape. But then we were trapped. We lured them inside and put up warning signs. We knew the hut belonged to a wit—healing woman, but we meant no disrespect."

"Witch?" The old woman's brows shoot straight into her hairline. "You think I'm a—"

"A respected elderly healing woman," I say quickly.

"She thinks that's your hut, Gran," one of the younger women says, struggling against a laugh. "You do kind of look like a—"

The old woman spins, a bony finger raised against the younger one, who makes no effort to contain her laughter.

The old woman turns on me. "If you mean the cabin to the south, it is indeed the abode of a healer. A young woman of twenty, who is *not* a witch. I am Yvain of Clan Hadleigh, great-aunt to the warlord."

"Clan Hadleigh?" I perk up. "That's the clan of my father, Armand of Hadleigh."

Her lined face darkens. "That is the father of the *princess*, and if you are still claiming to be her, I'll take a switch to your bottom to teach you respect. Armand—rest his soul—was my brother's grandson."

"And my father." I point at my face. "I have his eyes, see? I take after my mother more, but if you ever met your great-nephew, you cannot deny my parentage."

She snorts. "Yes, I can. I only need to look at you to know you are no princess."

When I squawk my outrage, Alianor says, "She has a point, Rowan. Your tunic is torn. Your face is streaked with dirt. And your hair . . ." She shudders. "You haven't had time to bathe since you left the castle, have you?"

I glower at her. "I bathed yesterday morning. It's damp in the forest, and my curls frizz, which is why I tie them back." I glance sidelong at a puff of hair on my shoulder. "*Usually* tie them back, when I'm not woken in the night by dropbears."

I stride up to the old woman, shoulders squaring. "Enough of this nonsense. You say I am not the princess? Ask me anything about court. About the queen. About monsters."

"Why are the dropbears on the move?" another woman asks. She's about my mother's age, and she's been silent until now.

"What?" I say.

"The dropbears are moving east. We've been tracking them to find out why. If you're an expert on monsters, tell us the answer."

"I have never even seen a dropbear until tonight. Hardly anyone does. Ask me another question."

"This is silly," the youngest says, stepping forward, her dagger out. "Enough stalling. You are a spy from Clan Bellamy, who thinks us fools."

"No, I'm the princess, and I'm—"

The young woman lunges. I grab for my sword, which isn't there, of course. No one else interferes, and I stand my ground as she moves forward, dagger pointed at my throat.

"Tell us who you really are."

I straighten. "Princess Rowan of Clan Dacre."

Her face twists with anger. "Lie to me again, girl, and—"

"I am Rowan, daughter of Queen Mariela of Clan Dacre and Prince Consort Armand of Clan Hadleigh."

She steps closer, dagger tip pressed to my chin. "You are an impudent little—"

An earsplitting screech rips through the quiet morning air. The young woman jerks back, her dagger nicking my chin. All the women back up, weapons raised as their gazes lift to the sky. A dark cloud appears, winging toward the clearing as that screech rings out again.

"Gryphon!" the old woman shouts as Tiera spots me. "Archers, prepare—"

"No!" I rush forward, waving my arms. "It's okay. She's with me." I race under the gryphon. "Tiera! Down, girl! I'm here!"

Tiera circles once as the women gape, their bows raised, arrows nocked. Tiera screeches in delight, lands beside me and gallops over to rub her head against mine. I scratch behind her ears and murmur, "Good girl. Such a good girl."

A figure bursts from the forest. Tiera hisses and ruffles her feathers as Dain rushes in, *my* sword in hand, Malric bounding along behind him.

"Finally," I say. "I thought you two had abandoned me to my fate."

"I was fetching your sword, princess. Malric showed me where it was. I thought you might need it to prove who you are." He nods toward the young gryphon. "But I guess Tiera does that."

The young woman with the dagger drops to one knee, her head bowing. "I'm so sorry, your highness. I wouldn't have threatened you if I'd thought you might actually be . . ."

"The royal monster hunter." It's the old woman, her voice a whisper. When I glance over, she's staring at the ebony sword.

"That's . . . ," she says, faltering. "That's Princess Jannah's . . ." Her gaze goes to Malric. "And the warg, too."

As I untie Alianor, I realize then that they don't know what's happened in Tamarel. It's been three months, but it will take longer for news of my aunt's death to reach every citizen, particularly those who live in the wilderness.

I bow my head. "I am sorry to bring news of my aunt's death, Mistress Yvain. She was killed by a gryphon in the spring."

"But . . . but it is your brother, the prince, who was to wield her sword. Is he—?" She swallows. "Your brother is—"

"Rhydd is fine," I say quickly. "His leg was injured in the gryphon attack, and the council decided that since we are twins, it was acceptable for us to trade positions. I am better suited to monster hunting."

"That is an understatement," murmurs one of the middle-aged women as she watches me pet Tiera. "We do not believe in magic, but if ever there seemed proof of it." She shakes her head. "That is a *gryphon*."

"A very young gryphon," I say. "I assisted in her birth. Her mother was the gryphon that killed my aunt and we"—I motion at my companions, both human and beast—"captured her, but since she was pregnant, I asked to allow her to give birth, so we could observe and learn. Unfortunately, she died in the process, and a baby gryphon," I say, looking at Tiera, "grows much faster than we expected. We're returning her to the mountains."

The women are all staring at me.

"Not alone," I say quickly. "We have companions. Adult human companions."

Yvain chuckles. "That is hardly the source of our astonishment, princess. I think it begins with 'we captured a gryphon' and continues clear through the rest. But as for your grown companions . . ."

She casts a questioning eye at the forest.

"We need to find them," I say.

"Or," calls a voice, "they can just follow that blasted gryphon and find you." Wilmot walks out, followed by Kaylein. "I released her to track you down, without realizing exactly how fast she can fly when she's looking for her momma."

He stops, his gaze on Alianor. "How . . . ?" He shakes his head. "I don't even need to ask, do I? Staying behind and studying." He snorts. "It's a wonder anyone believed that."

He continues forward, his hand extended. "Hello, Yvain. How long has it been?"

She clasps his hand in hers. "Too long. So you're the 'adult human companion' who lost these three?"

"I am, and thank you for finding them."

"Oh, we didn't find them. We kidnapped them, which I'm certain counts as a very serious offense when a princess is involved."

Wilmot lifts his brows.

Yvain shakes her head. "It's a long story, one I haven't fully pieced together yet. We can do that over breakfast." She turns to the other women. "Girls? Let's see what we can offer our royal guest."

CHAPTER TWENTY-ONE

It takes a while to sort everything out. As Yvain had said, she's Clan Hadleigh, and my great-great-aunt. The "girls" are all her relatives, too—one daughter, two granddaughters, and the youngest a great-granddaughter. They're an expedition team from a village located in a cleared region between the mountains and the Dunnian Woods.

I'd heard of the village from my father. It wasn't where he grew up—this is a different branch of his clan—but it's the most remote settlement in Tamarel, home to the last remaining mountain river guides. After the great river dried up, Yvain's people learned to ferry traders along a smaller network of rivers. Right now, she's leading an expedition to investigate the dropbear migration.

Last night, when the dropbears attacked us, Yvain and her troop had been hunting for that same pack, who'd slipped away in the trees a few days earlier. Instead, they came across us and recognized Alianor. They'd had a run-in with Clan Bellamy only days earlier, so they presumed we were spies. As for Malric, Yvain really *hadn't* noticed him. With his black coat, he'd disappeared in the night's shadows, and she'd presumed her first dart had gone astray.

Once Yvain finishes her story, she invites me to tell mine. I do, with relish. This is one thing I've discovered about being a monster hunter: No matter how terrifying an encounter is at the time, it will make an amazing story later. Also, Mom always said I had a knack for storytelling. I'm not sure she meant that as a compliment—I learned very young that if I made our misadventures entertaining enough, Dad couldn't bring himself to punish us. I learned *that* trick from him. No matter how dangerous—and reckless—his exploits, his retelling of them always made Mom swoon . . . and forget that he'd been in mortal danger at the time.

Dad always said that to tell a good story, you must resist the urge to embellish. Once you're caught doing that, no one will believe you. Instead, you craft and edit the story for maximum impact. You cut the boring parts and emphasize the exciting ones. Don't gloss over all your mistakes—use them for comic effect. Tell your story with passion and enthusiasm and emotion, dramatizing the tales with your tone and your expressions and your gestures.

"So now poor Cedany's hut is filled with dropbears," says Goscelin, Yvain's daughter.

The youngest, Swetyne, grins. "But they left a warning. On both doors."

They all laugh, and Yvain promises they will resolve the cabin-filled-with-dropbears problem before Cedany returns.

"So there really is a healer?" Alianor says. "I would love to meet her. I'm in training to be a healer, though I'm hoping to specialize in monsters."

Yvain's brows rise. "And what does your father think of that?"

"Whatever will bring his daughter closer to the princess," Goscelin murmurs. Then she realizes Alianor overheard and says, "My apologies, child. Despite our issues with Everard, he is your father."

"Oh, but you're right," Alianor says blithely. "He is delighted by my friendship with Rowan. I'll worm my way into her confidence, earn my place as her trusted companion, win the heart of her brother and become Queen Alianor of Tamarel, working on behalf of Clan Bellamy from the highest position in the land."

"Second highest," I say, suppressing my surprise that she's figured out her father's plan. "Rhydd would be king."

Her eyes dance. "But a king wants a happy wife, does he not?"

The women laugh, and Alianor stretches her legs. "My father has his dreams, and I have mine. While he imagines a crown on my head, he'll leave me be, and I can study and train to become the kingdom's first doctor of monsters, working alongside my friends and living single and carefree, surrounded by handsome boyfriends."

I choke on my tea, and everyone laughs, except Dain, who looks as scandalized as I must.

"We will introduce you to Cedany if we can," Yvain says to Alianor. "First, you have a gryphon to return to the wild, and I think we can help with that."

Yvain and her troop can indeed help us. They know of a gryphon aerie not far into the mountains, along a nearby river. They traversed that river themselves to track the drop-bears, and their raft is only a half-day's walk away.

After we eat, Wilmot heads out with Yvain's daughter and granddaughters to investigate Dropbear Cabin. I want to join them, but Wilmot insists we stay with Yvain and Swetyne.

"I'll already get a tongue-lashing from Berinon when he learns I let you wander off in the night," Wilmot says. "If he finds out I intentionally brought you *back* to a dropbear pack? That would earn me an *actual* lashing."

Not true, but I understand his meaning. After they're gone, Alianor and Swetyne talk healing while Yvain wants a closer look at Tiera, Jacko and Malric. I jump on the opportunity, and in Yvain, I find an enthusiastic audience. Soon we're chattering away over the beasts as I point out one feature after another. Dain sits close by, whittling an arrowhead as he listens, sometimes pausing to ask questions.

It is, of course, Tiera that we spend the most time poring over. My time with her is slipping past, and I want to use it wisely, as both scientist and companion, studying her and play-ing with her and enjoying our time together, while desperately trying to forget how short it will be.

"It's truly remarkable," Yvain says. "A warg, a jackalope, a baby gryphon . . ."

"Malric was Jannah's," I say. "I only inherited him."

"She also has a chickcharney," Dain says. "And a pegasus filly. She didn't inherit either of those. Monsters follow her home."

"You have a gift," Yvain says, stroking Tiera's feathers.

Dain shrugs. "She's kind to them, and she respects them."

I tense, waiting for the insult that will surely follow. Dain only returns to whittling, while Jacko snuffles the falling sawdust.

"I didn't mean to imply it's all her Clan Dacre blood," Yvain says. "She uses it well, and obviously she has an affinity for beasts. Have you spoken to your kin about that, child?"

"About what?"

She waves between the three beasts. "This is not normal, even for a royal monster hunter. Surely your mother realizes that."

I shrug. "I like monsters."

"As they like you. As Dain says, you're kind and respectful, and that's why they stay with you. But the bigger question is why they come to you at all."

I frown at her.

She chuckles. "Does this seem normal to you, child? That you just happen to stumble upon gryphons and pegasus fillies and baby jackalopes?"

"And wyverns and jba-fofis and dropbears . . ." Dain murmurs.

"The wyverns were hunting the chickcharney, which we were also hunting. We *did* stumble on the jba-fofi lair. The dropbears . . . ? I guess we accidentally crossed their path."

"I'm sure there are explanations for some," Yvain says. "But you should consider the possibility that you attract monsters."

My heart thuds. "Are you saying it's my fault the dropbears are heading toward Tamarel?"

She laughs and clasps my shoulder. "No, child. That would indeed be magical. Something else is driving the dropbears east, but I believe it's no coincidence that their path intersected with yours."

"She's a monster magnet," Dain says.

"She is indeed. If you're going to be her companion, you'd best be prepared for beastly encounters."

She says it lightly, but I tense. Dain obviously isn't sure he *wants* to be my companion, and he really doesn't need any excuses to decide against it. But he only shrugs, his gaze still on his work.

"It's not dull, that's for sure," he says.

"Good," Yvain says. "There are people who want nothing more than an easy and comfortable life, and I do not begrudge them that. But I'm not hunting dropbears at my age because I need to. As for you, Rowan, your mother will soon notice exactly how often you encounter monsters. She's just preoccupied, with your aunt's death and the change of heir. You should bring it to her attention."

When I don't answer, she says, "You need to tell her, child. You can't be the first member of Clan Dacre to have so strong a gift. You'll find help in your histories. Help that you'll need so you may learn to manage it and use it to your advantage."

"Is it an advantage?" I say. "I'm supposed to be scaring the monsters off, not attracting them. That sounds more like a curse."

"Yes," Yvain says, nodding at Jacko, now snuggled with Tiera, who has her head on my lap as she dozes. "It looks like a curse to me."

I make a face.

Before I can speak, she says, "I understand your concern, but a curse is only a misused gift. There are plenty of advantages to having monsters drawn to a royal monster hunter."

"So they aren't drawn to the rest of us," Dain says, still working on his arrow. "Well, unless you're *beside* her at the time. I might need to start wearing stronger armor."

"You jest, Dain, but it's true," Yvain says. "They'll come to her, and that will help her study them and learn their habits. Speak to your mother, child. She will help."

"Maybe you can tell her yourself," I say. "She should be told about the dropbears, too. Clan Hadleigh is coming soon for a meeting."

Yvain's eyes crinkle. "Is that an official invitation to the castle?"

"It is."

"Then I accept. I'd planned to make my way there to warn Jannah about the dropbears. We'll help you get this young gryphon to a more suitable home. Then we'll come to the castle with you and discuss this all with your queen mother."

CHAPTER TWENTY-TWO

"I could get used to this," Alianor says, lying on her back as our raft floats along the gentle river.

We're going upstream, which means we need to all take turns paddling, but the current is light and the water deep, and it feels like a pleasant midday row. The raft won't hold ten people and three beasts, so Yvain's granddaughters remained with their mother, Goscelin, guarding the dropbear cabin. That leaves seven humans and three beasts.

I'm stretched out with Alianor, my head on Tiera and Jacko on my stomach. Dain's taking a turn at rowing with Swetyne and Wilmot, while Kaylein sits beside me and Yvain perches atop a barrel seat.

I should probably be sleeping after my long night, but weirdly, I'm too relaxed to sleep. I'm lying on a raft, bobbing in the current, as I watch the late-summer sky above, the brightest blue with clouds as white as lambs. Around me gentle conversation drifts like the raft itself.

"Are there only women in your village?" Alianor asks.

Yvain chuckles. "No. Why do you ask that?"

"Because you're all women. Clan Bellamy women accompany expeditions, but there are always men, too."

"To protect the women?" Yvain asks dryly.

Alianor's quiet for a moment. Then she says, "I'm not sure, actually. Sometimes it's only men, but mostly it's both. There are still more men than women in an expedition, though."

"In our village, it's the women who hunt and explore while the men guide the river rafts. They may join us, if they wish, but this promised to be a long trip, and summer is our busiest time for the rafts."

"Is there a reason why you do different jobs?" I ask.

"Because people don't want women as their river guides."

I glance over, thinking she's joking, but she shrugs. "People feel safer with men guiding the boats. They don't mind a woman or two on the crew, but when it's mostly women, they'll pay double for a male crew."

Alianor looks over. "Then I hope you continue offering the female crews so you may charge double for the male ones."

Yvain chuckles. "You are indeed Clan Bellamy, child. Always looking for the trick."

"That's no trick. It's common sense. If they're foolish enough to pay double for men, they cannot claim you're over-charging them. It's their choice."

"She actually has a point," I say.

Alianor knocks my boot with hers. "Don't sound so shocked."

I look at Yvain. "But it doesn't seem right if it forces you to divide the jobs that way. People should do what they want. And what they're good at."

"Stop giving your customers a choice." That's Dain, his voice drifting over from where he stands with his paddle. We all turn his way, and he shrugs. "Wilmot told me once about a monster hunter who retired to the north, and no one wanted to hire her because their monster hunters had always been men. Those who *would* hire her offered less money. So she refused. Either they paid her full price or she didn't clear the monsters. Eventually, they had to give in."

"That only works if you're offering a unique service," Kaylein says. "We have the same problem where I come from. No one cares who catches the fish, but if they've come to go fishing themselves, they want men to take them out. And they want fishing poles and nets made by women, because we're supposedly better at that. If my family decided that my brothers should make nets and my sister should guide boats, people would just hire others. Even though the royal monster hunter has been a woman for three generations, people still tried to tell me I couldn't be a palace guard because I wouldn't be strong enough to lift a proper sword."

"What did your parents say?" Alianor asks.

"Do whatever I wanted," Kaylein says. "Whatever made me happy. Dad made my swords, after Berinon crafted the first. My mother sparred with me for practice, even though she's horrible at it."

We all laugh, and conversation continues, weaving through topics heavy and light, until the midday sun burns so bright that Malric jumps off the raft . . . and Jacko leaps up to yodel his alert cry.

"He's fine," I say. "He's just cooling off. In fact, it looks like an excellent idea."

I take off my sword and my breeches, letting my long tunic cover my undergarments. Then I jump in . . . and Jacko whips into a frenzy, racing around, screeching his alert, butting Alianor and Dain for not leaping in to save me.

"Thank you, princess," Dain says, as Jacko hangs from his pant leg, growling. "I hope you're nice and cool now."

"I am, thank you," I answer from the water.

Kaylein takes his paddle. "Go on and join her. The jackalope will figure it out." She plucks Jacko from Dain's pant leg.

Dain reaches for the paddle. "I'm fine."

"He can't swim," I call as Alianor dives into the water.

"I can, too," he says, turning to face me as I swim lazily upstream.

"Can't."

His face darkens. "Can."

Kaylein gives him a nudge between the shoulder blades, and he rocks on the edge for a heartbeat. He could catch his balance, but instead he lets himself fall into the river.

When he surfaces, he scowls at Kaylein.

"See?" she says. "You wanted to. You were just too cranky to admit it."

"I'm not cranky."

"And the sky is not blue," I say.

Dain turns on me, and I dive, slicing through the water and surfacing a few feet away. Jacko perches on the edge of the raft, quiet now that he's realized we haven't all accidentally fallen overboard.

I swim to Malric, who shakes his head, spraying me, and I laugh before I dive under. Alianor and I retrieve rocks and shells from the riverbed, competing for who can find the best and biggest. At first, Dain only swims, but when he does go under, he spots something. He surfaces, lifting a clam the size of my head . . . and Tiera swoops down to grab it.

"Hey!" he shouts.

She flaps her way to the shore, smashes the shell, and gobbles down the meat inside.

"Good girl!" I call. "Very good girl!"

Now Dain's "Hey!" comes my way.

"I'm praising her for finding food," I say.

"I found the food."

"And she found it in your hand."

He swings at me and I dive, laughing and getting a mouthful of water. When fingers brush my foot, I glance to see him coming after me, and I swim faster and deeper. He brushes against my side, and I twist, wondering how he got there so fast. Instead, I see a smooth, glowing flank.

I jet to the surface, breaking it and gulping water as a head rises right in front of mine. A head of that same glowing silver-white skin. It has a long, thin mouth and bright-violet eyes that watch me before the beak-like mouth opens and it makes a sound like a child's laughter.

I grin and tread water as it floats, watching me and making that burbling sound.

"Hello there," I say.

The encantado chortles and squeaks. I've met the river-dolphin beasts before. They're one of the most playful monsters, and as I talk to this one, another nudges me. I dive, and when I come up, both the encantados surface with me, chortling and tossing their heads. Dain swims a little closer, wary, and then he flails, his eyes round as a big encantado leaps up right under him, toppling him.

"Hello, little friends," Yvain calls. "I didn't even need to lure you in with minnows today, did I? Our monster hunter did that."

She reaches into a barrel and tosses a handful of tiny silvery fish. I catch two and pass one to Dain, who stares at it, and then at me, as if I expect him to eat it. I laugh and grab another to toss to Alianor, but Tiera snatches it mid-flight, and the encantados rear up, dancing on the river surface as they scold her.

Alianor sees me holding up minnows for the encantados, and she grabs another. Dain throws his in the air. Tiera swoops, but the biggest encantado leaps clear out of the water and grabs it first. We continue playing like that—Yvain tossing us fish, which we throw to see who can get them first: the encantados or the gryphon. When the water grows choppy, Swetyne calls, "Better climb on board. Unless you want to be encantado chow yourselves."

Once I've hauled myself onto the raft, I see what she means. Approaching the mountains, we're entering a section of rapids, the water growing rocky and rough.

As for becoming encantado chow, she's not entirely joking. Legend says that they lure humans into deep water, where they'll drown and then devour them. This is why villagers who live near rivers avoid the water at night.

The truth, as usual, is a mix of fact and fiction. Seeing those silvery bodies dancing in the night-dark water, welcoming human playmates, I realize it would be easy to follow them, entranced by their beauty. And if you drown while doing it, well, encantados *are* carnivores—they will eat what remains, and we can't begrudge them that. They've also been known to lure very small children into the river. Yet even realizing what encantados *can* do, I'm still happy to play with them. I just use caution, same as I would with a dog.

Encantados help people, too, as Yvain explains when we're all on board.

"We use the minnows to lure them in," she says. "Then they'll lead us through the rapids better than any of our guides."

Which they do. They swim at the head of the raft, silvery bodies leaping from the water, glowing visibly as they dart through the clear paths between the rocks. As we navigate behind the encantados, Yvain explains that this particular river is slow moving, with deep water and relatively few rapids, which makes it good for big rafts. The narrower, faster rivers require boats that are also narrower and faster, but can only hold a couple of people plus supplies.

That gets Kaylein talking about the boats they use on the ocean, which are larger and sturdier, suited for the tempestuous water.

"Speaking of tempests . . ." Yvain says, squinting at the sky.

Dark clouds roll from the mountains.

"Is that a storm?" I ask. "Or just the mountain weather?"

"Storm," Swetyne and Alianor say in unison.

Yvain nods. "The heart of the mountains is storm-tossed and fog-shrouded, but we're not going that far in. The aerie is at the edge. That's definitely a storm."

"What do we do?"

"Keep paddling for as long as we can. There's open land ahead. Once that storm is closer, we'll make for shore and wait until it passes. We have time, though, and I'd like to push on past the rocks."

I reach for a paddle, but Kaylein shakes her head. "We have this, your highness. It's deep water here. Deep and cold and rocky, and your oar can catch easily and topple you overboard. Just keep an eye on those clouds for us."

They don't need me to watch the clouds—everyone can see them—but it gives me something to do. When we hit a rough patch, Yvain has us sit. I do, with Tiera at my back and Jacko on my lap, all of us watching the silvery glow of the encantados, diving and leaping. The clouds are rolling in faster, and Swetyne curses under her breath, earning a warning look from her great-grandmother.

"I can ask Tiera to fly," I say. "If a lighter load will help . . ."

"We're fine," Yvain says. "We need only to pass . . ."

She trails off, and I rise onto my knees, following her gaze. I see black water ahead, and I squint up at the sky, wondering if that's the reflection of the clouds.

"Deep water," Kaylein murmurs. "The deeper it is, the darker it looks."

"Is that a problem?"

She shakes her head. "Deep means no obstacles. We can cross it easily, and then Swetyne says we'll be turning onto a tributary just up ahead. That'll be flowing away from the source, so we'll be riding *with* the current."

I nod and stare at that dark spot. That *is* where Yvain had been looking when she trailed off, and she's still staring at it, paddling in silence, her gaze fixed on that spot. It's black as night, the surface swirling, small white-capped waves rising around it.

I move closer to Kaylein. "But if it's deep, why is it swirling?"

"The storm. The wind's rising. We'll have choppy water everywhere soon."

As if on cue, a blast of wind rips past, bringing hard, cold pellets of rain.

"To the shore!" Yvain shouts. "Steer left!"

Swetyne pauses, her paddle raised. "But we're almost past the rocks. The tributary is right up—"

"To the shore! Now!"

The lead encantado shrieks a high-pitched warning. The smallest dives . . . and disappears into the black water. The others disperse, silver streaks through the gloom, swimming madly in every direction, abandoning us. I stare at where I'd seen that small one vanish. A moment later, the white-capped waves turn pink with blood.

"To the shore!" I shout. "Something's in—"

The very water itself rises up in a tremendous roar. A geyser of black water splashes over us, the raft rocking violently with the force of it. The rain pelts down, solid now, ice-cold balls of driving hail.

My gaze never leaves that geyser. The water falls away, and the shape is still there, a huge black shadow against the darkening sky. The beast throws back its head, and a whinny slices through the howling wind. Black hooves slash the air as the beast rears.

It's as big as a unicorn, and it looks black until foam sliding down its flank shows its coat as darkest green, like the water itself. Emerald-green eyes roll and white teeth flash as its black lips curl. That sound comes again, halfway between a horse's whinny and a scream.

"Ceffyl-dwr," I whisper.

CHAPTER TWENTY-THREE

I can grumble about unicorns being horrible, nasty beasts, but compared to the ceffyl-dwr, they are as gentle as old nags. These are terrible and terrifying, the only equine carnivores, with white teeth sharp as spades and hooves like razors.

An encantado will feed on a drowned swimmer; a ceffyl-dwr will rip live ones apart with tooth and hoof. Legend says that they entrance riders to mount their backs and then dive into the river's deepest pools to drown them. I always thought that just meant that anyone foolish enough to try riding one would be drowned. Now, seeing this nightmare beast, I cannot believe anyone would *try* climbing on its back.

"Tiera!" I shout. "Fly!" I motion wildly at the sky. She doesn't need another hint. She takes off, safely away from the raft while lightening the load.

Around me, everyone shouts orders. Yvain tells the

paddlers to make for shore, as fast as they can. Wilmot shouts for Alianor, Dain and me to get down. Kaylein echoes Wilmot's orders, saying to hang on to the ropes binding the raft together.

I grab Jacko and hit the floor, even as I cannot stop staring at the ceffyl-dwr. It rides the waves as two others appear behind it. They're coming straight for us. Three huge ceffyl-dwrs are making for our raft, and the royal monster hunter lies huddled on the floor, hugging her jackalope.

I push Jacko beneath me, rise to my knees and draw my sword. The hail beats down, frozen slush half-blinding me. An arrow whips past, and I glance to see Dain on one knee, Alianor beside him, her dagger at the ready.

I want to leap to my feet and defend our raft, but it lurches and sways, and I'd tumble off the side and be no use to anyone. I grip Jacko between my knees and ready my sword. The ceffyl-dwrs bear down on us, riding the storm-tossed surf, their manes whipping behind them. They are not slowing. Not slowing at all.

"Brace!" I shout. "Brace for imp—"

The lead ceffyl-dwr hits the boat. It pitches wildly. Yvain stumbles, and Swetyne goes to help her up, but the old woman shouts for Swetyne to paddle, just paddle. All three ceffyl-dwrs swim alongside the raft, too far away for me to strike. When Dain's arrows hit, they only toss their heads and snort.

Why aren't they attacking?

The biggest—a stallion—grabs the raft in his teeth, and I stare, uncomprehending, as the other two do the same. All three bite into the raft, those huge, sharp teeth slicing through rope.

I realize their plan two heartbeats before the stallion's rope snaps. One mare chomps through her rope, the second through another, and the raft begins to split apart.

Why fight the humans in their boat when you can bring them into the storm-tossed water with you?

I swing my sword at the nearest ceffyl-dwr, but it's out of reach, and the logs are spinning and rolling and slick with hail.

Over the roar of the wind, Yvain yells for us to grab a log. I hesitate. I want to fight. When I lift my sword again, though, a hand clamps my foot, and I glance to see Alianor mouthing, "Hang on!"

I nod and snap my sword into its sheath, my body shielding Jacko as I fall onto all fours. I wrap my hands around a log. There's a tremendous crack, and I look up to see Kaylein, her eyes wide as she lunges for me, someone grabbing her and hauling her back. A blink, and before I know what's happening, she's gone.

They're *all* gone.

The raft has split in two, taking Wilmot, Kaylein, Swetyne and Yvain, who were all on the far side paddling for shore. I see only a dark shape as their half of the raft swirls out of sight. Then I see another dark shape, this one in the water.

"Malric!" I scream.

He fell in when the raft broke, and he's frantically paddling toward our half as it bounces off rocks. I reach for him. Then another dark shape appears, one underwater, a huge form twice as big as Malric.

A ceffyl-dwr swimming straight for him.

Something flashes overhead. White and tawny brown. Tiera's talons stab the water and grab the ceffyl-dwr by its long dark-green mane. She swoops up, the seaweed-like hair caught in her talons. She stops short. The beast is too big to drag from the water, but she's diverted its attack.

Alianor and I pull Malric onto our raft. The ceffyl-dwr rises from the water, snapping. An arrow hits it square in the eye, and it falls back, shrieking. Tiera drops, too, but just a little, before untangling her talons and swooping into the air.

Malric huddles on the raft, and I cast a quick look around. It's Dain, Alianor and me, with Malric and Jacko. Tiera flies overhead. Somewhere from the fog comes a shout, and Dain's head whips that way, telling me it's Wilmot.

I tense, afraid Wilmot's in danger, but the tone says he's only calling to find us. They must be safe. We are not. We have two ceffyl-dwrs circling our raft. The third—the one Dain hit in the eye—has backed off, her screams sounding in the fog.

"The ceffyl-dwrs all stayed with our half of the raft," Alianor says, barely audible over the storm.

With *my* half of the raft.

I cast a guilty glance Dain's way, braced for his response, but he shakes his head and mouths, "No."

"It's my—" I begin.

"No," he says, louder, firmer as he moves up beside me. "They could rip our raft apart, princess, and they aren't."

That doesn't mean we're safe. They're circling like sharks, as if trying to figure out what to do with us.

"It's the storm," he says. "They wouldn't be so bad if it wasn't for the storm."

Without the tempest, we could fight them. We could get to shore. That also wouldn't mean we'd be safe. As the ceffyl-dwrs circle, the gills on their dark necks flutter with each breath, but they're breathing air right now. They won't suffocate on land. Still, they are creatures of the water, and on land, fighting them would be like fighting unicorns. Difficult, but we could have done it, especially if we'd had the adults. Out here, though, on the storm-tossed waves, we're barely clinging to our shattered raft.

"We've headed upriver," Alianor says. "The waves and the ceffyl-dwrs carried us past the rapids."

I ignore her. We're in the middle of a river thirty feet across. Even if we're past the rocks, we don't have paddles, and we certainly can't jump into ceffyl-dwr–infested water and swim for shore.

"We're upstream," she says again, louder. She pokes my arm and points, and I have no idea what she's talking about . . . and then I do.

It seems as if we've spun again, because the river now goes off in another direction, just visible through the fog. Except it doesn't. The river still stretches in front of us and behind us, but now it stretches to our right side as well.

I remember what Kaylein said about the tributary. We've been knocked just past it. Now, without paddles, we're floating downriver, back where we came from. In a few moments, we'll hit the rapids again.

We need to steer into that tributary.

As I'm looking around wildly for something to paddle with, the massive head of the ceffyl-dwr stallion appears in our path. He rears up, riding the water, hooves slashing as he waits for us to drift closer.

"Hold on," I say, as I make my way to that end of the raft.

"What—?" Dain begins.

"Hold. On."

I lift my hand, warding Dain off when he steps toward me. I get my footing. We're heading straight for the stallion as he rears and twists, his green eyes glittering with glee. His prey is coming to him, and all he needs to do is wait and then dash our broken raft to splinters with his flying hooves.

I stand on the edge, sword raised as the raft hurtles toward him. He snorts, tossing his mane, teeth gnashing, as if already tasting me. He sees my sword, but he's not backing down, and at the last second, he leaps straight at me.

I swing with all my might. The blade sinks into his shoulder, and when the raft strikes the stallion, I lever as hard as I can, using the sword to send the raft spinning to the right.

It works . . . too well, actually. We start to spin, and I almost lose my grip on the sword, but I wrap both hands around the hilt and yank it out so hard I stagger back. And that's when I *really* don't want to drop it, as I envision a razor-sharp blade bouncing around a tiny, crowded raft.

As the raft spins down the tributary, I manage to sheathe my sword. The storm is passing, the hail gone, only rain falling, the sky gray, the wind still whipping but no longer howling. That is good. The fact that we're not heading for the rapids is also good. The bad part? The three ceffyl-dwrs plunging through the stormy water after us.

I catch a glimpse of figures running along the bank.

Wilmot shouts, and I think Kaylein does, too. I don't know if they're telling us to come to shore or trying to distract the ceffyl-dwrs. The raft is roaring downriver, caught on the wild storm-tossed current. Even if we had oars, I don't think we could get to shore.

As for the ceffyl-dwrs, they're chasing us like horses driven mad by gadflies. The one Dain shot might be half-blind, but that isn't slowing her down. While I sliced the stallion deep in the shoulder, he's still coming, fresh fury in his green eyes.

There is a moment, when I stand on the back of the raft watching the three ceffyl-dwrs, that I am awed by their terrible beauty, my fingers inching for my sketching pen even as I'm struck by the impossibility of capturing what I see.

Sunlight pierces the storm clouds as the rain moves on. Rays strike the river, reflecting off the roiling dark surface and the white-capped waves. And the ceffyl-dwrs ride those waves, their front hooves coming up and down like beautiful toy horses.

They *are* beautiful, too. Beautiful and terrible, sleek and muscled with coats of darkest green, long manes, and fetlocks that flow like seaweed. White teeth. Shining green eyes. As breathtaking as a pegasus or a unicorn. Maybe even more so, with their otherworldly color and fluttering gills.

Awe-inspiring and utterly horrifying in their pursuit, each giant wave bringing them closer to the raft—while we have no way of moving faster, of escaping.

We cannot escape, so we must fight. Dain does, as soon as the wind dies enough for him to shoot, but the ceffyl-dwrs dive and duck, and the storm gusts scatter his arrows.

Alianor clutches her dagger. I have my sword. At my feet, Jacko bares his teeth and chatters. Tiera has been alternating between sitting on the raft and flying, and as the ceffyl-dwrs draw closer, she takes to the air. Malric stands beside me, completely silent, too busy watching the monsters to waste breath on a growl.

"If you fall overboard, swim for shore," I call to the others. "Do not try to fight in the water. It's too deep and too choppy. Get to shore. Forget us and swim."

"That goes for you, too, princess," Dain says.

When I don't answer, Alianor says, "He means it. Don't worry about us. Once you're in the water, *you're* the one in danger. Just swim."

I nod. The ceffyl-dwrs are less than ten feet away now. I grip my sword and adjust my stance. Then I pause and step backward. Everyone glances at me in confusion.

"They'll try to break up the raft," I say. "We need to let them try. Allow them to get close enough. Allow them to bite the ropes. That's when we strike."

They nod.

"The stallion's mine," I say. "Dain, go for the mare on my left. Alianor? Take the wounded mare. Malric will help wherever he can. Just be ready for—"

A massive wave hits, one that rolls right over the heads of the ceffyl-dwrs, and when it passes, the mare on the left is gone, leaving only the wounded one and the stallion coming at us. Was she pulled under? Where—?

Black shimmers beneath the water. Then the stallion dives.

"Hold on!" I shout. "Grab something. They're going—"

The raft rocks as the mare slams up under it. As I grab the ropes, I manage to smack my sword down to kneel on the blade. Then the stallion hits. It crashes into us, and the raft leaps from the water, wood cracking as the beast rises, its fish-stinking breath washing over me. One rolling green eye stares into mine. Then it swings its huge head, wet mane slapping me, jaws opening, teeth gleaming, so close I see the shovel shape of them, coming to that razor-sharp edge. One chomp from those teeth—

I punch the ceffyl-dwr in the eye. My fist hits hard, and the beast screams, falling back. As it does, a log under my leg rolls free, and I scramble, flailing, until Malric shoves me back onto what remains of the raft . . . just as my sword slides into the water. I almost grab it by the blade. Luckily, my brain kicks in, and I grasp the hilt.

I lift the sword just as a ceffyl-dwr lunges at me. It's not the stallion. He's right there, recovering from my blow, blinking and snorting. This is the uninjured mare, dodging in front of the stallion to get to me.

I swing my sword. It's too fast, and the blade strikes her in the neck, but tilted, slicing instead of cutting deep. As I pull back to try again, Alianor lunges beside me, sinking her dagger into the mare's front shoulder. The ceffyl-dwr rears, a deep wound in her shoulder, a cut across her neck, her eyes rolling, hooves slicing through the air.

I swing again, and this time she's too far away, but my blade still catches her in the shoulder. With a scream, she twists, and one of her front hooves hits the stallion. Blood sprays, and the stallion bellows and lashes out, biting the mare in her shoulder.

The raft hits a rock and ricochets off it, spinning us into the river, away from the fighting ceffyl-dwrs. We still have most of the raft, but a few logs have fallen free. Dense mist swirls around us, and I struggle to make out forms. Dain is behind me with Malric, both of them watching the dark shape of what must be the other mare, well back from the raft. I don't see Tiera, but I presume she's safe, having flown from danger. Jacko is by my foot, and I reach for him.

The rafts slams into another rock. A log cracks, the one right under Jacko. He leaps for me as I grab for him, but the log shoots away, his back legs still on it, and he falls into the swirling water ... just as a ceffyl-dwr bellows in the fog.

CHAPTER TWENTY-FOUR

"**N**o!" I scream.

Jacko writhes in the water, shrieking. I reach for him, but the raft is already hurtling away, leaving him thrashing, unable to swim, the ceffyl-dwr's dark shape bearing down. I spring to dive in, but hands grab me.

"No, Rowan," Alianor says.

I spin on her, snarling, but Malric's right there, snarling back. When I try to leap in again, he grabs my tunic, and I pound at him, twisting wildly, hearing the ceffyl-dwr coming closer, my jackalope in her path.

I must get to him.

I will get to him.

As I fight, Malric snarls at Alianor. She throws herself on me, and he turns, crouching as if to jump in. But before he can, there's a splash. Alianor releases me, and I scramble to the edge to see Dain swimming for Jacko.

Dain grabs the jackalope and starts back. The ceffyl-dwr appears right behind him. I steady myself on my knees, sword ready. Malric leaps into the water just as Tiera appears. She swoops, and Dain looks up, but she only seizes Jacko in her talons and continues on, depositing the jackalope on the shore and then settling in herself.

The ceffyl-dwr rises right behind Dain, and the gleam in her good eye says she knows he's the one who fired that arrow. Her hooves shoot up from the surf as she rears, and I tense to leap off the raft, having no idea how I can fight her in the water but determined to try if she gets any closer.

Dain keeps swimming as fast as he can, cutting through the choppy water. The current helps, but it's not enough. When the ceffyl-dwr drops from rearing, her front hoof slices through his breeches. Bright blood stains the leather for one heartbeat before his leg kicks underwater, the blood disappearing only to well anew.

I want to leap to his rescue, but my brain is like a ball caught between two walls, bouncing back and forth.

Jump in! Distract her! Do something before she gets him!

Stay where you are! You have your sword. He's almost to the raft. You can knock the ceffyl-dwr away while he climbs on board.

How fast is he swimming? How fast is *she* swimming? How fast is that gap between them closing, and how swiftly is the raft moving?

I rock on the edge. The ceffyl-dwr tears through the water. She's almost on Dain. Her head clears the surf, mouth opening, ready to bite.

I dive, and in midair, I spot a dark shape launching itself at her rear haunch.

Malric.

I forgot about Malric.

While I was watching the ceffyl-dwr and Dain, he'd swum behind the monster. Now he's biting it, and Dain's getting away . . . and I'm in the water. I thrash, trying to get my bearings. Dain's hand rises above the surface in a long breaststroke, and he's here. I help him clamber onto the raft. Then Dain and Alianor pull me up, and I draw my sword.

Malric has his powerful jaws sunk into the ceffyl-dwr's haunch. She's trying to bite at him, but each time she twists, she's only swinging him out of the way.

"Oh no," Alianor breathes.

I'm about to tell her Malric's fine—he's tiring the beast out by clinging while she fights uselessly. Then I follow Alianor's gaze to see a huge shape bearing down through the fog. The stallion.

"Malric!" I shout.

We all scream, but he doesn't seem to hear us as the mare whips him in and out of the water. Dain grabs his bow. I wheel toward Tiera on the shore where she's preening Jacko's bedraggled fur as he shivers.

"Tiera!" I say.

She looks up, decidedly unconcerned about what's happening over here.

I jab my finger at the approaching stallion. "Can you drive him off?"

She cocks her head, uncomprehending. Of course she doesn't understand. She's a monster and a baby one at that.

But sensing my panic, she rises and spots Malric. She takes wing and flies at the warg, her talons down, as if she can rescue him the same way she rescued Jacko.

"No!" I shout. "Fly at—"

She swoops up, realizing Malric is far too big to grab. Then she sees the stallion. With a piercing cry, she shoots into the air and then plummets. The stallion glances up. It's an unconcerned glance—just wondering what he spots out of the corner of his eye. Then he sees the gryphon.

There are few predators big enough for a ceffyl-dwr to fear, but a gryphon is one of them. In that second, I'm sure he doesn't notice how young Tiera is. He only sees a gryphon, and he rears, hooves slashing the air as he falls back. Tiera swoops past and flies up again with a screech of victory.

I open my mouth to shout for Malric, but he's seen the stallion. He releases his grip on the mare, and she sends him flying, skimming like a stone over the water. Then he swims for the raft while Tiera dives at the two ceffyl-dwrs.

Malric reaches the raft. We haul him on, and we barely have a moment to breathe before the raft strikes something submerged in the water. It knocks against the left side, sending us straight into a fast-flowing eddy, and we're spinning downriver so fast all I can do is hang on.

As we whirl, I do a lightning-fast tally. Tiera is in the air. My sword is in its sheath. Jacko is safely on the shore, and my body is wedged between Dain and Malric's wet forms. I spot Alianor and exhale. Everyone accounted for.

No one falls off. We're huddled in the middle of the raft's remains, and as fast as we're moving, it's a smooth ride, no rocks appearing to dash us to bits. Not that we'd stand any chance of spotting rocks. We're flying along, the trees a blur, until finally we crash into something, and we're all thrown into the air, flailing. I brace for water to close over my head. Instead, I splash down flat on my back.

I carefully lift my head. The smashed remains of our raft lie scattered around a tree trunk, half-submerged at the river's edge. I'm on my back, the water halfway up my sides. I rise shakily, looking around. The others are all fine, having landed in less than a foot of water.

Jacko leaps onto me, and I cradle him as he rubs his wet cheek against me, his heart racing from his run. Tiera lands beside Dain, who's on all fours, coughing. He glances at her and mutters, "I'm alive, no thanks to you."

"She took Jacko away so you could swim to safety," I call over.

"Rowan's right," Alianor says as she stands farther down the shore. "Tiera wasn't rescuing Jacko and leaving you to your fate. Not at all."

He grumbles, and I push to my feet, calling, "Malric?"

The warg is splayed motionless on the bank, but when I start toward him, my heart thudding, he rises and shakes and gives me a look like I interrupted his afternoon nap.

I walk around, assessing our situation. I have no idea how far we are from Wilmot and the others, except that the answer is "too far to easily walk back," especially when there are three ceffyl-dwrs between us. Farther down the river, small mountains rise, the larger ones behind.

Alianor comes up beside me. "We're close to where we needed to be."

She nods at the mountains. "The aerie is in those foot-hills. That's what Yvain said. Down the tributary river to where the foothills begin and then a quarter-day's walk into the setting sun."

"Do you know the area?"

She shakes her head. "Clan Bellamy never comes this way. Too many monsters. Encantados *and* ceffyl-dwrs. What are the chances?"

"With me around, pretty good."

Dain walks over. "Don't go taking the credit for all our monster encounters, princess." He glances at Alianor. "Yvain suggested that Rowan's affinity for monsters may also attract them. That means if they're nearby, yes, I think some-thing draws them to you. A scent or just a . . ." He shrugs. "A sense. But you didn't attract dropbears from a hundred miles away. As for the encantados, Yvain said they're often in that river."

"And the ceffyl-dwrs?" I say.

"Yeah, we can totally blame you for those."

I shake my head and walk toward the tree stump that wrecked our raft. It's a dead tree that fell long ago, a massive one, the trunk cutting partway across the river and forming a dark, deep pool. If we hadn't crashed against the stump, we might have ended up in that pool.

We're fine, though. Battered and bruised, but on our feet. Also completely without supplies. Still, we have our weapons, and we can get food and water. The question is whether to push on or try to circle back to the others.

I eye the mountains and consider our options as Jacko

snuggles in my arms. Alianor tends to Dain's shallow leg wound while I walk and think.

I'm wandering near the fallen tree trunk when a shape rises from the deep pool. At first, I think it's a turtle or an otter—it's dark and no bigger than Jacko. Then two points appear and flick. Ears? Yes. Black ears atop a black head. That's what I'm seeing—not the entire beast but just its head, rising from the water.

The ears appear first and then the top of a skull and then nostrils, each as big as my hand, rounding as the beast inhales air. That long head turns toward me . . . and a bright-green ceffyl-dwr eye meets mine.

CHAPTER TWENTY-FIVE

I freeze as Jacko hisses, his claws digging into my arms before he shifts them with a chirp of apology. His gaze, though, stays fixed on the beast. On that green eye. On the hair that had seemed black, but is actually darkest green.

One of the ceffyl-dwrs caught up to us. It swam underwater into that deep pool . . .

No, there's a white blaze on the beast's nose, and its head is only the size of my mare's. This is another ceffyl-dwr, a young one.

And where there's a juvenile, there will be adults. Ceffyl-dwrs live in small herds—family groups of a stallion, a few mares and their children.

We've escaped one family only to run straight into another, and I want to fall on my knees and weep with frustration and exhaustion. Dropbears, encantados, ceffyl-dwrs and more ceffyl-dwrs.

It's the Dunnian Woods, Rowan. At the edge of the mountains. This is where the monsters are. This is why people don't come here. Weeping about that is like heading to sea and crying about all the water.

I know this, but I'm just so tired. I'm not sure I can fight. I'm not sure any of us can. I should shout for Dain and Alianor, warn them, and prepare, but instead, I just stare at the young ceffyl-dwr as it stares back.

The beast snorts, its breath rippling the water. Then it makes its way toward the almost-submerged trunk separating us. The ceffyl-dwr looks like an alligator, half its head skimming over the water. When it reaches the trunk, it can no longer see me, and that head rises, very slowly, peeking over the log.

Jacko has stopped hissing, though his flanks vibrate with a low, steady growl. I glance around for the others. Dain, Alianor and Malric are all occupied fifty feet away. Tiera is farther down the river, fishing and ignoring us.

I look at the ceffyl-dwr.

"Hello," I say, my voice unsteady.

The ceffyl-dwr's ears flick at the sound. It tilts its head, as if waiting for more.

"I'm Rowan," I say. "A human. Have you ever seen one before?"

Another attentive head tilt. It doesn't know what I'm saying, but the sound of my voice tells it that I am reasonably calm, maybe a little afraid, but not aggressive, not threatening.

The beast swims alongside the log until it reaches the shore. As it emerges, I brace myself, fingers twitching for my sword as I calculate how close I can let it get before I draw my weapon.

It steps onto the shore and turns to regard me. It stays where it is, as uncertain as I am and twice as curious. Still growling, Jacko leans forward, his nose working.

"You're a beautiful beast," I say. "I bet you know that, don't you?"

The ceffyl-dwr tosses its head. *His* head. When it walked from the water, well, I could tell its sex. A stallion makes me extra nervous, but I remind myself I still have time to draw my sword, and he isn't any bigger than my mare. I see no other members of his herd. He might actually be alone—after a certain age, a stallion is driven from his herd to fend for himself until he is old enough and strong enough to fight another stallion and take his mares.

As the ceffyl-dwr watches me, I keep telling him he's beautiful. It's true. His coat is deepest green, the sun catching and lighting the incredible color. His eyes are bright emeralds. His hooves shine black, and his mane . . . I'm not sure whether it's black or an even darker green than his coat. It hangs twice as long as a horse's, a tangle that looks like seaweed. Barnacles cling to the ends of the strands, and when he tosses his head, they click like castanets.

I'm not sure what to do next. He isn't moving toward me, and I *know* I shouldn't move toward him. Even a wild horse is dangerous to approach. Yet I'm not certain I should back away either. He might see that as submission and attack.

I draw myself up taller and continue talking and—

The ground thunders behind me, and I glance to see Malric charging at the ceffyl-dwr, his head down, paws pounding,

Dain and Alianor behind him, running with weapons in hand as they finally see where I am and what I'm doing.

"No!" I shout. "It's fine. Don't—"

The ceffyl-dwr rears, whinnying. His hooves slash so fast I hear them slice through the air. I shout at Malric. The warg skids to a halt just out of striking range, and he bears down, snarling and snapping.

The young stallion paws the air and trumpets his battle cry. He doesn't attack, though. He stands his ground in a threat display, and Malric does the same. I move up beside Malric. He shoots a snarl my way, one that I'm sure translates to "Draw your blasted sword, girl!" I don't. I only move forward, Jacko hopping at my feet.

I stay beside Malric and call to the ceffyl-dwr softly, saying, "You're all right. Everyone's all right. We'll be leaving in a moment. We just need you to let us pass."

"He can't understand you, Rowan," Alianor says.

"It's her tone," Dain says. "He'll understand that and her body language."

The ceffyl-dwr watches them as they speak, and again he cocks his head, ears flicking. Those green eyes seem to shine even brighter, and I swear I see the beast processing. He may never have seen humans before, and now he hears us all making the same sounds, and all speaking in the same unthreatening tones as we communicate amongst ourselves.

"May we pass?" I ask. "May we leave you to your pool?"

I step sideways toward the forest. The ceffyl-dwr's gaze follows me, but he doesn't move. I take two more side steps while Malric stands his ground. I'm almost at the forest, and then the ceffyl-dwr prances toward me.

Malric lunges. His jaws snap an inch from the ceffyl-dwr's leg, and I know he's missed on purpose. It's a warning snap. The ceffyl-dwr snaps back, and they glower at each another, the stallion lowering his head to look right into Malric's eyes.

The ceffyl-dwr prances my way again. Malric growls. I don't need to tell him not to attack. The stallion's movements are light, no battle charge, just a pretty two-step inching closer to me.

Then the ceffyl-dwr rears, pawing the air and shaking his mane. His front hooves hit the ground and his back ones fly up as he bucks. I have no idea what he's doing until he lands and somehow, in that playful, twisting, bucking, seemingly innocuous movement, he's gotten himself right in front of me, and Malric lets out a snarl of pure rage at himself for missing the trick. The warg doesn't attack, though. He doesn't dare. The ceffyl-dwr is so close that his breath tickles my hair.

"Princess . . ." Dain says. "I have a shot lined up."

"Good," I say. "But please don't take it until I ask you to. No matter what he does."

Dain grumbles, and Malric echoes it. The ceffyl-dwr inhales, his nostrils rounding. Then he blows a breath, smelling of fish, the hot blast of it rippling through my hair. As he sniffs me, I carefully unsheathe my sword.

One last sniff before his mouth opens, just a little. He knows what I look like, what I sound like, and what I smell like. Now he's wondering what I'd taste like.

"No," I say in the firmest voice I can muster.

He closes his mouth, tilts his head, considers again. Those jaws open, just enough for me to see his sharp white teeth.

"No," I say again.

He blinks and pulls back with a whinny. Then his head darts forward, and he nips my shoulder so I fast I don't have time to do anything but yank away. It's a quick nip, testing me, and as he withdraws, I swing my sword. He sees it and prances back, but I catch him in the front shoulder with the broadside. I only mean to whack him in warning, but the obsidian edge is too sharp and it nicks his skin, blood welling. He prances away with an affronted whinny.

I lift my hand to my shoulder. When I press my fingers in, I wince, but his teeth didn't penetrate the wet leather of my tunic.

"Now you know what I taste like," I say, lifting my sword. "Obsidian and steel."

He continues his dance for a few moments, bucking and rearing and prancing, hooves striking the ground. Very clearly not pleased that this nasty human hurt him when all he wanted to do was see whether she was edible. His cut is shallow, though, and it certainly doesn't impede him, and after a lick at the slice, he stops and eyes me again.

"We would like to pass now," I say. "Please allow us to pass."

He tosses his head and whinnies. Then he charges.

"Princess!" Dain shouts.

"Hold!" I say.

The ceffyl-dwr charges until he's a few feet away from me. Then he stops short, clods of dirt flying. He stands there, head down, watching me.

"No," I say. "I'm not going to run away. I'm not going to attack you either. Now stand down, ceffyl-dwr, and allow us to pass."

Another head toss.

"Rowan," Alianor calls. "As entertaining as this is, it's taking time we don't have if we're going to reach the gryphon aerie tonight."

"We can't approach it at nightfall anyway," I say. "If going there alone is our plan at all. I haven't decided. As for this guy . . ."

"Let Rowan handle him," Dain says. "He's young, and he's curious, but he's a stallion and a beast, and he's testing her before he decides to let us—"

The ceffyl-dwr's head swivels toward Dain so fast, we all jump. The young stallion trumpets and charges, and I race after him, my sword raised, Malric lunging, Dain diving out of the way. Only the ceffyl-dwr isn't running at Dain. He's running at something behind him, something coming down the river.

The ceffyl-dwr stallion.

The older stallion leaps from the river and lands on the bank, his head down as he paws the ground. The young ceffyl-dwr gallops into his path and rears. The older one does the same, the two of them on their back legs, facing off. The young one strikes first, and that's a mistake. He's young and inexperienced, and he wants the first blow, and the stallion expects that.

The bigger ceffyl-dwr dodges and bites the young one's shoulder. The young one twists and kicks with his hind legs. One makes contact and the older stallion falls back with a screech—too much of a screech for what was only a glancing blow.

The stallion is in rough shape. I sliced him deep in the front quarter, and he has other cuts from his fight with the mare. Still, he's much bigger and stronger than the younger ceffyl-dwr.

"Rowan?" Alianor says. "We need to go while they're distracted."

I nod but don't answer, my gaze fixed on the battling stallions.

Dain steps up beside me and lowers his voice. "The young one isn't defending us. He's defending his territory and himself."

They're right. Yet the thought of abandoning the young stallion to his fate . . .

He'll be fine. With the older one's injuries, it's too even a match. The older ceffyl-dwr will realize that and retreat. He risks his herd if he loses this fight.

Still . . .

You were trying to escape the young ceffyl-dwr yourself. He's still a threat. You can't endanger anyone else by interfering.

"Retreat," I say, my gaze on the ceffyl-dwrs.

When Alianor and Dain hesitate, I wave and begin walking backward toward the forest edge. Once we reach it, I ask Dain if I may use his bow.

"For what?" he asks.

I don't answer, and he shakes his head. I'm about to ask again when he takes the weapon from his shoulder. He doesn't hand it to me, though. He waves for us to get farther into the forest.

"They'll have trouble following us in there," he says. "It's too thick."

He lines up the shot.

"I can—" I begin.

"No, actually, you can't, princess. You'll need more practice first."

"I wouldn't ask you—"

"You didn't."

He waves me back, and I take a few more steps, with Malric and Jacko both herding me. I don't go far, though. I wait while Dain shoots two arrows, in quick succession. One hits the older stallion in the shoulder, the other strikes his flank. Neither is anywhere near fatal, but they add to the older ceffyl-dwr's collection of wounds, giving him all the more reason to deliver a quick thrashing to the youngster and then retreat with his dignity intact.

Dain's right, too, that I could not have made those shots—not without serious risk of hitting the younger stallion instead.

We don't wait to see how the stallion reacts. That was the danger of doing this—the risk that he'd see who struck him and charge. Dain fires the arrows and beats a hasty retreat to where we wait. Then we all hurry deep into the thick forest, where the ceffyl-dwrs cannot follow.

When we're far enough in—and the stallions give no sign of coming after us—Alianor says, "So what's the plan?"

I glance at Tiera, walking behind Malric.

I don't know the right choice here. If I say we should press on, is it because that's genuinely the right move? Or because I want to prove I can do this myself?

If I'm worried about looping back and encountering the ceffyl-dwrs again, is that really any greater a danger than encountering unknown monsters if we carry on without Wilmot and Kaylein? Are we making things worse for *them* by forcing them to pursue us?

But I'm the royal monster hunter—if I wait for rescue when my goal is nearby, that's something Heward and Branwyne can use against me.

She was a quarter-day's hike from an aerie, yet she huddled in the forest like a frightened child. Waited so her guard and her trainer could take the risks in her stead. How will she ever survive the trials alone in the mountains?

"I say we press forward," Alianor says.

When I glance at Dain, he seems startled, as if he didn't expect me to seek his opinion. I don't outright ask, though. To ask is to put the responsibility on him. Yet I can wait to see whether he'll give me an opinion, and after a moment's contemplation, he does.

"Wilmot would want us to wait, but that means spending more time in dangerous woods," he says. "Finding him wouldn't be a simple matter of heading back in the right direction. He can't track us either, not when we came by river. He might find the remains of our raft and our sign but . . ." He shrugs. "He might not. Going forward is definitely dangerous. I'm not sure it's *more* dangerous than waiting, though."

"I am afraid if I stay behind, Heward will say it proves I'm not ready to wield the ebony sword."

"And if you push on, he'll use that, too, as proof you're impetuous and reckless."

"Like my father," I murmur, too low for them to hear.

"The truth, Rowan," Alianor says, "is that Heward and his supporters will find a way to use anything against you. If you're going to live worrying how Heward can fault you for it, you'll end up doing nothing at all . . . and he'll fault you for that."

Dain gives a slow nod, as if reluctant to agree with Alianor, but here he must, because she is indeed correct.

"What you must consider instead," she continues, "is how your people will view your choice. Will they want their royal monster hunter waiting for the adults . . . or completing the task on her own?"

Dain glares at her. "No, that is not what she must consider. Ever. It's like a boxer asking the crowd what he should do next. Whatever is most entertaining . . . and most dangerous. If she lives her life like *that*, she won't live it for very long."

He glances at me. "You need to do what you feel is right, Rowan. Whichever way you can argue was correct when you are questioned."

I nod. "Push on, then. If both paths seem to hold equal danger, I should complete my task."

CHAPTER TWENTY-SIX

Back at the riverbank, Dain and Alianor had left a sign for Wilmot to say we were fine and headed inland. Now we write another one, presuming Wilmot can find our trail from the first. I use Dain's dagger to write *Gone to aerie* on a tree while Alianor hangs a strip of her bright-yellow tunic from the lowest branch and Dain tramples the undergrowth, hoping it will mark a place Wilmot will find.

Then we hike out.

We stop before twilight makes it too dark to see our way. We could have gone farther, but we found a likely shelter: a cave we can all fit inside, with an entrance small enough to defend.

Despite my pessimism earlier, we do have a few supplies—items in our belts and pockets that survived the river dunking. Fire sticks in a waterproof container, for one thing. That lets us start a fire and begin to dry our clothing. As we do that, Dain announces his intention to hunt.

I want to join him, but he refuses, and so I ask Malric to accompany him, and the warg seems to understand and, more surprisingly, agrees. The two of them head off in search of dinner.

As soon as they're out of sight, Alianor says, "You really thought I refused to come along?" And it takes me a moment to realize what she means. So much has happened since last night that I've almost forgotten she hasn't been with us from the start.

When I shrug, she eyes me, her expression hidden in half-shadow under the campfire glow. After a moment, she says, "If I'd warned you, then you couldn't honestly tell your queen mother that you knew nothing of my plan. I didn't want to put you into a position where you'd get into trouble."

"Thank you." I scratch Jacko around his antlers, which makes his leg twitch with delight.

Silence stretches for a few minutes. Then she says, "Earlier, I joked about what my father expects me to do at the castle. I wanted to be the *first* to say it. My dad says that rumors fly faster than the swiftest arrow, and they're twice as deadly, and the higher your position, the faster and sharper they get. In the castle? That's as high as it goes. That must be hard for you."

I must look confused, because she smiles and says, "Or maybe for you, it's just normal. You may have enemies, but you have plenty of allies, too. In the castle, all I have are enemies."

She hurries on before I can protest. "I just mean that I'm an outsider from Clan Bellamy, so they're looking for my angle. If I'm with you, I must be ingratiating myself with the princess. If I'm with Rhydd, I must be hoping to win myself a crown. They're going to say it, so I say it first. Get it out in the open so we can talk about it."

She crosses and uncrosses her legs, as if trying to get comfortable. Then she looks at me. "Do you want to talk about it?"

I'm quiet, petting Tiera as the gryphon settles against my side. Rhydd didn't want me mentioning this to Alianor, but she already knows what people are saying, so I say, "I did wonder, when you refused my invitation to join the expedition. It felt like . . ." I shrug. "Rejection, I guess. Like maybe I thought we were better friends than we actually are."

I run my hands over Tiera's furry flank, and she leans into me so I can reach an itchy spot. "It's mostly just been me and Rhydd. There are other kids we play with but . . ." Another shrug. "It's hard, like you said. I appreciate that you brought this up. You're right. That makes it easier. You'll want to speak to Rhydd, too." I add, carefully, "He might already know, but . . ."

She grins. "He does. We spoke after you left. He thinks it's hilarious. He has agreed to marry me if I promise to handle all the really boring political dinners and meetings in his place. I have refused. So . . ." She shrugs. "No crown for me."

As we stretch out on the grass, she says, "Speaking of boys, have you noticed how cute Kethan is?"

"Heward's son?" I sputter.

"He's actually really nice."

"You want to marry Kethan?"

"Ugh, no. I don't want to marry anyone. I'm just saying he's cute." She purses her lips. "I wonder if he'd be a good kisser."

"Eww." I shudder.

"You'd say that about anyone, Rowan. Give it another year, and then we'll talk."

"Not if it's about kissing the guy whose dad wants to destroy my family."

"Oooh, star-crossed lovers! That is so romantic."

"Uh, no. No, it is not. Especially when he's *eighteen*. That's gross."

"Maybe not Kethan, then. How about . . ."

She begins listing other boys from the castle, and I close my eyes, resting as my mind fills with more pleasant thoughts, like what Dain will bring us back for dinner.

Dain and Malric catch a few birds, and we dine on those as well as some nuts I gathered close to our camp. Then it's bedtime.

We agree to a guard schedule. Dain will go first, and then Alianor, with me taking the final shift until morning. I suppose Malric could have a turn, but it being impossible for us to obtain his agreement, he gets to spend the night in undisturbed slumber, the lucky beast.

I fall asleep faster than I expect. I'm cuddled up with Tiera, Jacko at my stomach, and I drift off into a deep and dreamless sleep. I wake briefly when Dain and Alianor change guard shifts, and when I fall asleep after that, it's not nearly as deep or as dreamless.

I keep seeing Jacko in the water, thrashing, his eyes rolling my way, begging me to save him. At first, the dream reflects reality—I'm fighting with all my might to get to him. But then it changes, and I'm just standing on the raft, watching. I wake gasping from that one, and he wakes, too, his antlers knocking my face as I hold him tight and he cuddles in.

Next, I tumble into a dream where I'm at the aerie, only it's empty, with no sign of gryphons having been there in years. I tie Tiera by her leg shackle and walk away as she screeches in terror and confusion. I startle awake from that, and she's right there, against me, and I cuddle closer, shivering. When the beat of her heart rocks me to sleep, I only fall into a fresh nightmare, one where there *are* gryphons in the aerie, and when we drop off Tiera, they attack her . . . and I walk away, leaving her screaming for me.

I bolt upright, and I sit there, rubbing my arms as I shiver, despite the warm night and the even warmer bodies pressed against mine. I don't try to lie down again. There's no hope of sleep. So I creep to the entrance and tell Alianor I'll take over early.

She squints up at the moon, calculating the time.

"It's barely halfway through my shift," she says.

"It's fine. I can't sleep."

She peers at me. "Bad dreams?"

I shrug.

"About the ceffyl-dwrs?"

I give a noncommittal nod.

"While I'm sorry for your nightmares, I'm also a little bit glad you aren't as fearless as you seem."

"Oh, believe me, I'm not fearless. I'm just really good at faking it."

"Nah, even with nightmares, you're still frighteningly fearless, Rowan." She pulls me into an unexpected hug. "I won't insist on finishing my shift, but get me up early so I can take over and let you rest."

CHAPTER TWENTY-SEVEN

I settle in just outside the cave entrance, where a low fire
burns. Jacko takes up position on my lap. When Tiera
realizes I'm not returning to the cave, she comes out, too.
She tries to settle at my back, wrapping herself around me like
a soft chair. I kneel beside her instead, moving Jacko so I can
hug her, and when I do sit again, she lays her head on my lap,
and Jacko snuggles in by her stomach.

As I stroke Tiera's head, I think about the nightmare. I've
tried to be brave about letting her go, but inside, I feel as if I really
am abandoning her. I'm the closest thing she has to a mother,
and she's not yet grown, and I'm about to walk away from her
forever. Just thinking about it makes my chest hurt and my eyes
fill, and I want to hug her and tell her I won't abandon her.

But what are my other options? Tell my mother I'm keeping her? That's reckless and irresponsible and immature. I'd
need to keep her in a permanent cage, and I'd never do that.

The only other choice would be to run away with her and live in the forest. Which would be just as reckless and irresponsible and immature. I am the royal monster hunter. Giving that up would mean turning my back on my family and my kingdom.

Both options are unthinkable. So I must do something almost equally unthinkable. Abandon Tiera.

No, not *abandon* her. Give her back to her own kind. What happened in those nightmares is no more possible than me standing by and watching Jacko drown. I would have found a way to save him. And I won't leave Tiera until I'm sure she has a good home, with gryphons who accept her.

What if they don't?

Then I'll find gryphons who will. Or I'll come up with an alternate plan. I can say my only choices are to cage her or run away with her, but that's not entirely true. Ideally, she should be with other gryphons. If she cannot, then I'd need to figure out a way to keep her isolated in the forest with caretakers until she's able to fend for herself.

What I cannot do, though, is keep her as a companion. I know that, and yet I don't think I've fully understood what it will be like to leave her forever. I do now, and as we sit by the fire, I prepare for a time, mere hours from now, when all I will have of her are memories.

Over the last three months, I've taken pages and pages of notes on Tiera. Her habits and her growth and her changing appearance. Scientific observations. Now I don't just study her—I commit her to memory. What does her fur feel like? Her feathers? Her talons and beak and tail?

What does she smell like? What does her heartbeat sound like? Her shrieks? The odd little noise that tells me she is content? Most of all, what is it like to be here with her now, by the fire?

I curl up against her, my nose buried at the line between her head feathers and body fur. Then Dain clears his throat from the cave entrance. I glance to see Malric lying there, as if the warg has been silently watching over us all along.

"Is it your shift already?" Dain whispers as he walks over.

"I couldn't sleep, so I took over early."

"Is everything okay?"

"I slept really well, and then I didn't. I guess I'd had enough rest."

His gaze studies mine. He knows I'm lying, but he doesn't call me on it.

"Why aren't *you* sleeping?" I ask.

He shrugs and only says, "May I join you?"

I nod.

As he sits, Jacko hops over, stops a foot away and stares at Dain.

"Really?" Dain sighs. "I save you from drowning, and you still don't want me near your princess?"

"I haven't thanked you for that," I say. "I'm not even sure *how* to thank you for it. You risked your life for a beast." I manage a wry smile. "One you don't even like very much."

"I wasn't going to let you watch him drown, princess. Or jump in yourself after him. I would, however, appreciate a little gratitude from *him*."

I lean to look at Jacko's eyes, which are still fixed on Dain.

Then I chuckle. "He's not glaring at you, Dain. He's asking permission to come closer."

"Why would he need that?"

"Uh, because of that whole 'you don't like him very much' thing. He isn't going to hop onto your lap and risk being thrown off. That's just humiliating."

"I think you're wrong but . . ." He puts out his fingers. "If he bites these off, it's your fault."

Jacko sniffs the outstretched fingers while Dain holds himself very still, as if he expects a nip. Jacko sniffs and then takes another hop, bringing himself close enough for Dain to touch. Dain reaches out and tentatively strokes Jacko's head.

"He likes to be scratched at the base of his antlers," I say.

Dain tries it, still cautious, and while Jacko doesn't exactly hop onto his lap purring, he does settle in, a handsbreadth from Dain, and allows himself to be petted.

A few moments pass, then Dain says, his gaze on Jacko, "Earlier, when I went hunting, I didn't want you along because Alianor had asked for some time alone with you. I said I needed to talk to you, too, and I'd hoped that'd mean she'd give me some time in return but . . ." He shrugs. "It's Alianor."

True. Alianor isn't good at interpreting hints. If he wanted time alone with me, he needed to come out and say it.

"I wanted to talk about . . ." He rolls his shoulders, shifting in discomfort. "What Branwyne said."

"*Did* you tell her I'm only fit to be the royal zookeeper?"

"Not . . . exactly?" His voice rises at the end, as if this is a question. "I . . ." He trails off again and rubs his mouth, his gaze slinking toward the fire.

"Was she giving you a hard time about me?" I ask.

He looks over sharply.

I pull my knees in. "Rhydd is the diplomat. He knows how to dig around a problem to unearth it. I only know how to attack it straight on, and sometimes, that means being too blunt."

I shift, tucking my legs under me. "Earlier, Alianor said that her father wants her to befriend me and Rhydd because it helps her clan. Political advantage. She said she'd rather I hear that from her than have someone whisper it in my ear."

"Okay . . ."

"I've been told you're probably dealing with the same thing, but I shouldn't ask you outright, because you'll get defensive. I don't think that's helping matters, though, so . . . Are people giving you a hard time about being my friend?"

He squirms, as if wanting to duck back into the cave to avoid answering. But then he meets my gaze and says, "Yes."

"They're saying that you're trying to ingratiate yourself with me because you're thinking of becoming a monster hunter, and I'm the *royal* monster hunter."

"Yes."

"Are they also teasing you because I'm a girl?"

His cheeks darken. "It's not teasing," he mutters. "They mock me. Especially—" He cuts himself short and shakes his head.

"Branwyne?"

"She wants to be queen. But Rhydd isn't on the throne yet, so you're her target. She wants to make you look incompetent." He shifts again. "I don't understand court life. All the"—he flails his hands—"layers. Underhanded tricks and hidden motivations."

"What did Branwyne do?"

"I thought it was *me* she didn't like. That's how she acted. Who was I really? Where did I actually come from? What was Wilmot up to?"

He glances my way. "Alianor's dad wants her to get close to you and Rhydd. Branwyne made me feel like I was doing that for Wilmot. I defended myself, and then she said maybe I liked you in a different way. You're a princess, and you're the royal monster hunter, and you're pretty, and *that's* why I was always hanging around you, and I was a fool if I thought you'd look twice at me."

His fists clench. "She made me feel like some dirty peasant boy and . . ."

"And so you insulted me. To prove her wrong."

"I didn't—" He bites the word off with a sharp shake of his head. "Yes. I wanted her to leave me alone, and I said things I shouldn't have said, things I didn't mean. I grumbled about you and your monster companions. I said I didn't think you'd make a good monster hunter, that I didn't think you were pretty, that I didn't think you were as clever as everyone says . . ."

He rubs his hands over his face. "I was a jerk. I said awful things, things I don't believe, because I wanted her to stop making fun of me. That's all I thought about. Not that she might go around saying I don't believe you're fit for the job. I think you'll make a great royal monster hunter, Rowan. I really do, and I'll start telling people that."

"Then they'll think you have to, because I found out you've been saying otherwise."

He winces, his whole face screwing up. "Right. Okay. I ..." He throws up his hands. "I'm no good at this court stuff. I'm going to cause trouble for you, Rowan. That's what I've been thinking ever since Branwyne. When you chose Alianor over me, that seemed to prove it. Even you knew I wasn't worth the trouble."

"I chose Alianor because of what you'd said. Because I presumed you believed it." I meet his gaze. "I can't have a companion who'll insult me to save his *dignity*, Dain."

He buries his face in his hands. "I know. I've messed up so bad."

He lowers his hands just enough to look over his fingertips. "I'm not meant to be part of a monster hunting troop, Rowan. I belong in the woods, like Wilmot, where I don't have to deal with ..." A hand flail. "People."

"Is that what you want? To be left alone?"

"No. I want ..." He lowers his hands and looks at me. "I'm not sure what I want. To be a monster hunter, I know that. But with the royal troop or on my own? I don't know yet. Right now, I want to learn more. Wilmot is a good teacher, but he doesn't have all the skills I need. I want to train at the castle."

"Alone?" I lock gazes with him. "You can say yes to that, Dain. You don't need to hang out with me to get royal training. If you want to be left alone ..."

"I ..." He trails off, panic flitting across his face as his mouth opens and closes. Finally, he shuts it, squares his shoulders and says, "I don't."

I struggle against a laugh at how hard it is for him to make even this small admission. He glares at me, and I wipe a hand over my mouth.

"It's okay to say you want to be around other people, Dain. It's okay to say you're fine being around me. You don't even need to say you *want* to be. Just that you're fine with it."

I think my tone is gentle, but he fidgets like I'm shouting at him. I remember what Wilmot said about Dain's family.

Dain says he had to go into service, which makes it sound as if he'd been dragged from his sobbing family. But he never mentions them. Wilmot bought Dain's freedom, so after that, there was no reason he couldn't go home, at least to visit. He doesn't seem to, though, which means . . .

It means he doesn't want to go home. Or, worse, they don't want him.

I just had those horrible dreams of abandoning Jacko and Tiera. What would it be like to *be* the one who is abandoned?

Is that what happened to Dain?

My stomach clenches so hard I want to throw up. When I do leave Tiera, it will be with a new family. That wasn't what Dain's parents did. They left him with a horrible person, who expected him to live in the barn and work for a living when he was five. *Five.*

I've thought before about how different my life has been from his. That's one reason I don't just walk away when he's being a jerk. Even with Wilmot, Dain's life wasn't exactly princess-style luxury. But I haven't thought of how different it was in other ways.

When *I* was five, my parents had to go south for a winter wedding, and they decided Rhydd and I should stay home, where it was safe and warm. I'd howled, flying into a rage and accusing them of abandoning me.

Thinking of that, shame washes through me, so thick I almost choke on it. Berinon had taken me aside and told me, gently but firmly, that parents often have to go away, and if I was going to behave like that, maybe they'd need to go away more often until I got used to it. That shut me up fast. Then, after a week, they returned with presents and stories and hugs, and for two days they were with us from morning until night to make up for it.

What if they'd actually left for good? I cannot even imagine it. But Dain lived it. Even if it wasn't his parents' fault, he would have *felt* abandoned, and that's what mattered.

So now I'm amused because he struggles to admit he doesn't want to be alone?

I remember Wilmot laughing at Dain's version of how he came to stay with him. To Dain, he'd made a fool of himself, begging to be allowed to apprentice with Wilmot. In reality, he'd barely said a word. He just *felt* as if he'd begged. Because even saying, "Train me, please" had been hard. Like saying, "No, I don't want to be alone." Admitting that you want something from another person. That they have the power to say no, and it'd feel like your parents walking away all over again.

"Dain?" I say as he fidgets. He lifts his gaze, not quite meeting mine. "I usually call you my companion. Do you know why?"

More fidgeting, and a one-shouldered shrug.

"Because I'm afraid to call you my friend," I say. "I'm not sure you consider me a friend, and if I admit I think of you that way, and you don't feel the same, it'd be weird and awkward and embarrassing. But . . ." I shrug. "I need to get over that. Unless you don't want me to call you a friend . . ."

His gaze meets mine, and he shakes his head. Then his eyes widen. "I mean, no, I don't *not* want you—" A deep breath. "You *can* call me that. I'll never be weird about it. I do consider you a friend, so you . . . You know."

He makes a face and then shifts. "I'm hard to get along with. Wilmot tries to teach me how to be friendlier, but that's like . . ."

"A warg teaching a jackalope to fly?"

We both laugh softly.

"Yeah," he says. "Wilmot isn't exactly the friendliest person either. That's why we get along. I can be moody. Cranky, like you say."

"Nah, it's more . . ." I scoop up one of the nuts scattered over the ground. It's encased in a thick, spiked husk. "Prickly, like this. But the spines are meant to protect the nut, and once you get past them, you'll find a very sweet—"

"No," he says, glaring at me.

I grin. "Very sweet center. You just need to peel back . . ." I dig my nails into the green covering, but it's nearly as hard as a shell. I put the nut down and lift a rock.

"Smash it?" Dain says. "I don't think I like this comparison, princess."

"Crack it open gently." When a light smack doesn't do

— 240 —

anything, I smash the rock hard, and both the husk and shell break, the nut flying out, pieces shooting everywhere.

"*Really* not liking this comparison," he says.

"You get past the prickly outer husk and the hard shell within, and then there's a sweet—"

"Princess . . ." he says, his voice heavy with warning.

I grin, pop the nut into my mouth, bite down and—

I spit it out so fast Jacko leaps up in alarm.

"That's what I was trying to tell you, princess," Dain says. "A nut with that prickly green husk means it isn't ripe yet."

"Oh, *oh*," I sputter as I spit. I jump to my feet, flapping my arms and screwing up my face as I look around for something, anything, to get this horrible taste out of my mouth. And Dain is laughing, laughing like I've never seen him, rocking back and sputtering and shaking as I glower at him and finally locate a waterskin. I gulp and then spit. Gulp and spit.

When I finally sink to the ground, gasping, Dain says, "So if I have this right, I'm a prickly, unripe nut, and if you ignore my spikes and smash me open, you'll find I'm bitter and gross inside." He glances over. "Close enough?"

I glare at him. He laughs some more. When he catches his breath, he tosses me an honest grin and says, "I appreciate the effort, princess, but I might suggest dramatic comparisons are really not your thing. Prickly is a good way to describe me, though, even if I hope 'bitter and gross' *isn't*. I appreciate that you're making the effort to get past the spikes, though." He meets me gaze and sobers. "I really do."

I duck my head in a nod.

He continues. "I promise to be a lot more careful with what I say about you to others. I learned my lesson, and I'm truly sorry. I mean that. I will never insult you in front of anyone who wouldn't know I'm just teasing."

"Or you could just not insult me at all."

He stretches his legs. "I could. Let's make that a pact, then. We will never say anything even mildly insulting to each other again. That means you can't tell me when I'm being prickly or cranky or difficult. You can only tell me I'm awesome. You can't push me to spar with you by telling me I'm a lousy swordsman. You can only say I'm an amazing archer, and you hope to be as good as me someday."

He glances at me. "You could start practicing now. I'm ready for the compliments."

"You have really nice fingernails."

His brows shoot up.

I point at his hands. "Your fingernails are always clean and smoothly cut and really nice."

"Anything else?"

"Nope. That's all I've got. But they *are* nice fingernails."

He throws back his head and laughs.

"Okay, I get your point," I say. "Friends tease one another, and sometimes, that's a way to prod them to improve. You're free to tell me when I'm being reckless or irresponsible, because I am sometimes."

He makes a face. "You're never irresponsible, Rowan. That's not the same as reckless—not unless your recklessness endangers others. If you were like that, we wouldn't be returning her"—he hooks a thumb at Tiera, sleeping wrapped around me—"to the mountains."

"Okay, but sometimes when you tease me, it doesn't feel like prodding. It feels like an actual insult. As if I *am* irresponsible. Immature. Not terribly bright. Not worthy of this." I lay my hand on the hilt of my sword.

As I talk, his eyes widen. Then he shakes his head. "I definitely don't mean any of that. I'm just being . . . prickly, like you said. But I can see how it might sound. So I'll be more careful. A lot more careful."

"So will I. If I say anything that feels like a real insult, tell me."

He nods and leans back against a tree. "Not to change the subject . . ."

"Which you totally want to do."

A small smile. "True. I was going to ask about the ceffyl-dwrs. I don't know a lot about them."

"Well, thankfully, they aren't usually found near people, so hunters rarely deal with them. We do get called, though, maybe every few years, when a herd makes its way down one of the larger rivers. I remember one time Jannah and my dad were summoned to deal with . . ."

I trail off. "And that's not telling you facts about ceffyl-dwrs."

He shrugs. "Stories have facts. And they're easier to remember. Tell me what happened."

I smile and snuggle down onto Tiera as Jacko hops over, and we settle in for a story.

CHAPTER TWENTY-EIGHT

I fall asleep after telling my story. I don't mean to, but my eyelids get heavy, and I mumble something to Dain about just closing my eyes, not to let me fall asleep . . . and the next thing I know, it's dawn and Dain has magically transformed into Alianor.

I lift my head, blinking. "Alianor?" I croak.

"I came out to take over guard duty and let you nap," she says. "But you already were. I sent Dain inside to rest."

I rise, blinking hard. I'd been lying on Tiera, but she woke up hungry, so she's tearing into a bird Dain caught last night. Jacko hops away from my stomach and eyes the bird.

I stretch as I yawn. When I spot Malric behind me, I say, "I'm going to the stream to wash up. Will you come with me?"

The warg watches me in silence until I start to walk away, Jacko hopping at my heels. Then he lumbers after me.

"We'll let Dain sleep," I call back to Alianor. "But I'll want to get away before the sun's much higher."

"Agreed."

She doesn't offer to come with me. While we haven't seen any monsters, we can't leave Dain alone sleeping in the cave. We'll take turns washing up, accompanied by Malric.

The stream is a few hundred feet away. When we reach it, I refill my waterskin, grateful that I'd had it tied to my belt instead of in my pack. My soap and change of clothing are in that long-gone pack, so I have to settle for washing with water—cold water.

I'm bent over, raking my fingers through my curls when I ask Malric if he wants to hunt. We have food for breakfast, but it might be wise to get more, and dawn's a good time to do it. I think he knows the word *hunt*, and he definitely knows *Malric*, but when I ask, he doesn't respond.

I flip my curls back and see him standing a few feet away, looking in the other direction.

"I'm still dressed, if that's why you're turned around," I joke.

He doesn't move. Okay, so he's ignoring me.

"No hunting, I guess?" I say as I rake my fingers through a sleep knot.

I'm still kneeling, and when Jacko chirps anxiously, I look back to see him hopping back and forth over my feet. I quietly rise and pull my sword as I peer in the direction Malric is staring.

It's still dawn, the forest dark with shadow. Across the stream, though, I can make out yellow eyes watching Malric from a bush. As I adjust my sword, a dark gray muzzle slides out. A head follows, and I grip my sword tighter.

It's a warg. A gray one, about a hand's length shorter than Malric with a slighter build. A female?

The new warg pays no attention to me. It slides from behind the bush, gaze fixed on Malric, tail swaying, no submission in its posture, but no aggression either.

Malric sniffs the air and whines, deep in his throat, and I chuckle. Yep, it's a girl.

"I'll leave you two alone," I say, and I take a step back, but Malric turns on me, snapping.

"Or not . . ."

His head whips back to the female warg. He's gone silent, staring at her, his eyes narrowed. Then his lip curls in a growl, and that startles me. I almost tell him to be nicer—he's not going to make friends that way, and she's clearly interested in getting to know him better. But before I can chide him, the hairs on my neck rise. I'm learning to recognize this sense. It's the one that hisses "monsters" in my ear.

I swivel my gaze as I hold my body still. To my left, so faint I can barely make them out, another pair of yellow eyes reflect from deep in a cluster of bushes. As I keep scanning, I spot two more wargs, one by its eyes and the other by the tip of a tail flicking over the undergrowth.

"Trap," I whisper.

I don't know if Malric's smelled the other wargs—we're upwind of them—but he's figured out that this female isn't just being friendly. She's the bait.

Malric backs up until he's in front of me. The female keeps her gaze on him, still swishing her tail coquettishly. She's never once looked at me. She's doing that on purpose—pretending she doesn't see me.

Malric lowers his head and growls. The female has the gall to look offended, her eyes widening, head lifting as if in hurt surprise. She whines, and Malric's growl breaks into a snarl, his front feet planted, fur bristling, head lowered between his shoulders.

A warg bursts from his cover and charges, even as the female twists and snarls at him. He's a little smaller than her. Young and brave and foolish. He charges, and Malric spins on him, and I raise my sword, watching the other wargs. Then a brown blur shoots past me, and I barely have time to shout, "Jacko!" before he's launching himself at the young warg. He leaps clear onto the beast's back and sinks his teeth in.

The beast gives a very un-warg-like squeal of pain and surprise and starts bucking like a unicorn ambushed by fire ants. Jacko clings there, teeth and claws sunk in, riding along as the warg bucks and squeals.

The female stares, as if she can't quite believe what she's seeing. I'm sure she's spotted jackalopes before, maybe even eaten them. But I'm guessing they don't usually attack. So she has no idea what to do. Neither do the two other wargs, who step from their hiding spots, awaiting the female's signal.

I don't blame the wargs. Honestly, I'm not sure what to do either. Malric settles for snarling at the other three, muscles tense, ready to charge if any of them interfere. Otherwise, he seems to think Jacko is doing just fine.

I run forward, my sword raised, and I kick the young warg as he rears. He topples, Jacko still on him, and I slam my boot down on the warg's neck. Then I drive the tip of my sword into his throat, just enough for him to yelp.

The warg is much bigger than a wolf and much stronger than me. But Jannah always said not to think about that when you're fighting a monster. Think of it as an even match. *Act like it is.*

With both Jacko and my sword, I *can* fight this warg. So I channel that certainty into my expression as I glare down at him and press my sword into his neck. His eyes roll my way, and then he goes still, waiting and watching.

Jacko releases his hold and leaps onto the downed warg's side, throwing his head back in his victory cry.

"Yes, yes," I say. "But please be aware that there are three larger ones, right over there."

I gesture. Jacko follows my gaze and stops his cry but still puffs up and chatters at the others, who stare at him uncertainly. They look at their pack mate under my boot, and the female sniffs in disgust. They don't attack, though. They just watch. Watch Jacko, watch me and watch Malric, snarling between us.

Then the female—the pack alpha, it seems—sits. She lowers her rump to the ground, like a sword fighter lowering his weapon and saying, "Enough."

It's a trick. I know it is. There are three of them, plus the barely wounded young one under my boot. But from the way she's eyeing my sword, this might not be her first encounter with a blade. Monsters are smart, and this one has assessed her odds and decided we aren't worth the risk. At least, not worth attacking outright. If we stay on her territory, though . . .

"Malric?" I say. "Let's retreat."

I wave Jacko off the young warg. Then I back up slowly, sword tip still pointed at it. When the beast tries to rise, I slash, just enough to cut its front shoulder, and it falls back with a yip.

"My blade is sharper than your teeth," I say. "Remember that."

I start backing toward camp, sword raised, Jacko hissing at my feet. When we're a safe distance away, Malric follows, his gaze fixed on the four wargs. I get two more steps before I nearly bash into Alianor, hidden in the bushes, dagger in hand. Beside her, Dain crouches with his bow ready. Tiera sits off to the side, watching.

"We heard Jacko," Alianor says.

I nod. "They seem to be letting us leave, but we need to get out of here. Fast. The alpha's only standing down until she can mount a sneak attack. Fortunately, it's a small pack."

"Actually, it's not," Dain says.

I glance over at him, his attention still on the wargs.

"I've seen her before," he says. "She travels too close to Tamarel in the winter, when cows and sheep make tempting prey. She's got a pack of about ten. I'm guessing this is just a scouting party."

"All the more reason to leave," I say. "If she'll let us."

The wargs do let us leave. It's late summer, with plenty of food that *won't* put up a fight. Now Malric is off their territory, they seem satisfied.

Yvain said the aerie was in a mountainside. Technically an aerie is a nest used by a bird of prey, built in a high tree or on a mountain. Travelers have long reported finding such nests for gryphons, filled with the rotting corpses and skeletal remains of their victims. It makes a deliciously horrifying story, but the truth is that no monster hunter has ever come across a gryphon nest. They might be half bird, but why would they perch in a tree that wouldn't support the weight of their feline hindquarters? A nest also doesn't make sense when they don't lay eggs. As for those stories, Jannah would point out that no person, however adventurous, climbs to what looks like a massive predator's nest.

That last part holds true for monster hunters, too. No matter how curious we might be, we don't go *looking* for gryphon nests. Clan Hadleigh only knows of this aerie because they've spotted young gryphons in the area and therefore avoid the region. No one, including them, has ever seen an actual aerie. We are going to be the first.

We have a rough idea where to find it. When Yvain had mentioned landmarks, Alianor was paying close attention. It would have been a quarter-day's walk from the river if we'd gone as far as we were supposed to. From where we crashed, we figure it's a half-day hike, and we'd covered part of that yesterday.

Now we're off to an early start—earlier than we'd expected, thanks to the wargs—but that's good, because I soon realize it won't be like following a road. We're guessing, really. Wandering through the foothills in the right direction while looking for landmarks.

"If we don't see any by midday, we'll head for the river," I say. "This is too dangerous a spot to be in when it gets dark, and we have no idea how long it'll take to leave Tiera—to be sure she'll be accepted."

"How exactly do you plan to do that anyway, princess?" Dain asks.

My heart thumps double-time, and when I try to speak, my mouth is dry. "I . . . I'm not sure. I had been hoping Wilmot would have an idea. I should have talked to him more about the specifics . . ."

"I could have done that, too," Dain says. "I never thought of it."

My heart rate slows a little. His first question sounded like a challenge, but I realize he didn't mean it like that.

"I did speak to Wilmot a bit," I say. "The biggest concern is making sure the gryphons will accept her." I glance at Tiera. "Monsters aren't as likely as regular animals to hurt their own kind, especially young ones. If it was hard weather, they might shun her, because they don't want to share food, but if they accept her while we're there, they won't turn her out later. The problem is . . ."

"Making sure they accept her?"

I nod. "We can't get near the aerie, of course. That's asking for trouble. But if we can get *her* near it, then hopefully . . . Well, we'll figure something out. We just need to find those landmarks."

"Or we could just follow that," Dain says.

I squint into the sky, following his finger. There, in the distance, is a gryphon, flying toward a mountainside.

I grin. "Let's get higher and see where it lands."

We take off, scrambling up the hill, gaze fixed on the distant gryphon as it makes its way home.

CHAPTER TWENTY-NINE

We've located the gryphon aerie. It's on the mountainside, as Yvain had thought. Not a nest, but a cavern. That was what Jannah had always theorized—that gryphons would embrace their feline side and raise their young in dens.

When the adult gryphon flies into a huge hole in the mountainside, my insides ignite with a joy I can barely contain, and all I can think is that I cannot wait to tell Jannah ...

Nothing. I will tell my aunt nothing. I can't.

How much would she have loved to be here? How much would I love to have her here? Dad, too. He might not be as interested in the scientific aspects, but after a monster hunt, his eyes used to glow, his whole body thrumming with excitement. That's how he'd be, seeing an aerie.

What would it be like to have them both here? I shouldn't

think that. It makes my heart clench and my eyes fill. But it makes me feel something else, too. Something good.

I think back to the first time I fell off a horse. I broke a rib, and it hurt to breathe. Dad sat by my bedside all night, and when I woke in pain, he'd ask if I remembered what I'd been doing when I fell. Jumping over a log for the first time. What had it felt like, he'd asked. What happened just before that? I breathlessly told him how I got my pony up to a canter, and how incredible it felt to be riding so fast and when she jumped . . . It was the most amazing feeling ever. So, he asked, was I going to do it again, now that I'd fallen? Yes, I would, and when I thought of the good parts, even the pain wasn't so bad.

That's what it's like, wishing Dad and Jannah were here. It hurts, but it also makes me think of all the times they *were* with me. When I imagine how they'd look, what they'd say, it feels good, because it reminds me that I haven't forgotten them. I know exactly what Dad would say, seeing that gryphon fly into the aerie. I know exactly what Jannah would do. Mom always says Dad's still with me. Jannah, too. They're with me because I can imagine them here, and that makes me happy, even when it hurts.

Thinking of Dad, though—and especially of Jannah— means I realize something I need to do. Something they'd both insist on, if they were here.

I wait until we're partway up the small mountain. Climbing it isn't easy—while it's not steep, there aren't trails either. The mountain is thickly forested at the base, but quickly becomes rock. That's where I stop and turn to the others. Tiera immediately curls up with her head tucked under one wing. She's been alternating between flying and walking, and too much of either is exhausting at her age.

Jacko snuggles with her while Malric grunts and casts a meaningful look up the mountain, telling me we need to keep moving.

"Clan Bellamy recognizes the throne, right?" I say to Alianor. "They may not be the happiest of subjects, but they do consider themselves subjects, especially after the recent treaties."

"Uh, yes . . . I'm guessing you aren't stopping here for a political discussion, though. What's up?"

I turn to Dain. "Wilmot considers himself a loyal subject, whatever his issues with the throne. Do you, too?"

He tenses, and I'm ready for him to say no, he does not, considering he still blames the queen for his servitude. Instead, he says, carefully, "I know I've made mistakes, princess, but if you still have reason to doubt my loyalty . . ."

"I don't. I'm just confirming that, as subjects, you recognize the authority of the throne."

"Yes . . ." Dain says. "And to echo Alianor, what's up?"

"She's going to give us an order," Alianor says. "We admitted we're the queen's subjects, which means we're the subjects of both Princess Rowan of Clan Dacre and the royal monster hunter of Tamarel. If she gives an order, we're bound to obey it."

"I'm not carrying you up the mountain, princess," Dain says.

I shake my head. "As tempting as that is, no. I'm going to ask"—I take a deep breath—"*insist* you both stay behind."

"What?" they say in unison.

"We're not letting you walk into a gryphon's lair by yourself, princess," Dain says.

I lift my hands. "My plan is only to take Tiera close enough for the gryphons to smell her. I see a patch of forest up ahead. It's too thick for the adult gryphons, so I'll take Tiera in there. They'll hear us and come out, and hopefully I can hand her over without getting any closer."

"It's still dangerous," Alianor says. She pauses. "Which is why you don't want us there, right?"

It is, but I know better than to say that outright. I need a reason they can't argue, as my queen-in-training lessons taught me.

"The more people we take, the more likely we are to spook the gryphons. There may be young gryphons there, and the adults will be very protective. I need to take Malric—he won't let me go without him. That's bad enough. Add two more humans to the mix . . ."

I shake my head. "Three humans and a warg seem like an attack party. I can't risk that. I also need you to look after . . ." My gaze slides to Jacko. He's watching us, and when I look his way, he bolts over and stands on my boots.

I glance at Dain and Alianor. "He attacks everything that threatens me. He went after the wargs earlier. He attacked Tiera's mother. He could make things worse. Also . . ." I look down at him.

"He's bite-sized for a gryphon," Alianor says. "One chomp . . ."

When I shudder, she says, "Sorry."

"No, that is exactly what I'm afraid of. He's prey to them." I look at both of my friends. "So you'll stay behind?"

"Alianor can watch Jacko," Dain says. "I'll go with—"

"No."

His eyes flash. "We aren't letting you—"

"I'm within screaming distance."

Alianor says, "Meaning that if you need help, we might be able to get there in time, but if we can't . . ." She shrugs. "We get to hear the horrible sound of our friend dying." She glances at me. "Right?"

"Er . . . if I do die, I promise to do it quietly."

She snorts. "Somehow, I don't think if you're being torn apart by gryphons, you'll be thinking about saving us from nightmares."

"Knowing Rowan, her last thought really would be 'I can't inconvenience others,'" Dain mutters.

"I think my death *would* be an inconvenience for the kingdom," I say. "At least a minor one."

He gives me a hard look. "Alianor can joke, because we both know she's not really joking. *You* don't get to joke. Alianor's right—you're asking us to stand by and listen to you die, Rowan."

Alianor shakes her head. "I was needling her, but I don't think dying is quite what she has in mind." She looks at me. "Is there room for negotiation?"

When I hesitate, she leaps on it and starts negotiating how close they can be. We decide on a spot.

"That'll work," I say, "but I really am ordering you both to stay back. This isn't like being told you can't come with me, Alianor, and finding a loophole. It's also not me saying I don't want you along when I'm really hoping you'll come anyway."

She nods. "I know. You have my word."

She looks at Dain, who crosses his arms.

"Dain . . ." she says.

"I'm not giving my word because I don't have to. If I say I'll stay, I will." He shifts his weight. "I'm not happy about it, though. Really not happy."

"Understood."

We find the spot where they'll wait. Jacko knows something is up. I need to respect him and not try sneaking away. So I talk to him, and I cuddle him, and I promise I'll be back. He might understand, but he's still not about to let his human go off to battle without her trusty jackalope squire.

Alianor tries to hold him, but he wriggles free and tears after us. Malric turns and lifts a paw. The warg doesn't pin the jackalope—he just lifts that giant paw in warning. Jacko chatters and hisses, and then casts an accusing look at Tiera, as if to say, "Why's *she* allowed to go?" He'll figure it out when I return without her . . . and I doubt that'll make him any happier with me.

Dain walks a part of the way with me. When I insist that's far enough, he tries to give me his bow.

I shake my head. "You'll need that."

"I have my dagger."

"If I'm in trouble, I'd rather you had your bow."

He hesitates and then nods and gives me his dagger instead. I accept that, and with Malric leading and Tiera tagging along behind, I continue up the mountain.

CHAPTER THIRTY

I'm aiming for that forest grove near the cave entrance. It's on a plateau, lush and green and striking amidst the craggy rock of the mountain. It definitely looks too thick for a gryphon, which makes it a good place to hide.

As I approach, I realize I'm not the only one who thinks that. The patch is larger than I expect, and as I near it, a hare zooms from behind a rock and races into its forest sanctuary.

The hare must startle a bush of birds, because about a dozen mountain ptarmigans erupt from the forest. Tiera flies after a straggler. As I'm watching her go, the hare races back out, as if startled by the birds that *it* startled. I chuckle at that. Malric watches the hare zip past and seems to consider giving chase, but then lumbers ahead of me into the forest.

When we step into the cool darkness, Malric lifts his nose and snuffles the air. I try to pass, but he growls, and I sigh and lean against a tree. I give him a few moments to sniff and then I push past. He only grumbles and follows.

I head for Tiera, who's up ahead, having caught one of the ptarmigans. She's crouched over it, ripping it apart, feathers flying.

"Good girl," I say. "That's a very good girl."

Her head whips my way, as if I startled her. Bits of bird hang from her beak, which is kind of gross, but I can't let her know that. I need to praise her for catching her meal. It's the first time she's brought down a bird in flight, and I'm impressed.

"You're going to be fine, aren't you, Tiera?" I say.

She stares at me, nictitating membranes flicking over her amber eyes. I'm moving through the forest to get to her, and before I push past the final branches between us, she hisses, her wings flying up, head ducked low, tail whipping.

I stop short, shocked and hurt. "I'm not going to steal . . ."

I trail off. There are still leaf-laden branches between us, obscuring my view of her, but as she hisses, my heart thuds with a terrible certainty.

This is not Tiera.

No, it must be. She is a predator, after all. It's understandable that she'd complain if I get too close while she's eating.

Except Tiera has never done that. She's fed from my hands since her birth. On this trip, she's brought me food to share, and I've had to take mangled fish from her and pretend to eat it.

Full-grown gryphons won't fit in these woods. But that doesn't mean we won't find a gryphon from the aerie here . . . a juvenile like Tiera, also learning to hunt.

A crash sounds in the forest, and then Malric's there, grabbing my tunic and pulling me back.

"I know," I whisper. "That's not Tiera."

I retreat carefully as the young gryphon watches me. When I bump into Malric, I absently lay my hand on his head, reassuring myself he's there. I realize my mistake, but he only moves closer, his shoulder against my hip.

The young gryphon takes a step toward us. I stand my ground. It takes another. Then it sees Malric, and its beak opens in a hiss, fur and feathers puffing.

"We're sorry," I say, my voice calm but firm. "We didn't mean to disturb you. We're going to—"

The gryphon rears, front talons slashing. Then a squawk of challenge ... coming from my left. I wheel, my mouth opening to warn Tiera back. There, charging through the undergrowth is yet another young gryphon.

Seeing us, it stops short and lets out a shriek. Another answers from behind us, and then another, and before I have time to do more than pull my sword, we are surrounded by five young gryphons, three of them bigger than Tiera ... all of their beaks bloodstained from hunting.

It wasn't the hare that startled those ptarmigans.

It wasn't the ptarmigans taking flight that startled the hare.

I'd marveled at this little forest, so conveniently located near the aerie. Such an unlikely location for a patch of forest, especially one that the gryphons couldn't even use.

Not the adult gryphons, maybe. But young ones? Juveniles just learning to hunt and in need of a safe place to do so?

There's a forest contained within our castle walls. That's where Rhydd and I learned to ride and to hunt. That's exactly what this forest is. A training ground for young gryphons.

It's one thing for an animal to choose a nesting spot in a good location, easily defensible and near water and plentiful food. But what kind of intelligence did it require to see a patch of woods on a mountaintop and think, *That would be a good spot for our young to learn hunting?*

What if they actually built it? Saw a patch of earth and scrubby trees and brought seeds, growing trees that would attract hearty mountain animals and birds. Maybe that goes too far, but it *is* possible and if so . . .

I'd spent weeks studying Tiera's mother, but with her in captivity there'd been little opportunity to assess her true intellect. I'm not even sure how to comprehend this degree of intelligence in a beast, and I live with Jacko and Malric, excellent examples of just how clever monsters are.

All this wonderment, though, passes in a few heartbeats before reality knocks me in the back of the head . . . or in my back*side*, as Malric thumps me. The warg is reminding me that, instead of marveling at the intelligence of these creatures, I should be thinking about the fact we're currently surrounded by five of them, each big enough to kill me.

The smallest gryphon steps our way with a curious chirp, but a bigger one flaps into its path, hissing at it.

I raise my sword. To my left, a gryphon shrieks, and when I look, it's bristling, beak snapping, amber eyes fixed on my sword.

So I sheathe it.

Malric snarls at that, but I don't know what else to do. I cannot fight five young gryphons, even with Malric by my side. Nor can I tell them I'm not here to hurt them . . . while wielding a sword. I just got finished thinking how intelligent they may be. I need to respect that.

Is it easy to put my sword away? Absolutely not. No monster has earned my fear more than gryphons, and my time with Tiera has only tempered that fear with respect.

I look at these five gryphons, and I don't see five Tieras. I see Jannah, coming home with the head of a gryphon . . . and my father's body slung over his horse. I see a gryphon bursting through a barn roof, grabbing my brother by the leg and snapping it like a twig. I see that same gryphon dashing my aunt against a rock and killing her. I see all of that, and when I sheathe my sword, my hand shakes so badly I can barely get it in.

As I do, a voice inside screams at me that I'm a fool, a reckless fool, and I'm going to die, just like my father, just like my aunt. But there's another voice, one I feel more than hear, and it says this is the right thing to do, and when I look across at the gryphons, I swear I see Jannah there, nodding her approval.

I remember my mother, telling me how much I've learned from Tiera and her mother. I remember her telling me how much she's learned, her hatred for an entire species finally fading. I know so much more now, and I must trust my gut. That's what Jannah would tell me. Trust my knowledge and my gut.

"I'm unarmed," I say. "I apologize for trespassing. We're going to leave now."

I lift my hands to show that they're empty. Then I lay my hand on Malric's head.

Stop growling, Malric. Please stop.

To my shock, he does. He gives a grunt, one that says he doesn't approve of my strategy, but he'll go along with it. For now.

I raise my hands again, slowly. Then I glance over my shoulder and see the biggest opening between gryphons. I start backing that way. One lunges at me, and I grab the hilt of my sword. Just grab it, still sheathed. The gryphon stops, head tilting in a way I know from Tiera and her mother. Assessing. Considering. Then the beast stands down, almost as if it had been testing how fast I could go for my weapon.

I keep my gaze on the gryphons and I trust in everything I have learned about their body language. As I back out, the gryphons follow, their wings tucked in, their tails twitching. Like our cats when a fox invades their barn and realizes its mistake. It retreats, and they follow, ready to pounce at any provocation.

As they follow, they slide together into a solid wall of gryphons, a semicircle around Malric and me. Five more steps, and an earthy mountain breeze wafts past. Almost there. Then the trees overhead crackle and crash, and an ear-splitting shriek slices through the forest.

I look up to see Tiera—undoubtedly Tiera—diving, screaming in rage, her gaze fixed on the largest of the young gryphons.

"Tiera, no!" I shout. "No!"

My voice startles one gryphon, and he flies at me, his front talons grabbing my left arm, ripping through leather, slicing into me. I yank out my sword and shout, "No!" as loud as I can. I shout as if this simply is Tiera playing too rough and the gryphon lets go.

Beside me, Malric snarls, front paws planted, head between his shoulders. Tiera veers at the last second and heads for me, shrieking at the gryphon who'd grabbed me. I leap between them, and she crashes into me, and we tumble into a heap.

I spring up, hand going for my sword again, but the gryphons are all staying back, staring at Tiera. And Tiera, recognizing her fellow monsters, bounds over in greeting . . . No, not exactly. She doesn't recognize them at all, having never seen another gryphon. To her, they are strange predators who attacked her mother, and she hisses at them, feathers ruffling as I put my arm around her and rub her neck and tell her it's fine. Which makes the five young gryphons stare even more.

I play it up, petting Tiera and cooing at her, and she nuzzles me and then hisses at the young gryphons again. When she lowers her head, I scratch behind her ears.

"Good girl," I say. "Such a good girl."

Great. You've stunned five baby gryphons. Now I suggest you take advantage of that . . .

I start to back away again. Tiera stays where she is, snapping and hissing at the gryphons. A warning display, one that keeps them where they are, while Malric and I back out of the forest. I glance over my shoulder to see a wide expanse of rocky ground. Then I look forward again and call to Tiera. She begins her own retreat.

My boot finally touches down on rock, and then sun warms my back for an eye blink before it disappears, as a cloud rolls overhead. Then a thud sounds behind us, and every muscle in my body freezes.

I turn, ever so slowly . . . to see a wall of white feathers blocking my view.

I lift my gaze . . . straight into the amber eyes of an adult gryphon.

CHAPTER THIRTY-ONE

I fall back. My heel hits a rock and I trip, landing flat on my back. I lever up just as the gryphon lowers its massive head, beak coming so close I smell its honey-sweet breath, feel the blast of hot air as it exhales. That beak opens, and I reach for my sword, but the sheath is caught under me.

Malric snarls and lunges onto me. The gryphon shrieks, the sound deafening. Its beak opens to snap—

An answering shriek sounds from the forest. Tiera charges out, screaming a high-pitched gurgle of rage. She flies straight at the adult, her wings extending, beak snapping. The gryphon falls back, blinking. Tiera leaps between Malric and the giant beast. She rears up, hissing and clawing the air. The adult only blinks again. Then it lowers its head, carefully staying out of range of those slashing talons.

A whoosh of inhaled breath, a loud sniff. Then the adult sits on its haunches and looks at her. The five juveniles tumble from the forest, making the yipping sounds I'd heard from Tiera when I'd come to see her in the barn. They scramble over to the adult, who flicks her huge head at them, telling them not to bother her.

I think it's a her. Both females I've known—Tiera and her mother—have light-brown fur. Two of the juveniles, including the biggest, are darker brown. This adult is at least as big as Tiera's mother, but now that she's sitting back on her haunches, I see grizzled gray in her fur, scarring on her chest and a beak worn with age. An old gryphon that the juveniles obviously know well. Teacher? Caretaker? Nursemaid?

The big gryphon eyes me. Then she looks at Tiera. I slowly rise and lay a tentative hand on Tiera's shoulder. She keeps her gaze on the adult, but lets me pet her and leans against me as I scratch. The big one tilts her head as she watches, thinking.

I straighten, as best I can, and meet the old gryphon's eyes. "I brought her for you. To leave with you." I gesture between Tiera and the gryphon. "I can't keep her, and her mother's dead. She needs to be with her own kind."

The gryphon doesn't understand what I'm saying. I'm talking for my own benefit, hoping that my tone and my gestures and maybe the fact I'm here—a human bringing a juvenile gryphon to the aerie—will tell her what she needs to know.

In my head, I hear Jannah's voice.

Look at Malric. Take your cues from him.

The warg is on guard, but his posture is neither aggressive nor submissive. Whatever body language he reads from the gryphon tells him there's no immediate threat. When I stop freaking out, I can see that myself. She's calm and attentive, and also very aware that she could kill either of us with a snap of her beak.

As I talk, Tiera sniffs my wounded arm, her beak clicking with concern. Blood has soaked through my tunic. I roll the sleeve to see a gash. Shallow, but bleeding.

"Just a moment," I say to the adult gryphon. Then I use Dain's dagger to cut off my shirt sleeve, slit it up the middle and use it to bind the wound shut.

When I look at the gryphon again, she's staring at my arm.

"It's fine," I say, lifting it.

I'm ready to launch back into my appeal when she moves toward me. It's an easy step, not a lunge or a dart, and I force myself to stay still. Her gaze remains fixed on my arm. Does she smell the blood? I know that can drive some monsters to a frenzy, but I've never heard that about gryphons, and she certainly doesn't seem frenzied. If the blood were to catch her attention, it would have done so when I first walked out.

She approaches and lowers her head toward my arm. I steel myself, planting my feet and holding my breath as I lift my arm for her to see. She sniffs it, eyes it and then backs away as I exhale, my heart tripping with relief.

"I'm hoping I can leave Tiera with you," I say. "To raise with the others." I gesture from Tiera to the young gryphons. "I'd love to keep her. I just . . ." I swallow. "She belongs with her own kind."

Why are you explaining? She can't understand you.

This is pointless. It's never going to work.

Even as I think that, I hear Jannah's voice at my ear.

She's smart. Very smart. Even if she can't understand your words, she hears your tone. She also knows you aren't here to steal a baby. You brought one to her. Trust that she'll understand.

"Will you take her?" I ask, with plenty of motioning between Tiera and the gryphon and the other juveniles.

She walks to Tiera again and lowers her head for a sniff. When Tiera hisses, the gryphon bats her with one front paw, talons curled under, and makes a noise in her throat like a growl.

"It's okay, Tiera," I say. "She won't hurt you."

Tiera grumbles and squawks, her wings fluttering. Then she sidesteps over, close enough for me to pat her reassuringly as the gryphon sniffs and prods Tiera with her beak. She walks around the young gryphon, still sniffing and prodding, as if making sure she's healthy. Then she prods *me*, and I jump with a little yelp. She gives me a hard look, like I'm a baby who has complained at a gentle poke.

"Sorry," I say. "You just startled—"

She nudges me again, harder, her head down, and it's like what Tiera does when she's trying to herd me. Except the adult gryphon's head is the size of Tiera's entire *body*, and even a soft nudge has me tripping over my feet. Malric rushes over to plant himself beside me.

Beside me, not between us. I notice the difference, even as he growls at her. He's warning her to be gentle with me, but he isn't trying to stop her.

I turn to face her. "I don't under—"

Another prod, in the same direction. Then a look that wonders if I'm not terribly bright.

— 270 —

"You want me to go . . ." I glance over my shoulder . . . at a sheer drop, twenty feet away.

I shake my head. "I can't fly, and if you're trying to push me off the edge—"

She nudges again, with another look that's harder than the prod. Okay, logically, if she wanted to push me off the edge, she could just drive me there before I realized what was happening. Also, she hardly needs to force me over a cliff to kill me.

I take a deep breath and trust my gut, which says I still don't understand what's going on but "marching me to my doom" isn't it. I walk as close as I dare to the edge, look over it and . . .

There's a ledge about twenty feet below, strewn with gryphon feathers. The aerie.

"You want me to go . . ."

She lifts off with a great flap of her wings, the whoosh of air making me stumble. She lands on the ledge below, all four legs thumping down, her wings folding, and I am struck by her beauty and grace.

The only times I've seen a gryphon in the wild, I've been too busy staying alive to actually *see* it. I remember my father coming home from every manticore hunt sighing because it wasn't a gryphon. I've hated remembering that, because the memory drags with it the reminder of the first time my father finally saw a gryphon. The one that killed him.

"This is what you wanted to see, isn't it, Dad?" I murmur as I watch the gryphon land, see the muscles ripple under her fur, the sweep of her tail, the settling of her feathers.

I watch for a moment. Then she looks up, squawks and bobs her head toward the cavern.

"Oh," I say. "You want me to bring Tiera."

That makes sense—it will be easier for the gryphon to keep Tiera from following me if she's in an enclosed space.

"Tiera?"

I glance over my shoulder to see her watching the other juveniles chasing a snake through the rocks. Her hindquarters wiggle, tail whipping, like a kitten about to pounce. She stays where she is, though, and when I look at her, old emotions well up, memories of all the times I stood on the sidelines watching other children, knowing it'd spoil the game if "the princess" joined in.

"You can play with them soon," I say. "Come and see this first."

Am I tricking her? I hope not, and I'm glad when she scampers over to me.

I point at the aerie ledge. "We're going down there, okay? Fly after me."

I make my way down. Malric paces above, grumbling, and I grumble back as his pacing showers me in pebbles and dirt. He knows he has to wait for me to get down first, and he's not happy about that. As soon I climb down onto solid ground, he descends, slipping and sliding until he's beside me on the ledge. Tiera lands with us.

The cavern door isn't as big as I'd thought, and the gryphon needs to duck her head to get inside. We follow and . . .

I am in a gryphon's aerie. An actual aerie.

I might be the first person in all of Tamarel's history to see this.

I stand in the light beams falling through the entrance and peer around.

All those stories about gryphon nests littered with bodies and bones are, as Jannah had expected, nonsense. There are bones, but they're in one corner, and there's no more than a dozen—big bones like the thighs of deer. Marks suggest the juveniles have been gnawing on them. Dinner brought by their caretaker, now turned into toys.

There are molted feathers, too. They're also piled neatly to one side, in heaps that make my finger itch, imagining arrows with gryphon-feather fletching. I hadn't been able to bring myself to pluck any from Tiera's mother, and the stable hands had snatched up any that fell. Here there are whole heaps of them, in every size from baby fuzz to adult feathers the length of my arm.

There's dried grass, too—low heaps of it that suggest beds. I see sticks in amongst the grasses, keeping the beds in shape. Less structured nests, more of a sleeping mat between the gryphons and the cold stone floor.

The adult gryphon stands by one of the smaller heaps. Beside me, Tiera chirps anxiously, her talons clicking as she shifts her weight. The gryphon's beak nudges the bed . . . and something inside peeps.

The gryphon looks at me, and then back at whatever is in that nest. She repeats the gesture, and I know she wants me to come over there. As I take a step, I catch a whiff of cave smell, that musty, cool, damp scent, this one mingled with the sweeter smell of gryphons.

I look into that alcove, and in my memory I see another cavern, another gryphon, another cave tucked at the back, me and Alianor and Dain and Jacko in it, Tiera's mother terrorizing us. There were moments when I thought I'd never get out of there alive . . . and now I'm voluntarily in a cave with a gryphon?

My legs shake so hard they seize up, and I'm frozen there, my heart slamming against my chest as the terror from that day rolls over me.

The gryphon clicks her beak. Then she prods whatever is in the nest. Two small tufted ears appear. Then a white-feathered head and yellow beak. It's a gryphon smaller than Tiera, its head wobbling, eyes dull with sickness.

CHAPTER THIRTY-TWO

"O h!" I say, and I run forward before I can stop myself.

The adult gryphon pulls back, shaking her head and squawking, but she overcomes her surprise as I slide onto the rock beside the nest. Inside is a dark-furred male a little younger than Tiera.

When the adult's beak lowers into the bed, I don't have time to jump back. Then I see a gash on the juvenile's rear leg, a deep and ugly wound seeping pus. The adult gryphon licks away the pus as the young one mewls weakly.

Tiera appears at the side of the nest, chirping in concern and nudging the young gryphon. The adult makes that growling noise, but it's a soft warning, telling Tiera to be careful. Then the adult gryphon looks at me. At the wound. Back at me.

"You . . . you brought me in here . . ." I glance at my bandaged arm. "You want me to fix him."

She saw me bandage my arm, and she wants me to heal this young gryphon, who has a similar injury. Except it's not really similar. Mine is a shallow cut. This is a deep slice through skin and muscle, and it's already festering.

Don't panic. Just do what you can.

I examine the cut. When the young gryphon fusses, I absently pet him, not realizing what I'm doing until I see where my hand is . . . rubbing the belly of a gryphon that is not Tiera. He only makes a noise in his throat like Tiera's rumbling contentment, and he collapses back onto the nest. His skin is hot. He needs water for his fever, but I have no idea how to get that. I look around . . . and spot a big upside-down turtle shell, half-filled with water.

I stare at the adult gryphon. She brought him water, in a container that would hold it. I've seen monsters use tools—for cracking open nuts and shells—but this is a whole other level of intelligence.

I lift the shell to the young one's beak and help it drink. Then I rip off my other sleeve and use the remaining water to clean the wound. The flesh is still firm, with no signs of necrosis—where the flesh begins to die. Binding it won't be enough, though. It needs stitching.

I could probably break off a splinter from those discarded bones and take a thread from my tunic. I do have a much better idea, though . . . if the gryphon will allow it.

There's no way of explaining what I need to do. She'll need to see what I'm asking.

I go to the mouth of the cave and shout until I get a response. Then I hurry back into the cave and resume cleaning the wound.

The water is gone, and I look around for more. There isn't any. I rise, empty shell in hand, still searching for water, when Malric walks over to the nest and puts his front paws on it, peering in. The adult gryphon hisses, and the young one squirms at the smell of a strange predator. I pet Malric, and thankfully he allows it, as I assure the gryphon the warg won't hurt the baby. She stays right there, her gaze glued to him, front talons scratching the floor.

Malric sniffs the wound. Then he looks at me and gives a deep put-upon sigh. When he lowers his head to the wound, even I tense. His tongue extends, and he begins cleaning it, better than the gryphons can manage with their beaks and shorter tongues.

Tiera crowds in to watch, ignoring his growls. When he pulls back, he gives me a look, as if to say, "I hope you appreciated that."

I nod. "Thank you, Malric. I know that was, well, gross, but thank you."

He grunts, satisfied, and backs away to stand watch. I'm examining the wound when a sound comes, the scrape of boots climbing the mountainside. The adult gryphon's head shoots up, her amber eyes narrowing.

I run ahead of the gryphon to the ledge. Below, Alianor has reached a gentle slope, and she's racing toward the cave, Dain still climbing below her. When she sees me, she waves her arms.

"I have my medical supplies!" she calls. "What happened? Where are you hurt?"

"I said I was fine!" I shout back.

Dain says, "Which from you, princess, only means you're still alive."

"Is it Malric?" Alianor calls.

I shake my head. "It's a young gryphon."

"Tiera?"

I wave for them to get closer, and then stop them below the ledge . . . where they can't see the adult gryphon yet. I explain as quickly as I can.

"A gryphon wants you to heal her baby?" Dain asks.

"He's not hers. I think she's the caretaker. The nanny or nursemaid."

"Uh . . ." Alianor says. "You didn't eat any weird mushrooms in the forest, did you, Rowan?"

"Ha ha. No, there's a young—"

They both stumble back as a shadow passes over me. The adult gryphon walks to the edge, head lowered as she peers at the two new humans.

"These are my friends," I say. "Alianor is going to come and help the little one. She's a healer. She can sew him up."

Tiera appears, walking to the edge and peering down. The adult nudges her back with a scolding click of her beak.

"That's . . . a gryphon," Alianor says. "You're talking to a gryphon."

"She doesn't understand me. It's the tone that matters."

"Uh-huh . . . there's a *gryphon*. Right beside you."

"You don't need to come in if you don't want. I'll climb down and get your kit."

"You're asking me to come into a *gryphon aerie*. I wouldn't miss that for the world."

She starts climbing, and I tell her to approach carefully, while I watch for any signs that the nanny might have a problem with that. She just watches, wary but calm.

As Alianor climbs onto the ledge, my heart suddenly seizes, and I call down to Dain, "Wait! Where's—?"

I don't even get the rest out before Dain's back starts wriggling. He mutters and pauses on the mountainside. As he half turns, I see Jacko in a sling on his back. The jackalope must have been asleep. Now he's heard me, and he's antler-butting Dain to let him down.

"You're welcome!" Dain calls as Jacko bounds free and starts up the mountainside.

The jackalope races to me, and I bend, and he leaps into my arms. Then he sees the gryphon and hisses . . . and she hisses back. Tiera hears her playmate and comes galloping over. She nudges him with her beak, and he rubs against her cheek.

I tell Dain to wait and then I put Jacko onto Tiera's broad back and glance at the adult gryphon, hoping that will prove the jackalope isn't a threat . . . or dinner. She's staring at the sight, and I have to chuckle at that.

As strange as this all is for us, it must be just as weird for the gryphon, meeting a new juvenile, who brings along human, jackalope and warg friends.

"So I guess I'm staying down here," Dain calls from below.

When I don't respond, he squares his shoulders. "That's fine. Alianor is the healer. You're the royal monster hunter. There's no reason for me to come up."

"Give it a few minutes. Let her see Alianor at work." I pause. "Oh! Actually, I have a job for you."

"Of course you do." He sighs. "What is it, princess?"

"Hold on."

Alianor stands on the ledge gaping at the gryphon. I lead her over for an introduction, and as the gryphon sniffs her, Alianor stands a whole lot firmer than I did.

"I want to pet her," Alianor says as the gryphon moves beside her for a sniff at her back. "That would be wrong, wouldn't it?"

"I don't know. Does a healer need both her hands?"

She laughs. The sound makes the gryphon back up and study her. Then the nanny steps far enough away that I take that as permission to lead Alianor inside.

As we walk through the cave, it's a good thing I have hold of Alianor's arm, because she's so busy looking around, she'd trip over her own feet otherwise. I take her to the bed, and she marvels at it. Then she sees the wounded gryphon.

"Oh!" she says. "Poor baby." She kneels and peers in as I scratch the juvenile's ears. "You did a good cleaning job."

"Malric helped."

"Did he?" She glances at the warg. "Good boy."

He gives her a hard look, and she chuckles.

"Sorry," she says. "That made you sound like a dog. Thank you, Malric." She turns back to the young gryphon. "My full kit went down with the raft, but I kept a few things in my pockets. Needle and thread, luckily. Also a bit of healing salve."

"Good. Just hold on a moment, and I'll get us more water."

I run the shell to the ledge and call down to Dain. Inside the cave, the gryphon watches with suspicion but doesn't complain as he climbs. He stays on the ledge and looks around as best he can as I hand him the shell and explain what I need.

"There's a spring over there," I say. "Maybe a hundred feet west. Stay away from the forest and watch out for young gryphons. There are five of them up there. It's their training grounds."

"Training . . ."

"For hunting. Either the gryphons picked this spot because of that forest or they expanded it to suit their needs. It's the perfect hunting area for young gryphons."

"That's . . ."

"Unlikely?"

"Amazing. Wilmot is going to be so mad he missed this." I smile. "His fault for being on the wrong side of the raft."

Dain returns my smile and then heads down the mountain to fetch water.

CHAPTER THIRTY-THREE

Dain leaves, and I return to Alianor. I comfort her patient as she works. I worry about how the young gryphon will react to the stitching needle—if he cries out in pain, it might make his nanny think we're hurting him. But he's so exhausted by the fever that he only flinches and chirps, and the older gryphon isn't alarmed by that. She's too busy watching, her huge head right over Alianor.

"No pressure," Alianor says, glancing over at the eye . . . which is almost as big as her head.

That hovering eye isn't a threat, though. The gryphon is fascinated by the process, following the needle as it darts in and out, closing the wound. Jacko has come over to watch, too, and the gryphon is thankfully ignoring him. Tiera settles in with one of the bones, worrying it with her beak.

At a sound, I glance over to see that one of the younger gryphons has returned. It's the smallest—the most curious.

He's watching Tiera with the bone, and the older gryphon divides her attention between them and the stitching. When the younger gryphon gallops toward Tiera, I tense, but he only snatches another bone and flops down to gnaw alongside her.

Alianor has just finished stitching when Dain whistles. I hurry out. The younger gryphon follows, and Tiera trots after him. When she sees it's only Dain, she grumbles and flounces back inside, but the other one trails after me.

"That is . . . not Tiera," Dain says as he crests the ledge.

"I think it's a male. My theory is that the dark-haired ones are male and . . ." The gryphon walks past, giving me a rear view. "Yep, male." I take the shell from Dain. "Just wait here. He'll probably stay with you. He's curious."

"Or hungry."

I grin. "Guess you'll find out which."

I jog off with the water. As Alianor washes the wound, I gesture for Dain to enter, my gaze on the nanny gryphon, making sure she sees what we're doing. She eyes him and then prowls out as Dain shrinks back.

"She's going to sniff you," I say.

He nods, his face tight, and stands like a warrior at attention, only his eyes betraying his anxiety. When she reaches the bow on his back, she sniffs more, her wings tips fluttering, as if that's her sign of concern.

Before I can speak, Dain steps away from the gryphon, removes his bow, looks at her, and lays it on the ground. His fingers tremble as he does that, but he keeps the rest of his body steady.

"Now may I enter?" he asks, his gaze flicking to me.

One last snuffle of that massive beak, and then she returns to Alianor and the injured juvenile.

"I think that's a yes," I say.

As we enter the cave, talons skid over the rock behind us, and we turn as another young gryphon lands.

Dain goes still, a vein in his neck throbbing as a light-brown juvenile approaches. She gives Dain a quick sniff. Then she sees her nanny in the cave, decides it's all right, and goes to join Tiera and the young male with the bones.

"No one's going to believe this, you know," Dain murmurs. "They'll think we're children making up wild stories."

"Are you suggesting we shouldn't tell anyone?"

He shakes his head. "No, just . . ." He looks around the aerie. "It's like something out of a dream."

As I take him further inside, I point out the bones and the rough nests. "The adult barely fits in the cavern, so I'd theorize she's the only one who stays with the young. Maybe the parents leave them with her once they're old enough. Like a governess more than a nanny. She's teaching them as she looks after them. Did you see any sign of other gryphons around?"

"No. She's the one we saw flying earlier. I bet the others aren't far away. Just far enough, I hope, that we won't run into any."

His gaze moves to the pile of feathers, and his eyes gleam.

I chuckle. "That's what I was thinking. Imagine gryphon-feather fletchings for *all* your arrows."

He walks across and bends over the pile. He doesn't touch any of the feathers, and the older juvenile ignores him, though the youngest walks over to watch. He nudges Dain with his beak.

"Telling me to get away from the feathers?" Dain asks.

"No, I think he's just curious. Getting your attention."

Dain rises and puts out a hand, like you would with a dog. The young gryphon sniffs it and then rubs against it and Dain tentatively strokes the beast's cheek.

"See, there are monsters who like you. You just need to like them back."

He snorts.

I shrug. "Kinda true, Dain. Nobody wants to be around someone who doesn't *want* them around."

He shifts and looks uncomfortable, and I guess he's thinking I mean myself, too, which wasn't what I intended, but it fits. As he pets the young gryphon, I say, "As for Tiera, I can't explain that. She just doesn't seem too keen on guys."

"Yeah, but I didn't exactly go out of my way to be nice to her. When she was born . . ." Another uncomfortable roll of his shoulders. "I wasn't there."

He means I didn't bring him there. I didn't wake him up, and he felt the sting of that, and it affected his attitude toward Tiera. It's only now, seeing his expression, that I realize how much that had hurt.

"It happened so fast," I say. "Alianor brought me, and I was afraid of getting caught because I wasn't supposed to leave my room. I didn't even wake Rhydd—Jacko brought him. I'm sorry I didn't think to get you."

His gaze dips, and he says gruffly, "No, you're right. Of course you wouldn't. I just . . ." A deep breath, his gaze on the young gryphon as he says quickly, "I took it personally, and I shouldn't have. I jumped to the wrong conclusion."

The adult gryphon walks over to see what we're doing. She eyes Dain petting the smallest juvenile but doesn't interfere.

I point to one pile of feathers. Then I carefully approach it and scoop up a handful, my gaze on hers. I tuck the feathers under my shirt, watching for any sign she disapproves. She stares at me and then nudges an entire pile to my feet.

Alianor walks over. "I think she's saying, 'If you want my garbage, kid, take it all.'"

I chuckle. "They use some to line their beds, but I guess the rest is just trash that doesn't smell bad enough to haul outside."

Watching the gryphon, I give a handful of feathers to Dain. She only heads back to the wounded juvenile.

"If she honestly doesn't care, I'm loading up," Dain says.

"Take some for me."

He arches his brows, and I motion at my now-sleeveless tunic. "I'm a little low on shirt space. You can carry them."

"Is that an order, princess?"

I sigh. "Take all you want, plus a few for Wilmot, and then if you have space, some for me, please."

"I was joking. I'll take plenty for you, and I'll make arrows to go with them."

"If the others managed to rescue my pack, I have those firebird feathers. I'll give you some."

"Aww," Alianor says. "I love it when you two are getting along. Now give each other a big hug . . ."

Dain and I both stiffen.

She chuckles. "Don't push it, huh?" She plucks a few choice feathers from the pile. "I am going to have gryphon hair clips, along with the most amazing story ever."

"How's the little guy?" I ask.

"Stitched, cleaned and salved. He should heal. The cut didn't do too much damage, but he probably would have died from the infection. We saved a gryphon today, Rowan. So in a few years, when farmers report their livestock being snatched by a gryphon with a scar across his hind leg, we can drink a toast to our success."

"Uh . . ."

She throws an arm around my shoulders. "Kidding. Next time the kingdom is ravaged by a gryphon, you can just go out and have a talk with it. Persuade it to leave quietly in return for an ox or two."

I know she's still joking, but I do feel as if we've made a breakthrough here. Gryphons are fearsome predators *and* intelligent beasts, and we need to remember that in our dealings with them.

Even as I'm thinking that, the other young gryphons return to the aerie with food for their sick playmate. For most animals, a wounded comrade is a weak link, best left to die quickly. At most, the adults might feed him. Yet here, the other juveniles bring a hare, tear it up and feed their wounded friend.

The nanny gryphon is pleased with Alianor's surgical work, and it's time for us to go. Time to leave Tiera. I don't even remember that until I scoop up Jacko, who had wisely taken refuge with Malric as the cavern filled with young gryphons. When we start preparing to go, Tiera grabs her bone and comes after us . . . and the adult gryphon stops her.

"I guess that means she's allowed to stay," Alianor murmurs.

I nod, my throat closing.

"Do you want a minute with her?" she asks.

I nod again. I take Jacko over, and I pet and scratch Tiera, and Jacko rubs against her cheek, purring raggedly, as if he knows what's coming. I set him on her back for a moment.

"I need to leave you here," I say to Tiera. "This is where you belong. It's where you should have been, with gryphons who can look after you and teach you and play with you much better than I can."

My eyes fill, and I throw my arms around her neck in a fierce hug. "I loved getting to know you, Tiera. You're a part of my life I will never forget."

I bury my face in her neck. Then I take Jacko, and I start to go. Tiera tries to follow. The adult gryphon stops her, and she fusses, confused but more annoyed than anything. It isn't until I'm climbing down from the ledge that she begins to scream, her anger turning to fear as she realizes I'm going and she can't follow.

I want to just leave. Leave and not look back. But if I do that, she'll think I forgot her. That we all left, and this nasty creature wouldn't let her follow, and we didn't even realize it, didn't care. Like my nightmare of Jacko drowning and me ignoring him.

Before I've disappeared below the ledge, I turn, tears streaming down my face as I look at her, now pinned under the gryphon's taloned paw.

"Goodbye, Tiera," I call. "I'll miss you." Tears clog my throat. "I don't think I'll ever stop missing you."

I make eye contact with her, as hard as that is, so she knows she wasn't left behind, that I've done this intentionally.

Then I turn and hurry down the mountain, my vision blurred with tears, nearly tripping twice before Alianor takes my arm and insists on helping. When we finally reach the bottom and I'm still crying, I say, "I need a moment. I'm just . . . I'm just going over there."

I point blindly.

"You can cry in front of us," Dain says.

Alianor shushes him and tells me to take as much time as I need, and I stumble into the forest until I'm far enough away to break down in sobs. Jacko hops onto my lap, and I hold him close, promising I'll never do that to him, hoping he doesn't think I'm a horrible person for doing it to Tiera.

Jacko purrs raggedly and rubs against me. When I feel something brush my arm, I look to see Malric. Without thinking, I throw my arms around his neck. He doesn't back away. Doesn't even flinch, just leans against me as I bury my face in his ruff and cry until I can't cry anymore.

CHAPTER THIRTY-FOUR

We're on the move again. It's late afternoon, and I knew I couldn't indulge in my grief for long. Wilmot and Kaylein won't head home without us, which means our primary goal is finding them. I decide we'll head north and follow the river.

We're walking along the bank. Jacko is on my shoulders, Malric behind me, Dain and Alianor taking the lead. I'm quiet but feeling better. I've done the right thing. I try to focus on the wonders we saw, the new information we have on gryphons.

"You should write a paper for the university in Kandos," Alianor says.

I frown over at her.

"That's where my sister is. She's studying . . ." Alianor flutters her hands. "I'm not even sure what she's studying. Some kind of science."

Now I'm staring. "Your sister is studying science in Kandos, and you never mentioned it?"

She shrugs. "If it's not medicine, I'm not interested. It's probably not even practical science. She just likes to learn stuff."

"Weird," I say, my voice heavy with sarcasm.

She grins at me. "Yep. You guys would get along great. Anyway, she's studying in Kandos, and she says people who discover new things write papers and present them at the university. You should do that."

"Sure," Dain says. "Except for the fact that Kandos is on the other side of the *mountains*. In a whole different kingdom."

Tamarel doesn't have a university. We're a country with a lot of land, but not a lot of people. Jannah has told stories of nations across the mountains, cities of tens of thousands of people. Our biggest town has a thousand.

We have schools and scholars and libraries, but if you want to learn medicine or law, you apprentice under someone who teaches you. Other studies are mostly done as a hobby.

"You could still write a paper," Alianor says.

"I'll need to write something," I say, "and present it formally at court, for anyone who's interested. That's what Jannah did. She—"

Something catches my eye, a motion in the sky, something bigger than a bird. I squint up, but I'm looking straight into the late-day sun, and all I catch is a flash of white wings. My stomach clenches. I can tell by the size it's not an adult gryphon. Those wings, however, are the same size and color as a young gryphon's.

"Oh no," Alianor says, following my gaze. "Tiera came after you."

"No . . ." Dain says. "That doesn't look like . . ."

A streak of white shoots down, heading straight for Malric, who glowers at it until the last second before he steps to the side, and Sunniva whinnies and skids to a halt. Jacko jumps off my shoulders and chirps in greeting, and Sunniva nudges him. Then she looks at Malric, who backs up with a "Don't even try it" glare . . . so of course she tries it, prancing after him until she delivers a playful nip in the butt. Jacko tears off, and they whip along the riverbank as Malric stalks back to me, his look accusing.

"I didn't call her," I say. "I can't shout across the kingdom."

"You don't need to," Alianor says. "She sensed her person was upset and came flying to comfort her."

"Yeah, she hasn't even glanced my way yet," I mutter. Then I call, "Hey, Sunniva."

She keeps playing with Jacko. When I call again, her ears twitch, telling me she hears me, but she continues to ignore me.

"Oh," Alianor says with a chuckle. "Someone is *annoyed* with her person. You abandoned—" She clears her throat fast. "Hey, Sunniva! You could have followed at any time, right? Since you aren't confined to a stall. And have wings. You could fly across the entire country if you *wanted* to."

"She didn't want to," Dain says. "She was perfectly happy in her pasture . . . until she realized Rowan wasn't coming back quickly to brush her and give her apples. Now she's pouting over a choice *she* made."

"I don't have an apple or a currycomb," I call. "So you came all this way for nothing."

She keeps running with Jacko. They tear off down the river-bed, and Jacko veers into the forest, Sunniva following.

"I'll give them a few moments," I say. "Then we need to get moving."

Malric grunts, as if I'm being far too generous with the youngsters. He starts along the riverside, lumbering slowly, but making his point nonetheless.

"Maybe we should pause here to fish," Alianor says. "It seems like a good spot and—"

Sunniva screams. A bloodcurdling scream that has me racing down the riverbank, shrieking her name. Dain and Alianor race after me, and Malric's thumping paws follow. I barrel through the forest. Then Malric snarls and tears in front of me. I snarl back at him, but he's still running, just keeping me in check.

We burst past a cluster of trees, and there's Sunniva on the ground, hooves flying, a dark-brown warg on top of her. Jacko is on the beast's back, ripping into it with his teeth, and that's the only thing stopping the warg from tearing out Sunniva's throat.

I already have my sword in hand, and I'm charging, yelling, "Jacko!" for him to get out of the way. He leaps off the warg at the last moment, and I strike with all my might. The warg falls from Sunniva, yowling in pain. Another blow and the beast races into the forest, blood trailing behind it.

Alianor and Dain run over, and Alianor gapes at my bloodied sword before returning to Dain. "Apparently she can do more than cuddle monsters, huh?"

I expect him to grumble, but he's staring after the warg, still crashing away through the forest. Then he turns to me. My arms are shaking. My entire body is shaking. I want to collapse to the ground, but instead I spin, blade rising.

"There's never just one warg," I say.

Malric knows that, too, and he's already scanning the forest. As he does, he sniffs the warg's blood, and the rumble in his throat tells me what I already guessed.

"We've been tracked," I say. "That was one of the wargs we encountered this morning."

I back up to Sunniva and stroke her neck as she rises. She presses against me, shuddering.

"Oh, *now* she's happy to see you," Alianor says, but she's surveying the forest, too, her dagger out. "I'm going to check her out, okay?"

I nod. Alianor circles Sunniva, who's on her feet, the breath streaming from her nostrils hot against my neck as she presses her head into my shoulder, as if she can hide there.

"She's shaken, but there aren't any wounds," Alianor says.

"And Jacko?" I can feel the jackalope at my feet, but I don't dare tear my gaze from the forest.

"He's fine. He's a good little pegasus buddy. Aren't you—?"

Alianor stops. I follow her gaze to see a gray-black muzzle poking through the bushes. Malric growls, and I glance to see he's looking in a different direction . . . at a different warg.

"Princess?" Dain says.

He's spotted a third warg, and when I scan the trees, I count a half-dozen of them, including the gray alpha female, leaving no doubt it's the same pack.

"There were only four at the stream this morning," I say. "But you did say they were part of a larger pack."

"They brought reinforcements this time." Alianor tries to keep her tone light, but her voice quavers.

"How many do you count, princess?" Dain asks.

"Six. No, wait, seven. Uh . . . eight." I keep looking. "Nine. I count nine."

Dain curses under his breath. Even that curse comes out shaky.

"I don't suppose you can talk to wargs, too," Alianor says.

I want to joke back that even Malric ignores me, but the words won't come. Of all the predator beasts in Tamarel, wargs are the one we know best. Like their wolf cousins, they prey on livestock in harsh weather, and we're called to deal with them several times a year. They're smarter than wolves, but that only means they're harder to deal with, being nearly impossible to trick.

When Jannah was called to a warg sighting, she would take her entire troop, plus horses. Even driving them back to the forest never comes without injury. Gryphons may strike terror into our hearts, but the beast that has killed the most hunters is the one right in front of us.

With the four wargs this morning, we stood a chance, especially once Dain and Alianor had come to help. With *nine*? That is not a fight we can win.

I glance toward the river.

"Uh, they can swim, Rowan," Alianor says.

"Yes, but can they swim and fight at the same time?"

She shoots me a quizzical look.

"Sunniva?" I say. "Can you fly?" I point at the sky.

She whinnies.

"Okay, then I need you to—"

She drops, startling me, but she's only bent her front legs. Then she nudges Jacko.

"You want . . . ?"

I lift him up with one hand, the other still clutching the sword. I know she's saying to put him on her back, but the thought terrifies me. What if he falls? I won't be there to save him.

"He can't swim, princess," Dain says. "And you can't fight with him on your head."

Jacko hops on Sunniva's back before I can make up my mind. He takes up position, like he would with my mare, at the base of her neck, claws dug in. Then he grabs her mane in his teeth and glances at me as if to say, "See? I'll be fine."

I open my mouth, but just then, one of the nearest wargs feints our way, and Sunniva runs. He tears after her, but she's in the air long before he gets close.

"River!" I say. "Retreat to the river!"

We back up, weapons at the ready. The wargs match us step for step. When one breaks ranks, an arrow clips it in the shoulder and the beast stumbles.

We reach the river, and with it comes the most dangerous part of my plan. The wargs can't fight in the water, but neither can I. I scoop up a rock as I sheathe my sword. Then we're in the river, still backing up until, over my shoulder, I see deep, fast-flowing water.

"Find something to hold!" I say. "Don't let yourself be carried away."

There's a partially submerged log to my left, and I sidestep there. I grab it and ease into the deeper water. Alianor does the same. Dain finds a rock he can brace himself against. Malric stays out of the deep current.

The wargs approach with care. They're in the water, making their way toward us. The river swallows their legs and then reaches their chests.

They sense a trick, but they can't figure out what it is. Finally, the one Dain struck with an arrow gets impatient. It lunges at Alianor as another comes at me. The current grabs them both and sends them whirling downriver. Another warg lunges at Dain and then swirls away.

I move along the log as fast as I can. I'm at the end of the log when Alianor yells, "Rowan!" I turn as the alpha female hits the log. She leaps and hits me in the shoulder, and I tumble into the river.

Before I can blink, the current grabs me. I thrash, trying to catch a log, a rock, anything, but I'm in free-running water, and all I can do is gasp for breath.

Just breathe. That's enough. Breathe and wait. You'll hit a shallow spot where you can get out. Don't panic. Just—

A hand grabs my leg, and relief washes through me. I must not have been moving as fast as I'd thought, and Dain or Alianor has caught my—

Teeth clamp down on my leg, so hard I scream. Water rushes into my mouth. I choke, sputtering and kicking, and

I'm still slamming through the water, the current rushing over my face.

Whatever has my leg . . . is in the water with me.

Visions of the ceffyl-dwrs flash, and I have to fight not to rip my leg free. There are teeth embedded in it, and I do not want to tear it away, but if I don't, the beast will devour me and—

It is with a flicker of relief that I catch a glimpse of gray fur. Not a ceffyl-dwr.

Then I realize what it is. The alpha female. She fell in with me, and she has my leg clamped in her powerful jaws as hot blood wells over my ice-cold skin.

While we hurtle downstream, I use my free leg to kick at her head. It makes contact, and fresh pain rips through me, but I kick again. She lets go, only to grab my tunic instead.

I yank the rock from my pocket and bash the top of her head. Then, out of the corner of my eye, I see a black warg racing along the shore. I want it to be Malric. I desperately do. But I know at the speed we're going, he couldn't have caught up. It's one of the wargs that fell into the river.

I lose sight of him as I'm tossed and turned, barely able to keep my hold on the rock, much less aim it at the alpha warg. Luckily, she seems to be scrambling, too. Panicked claws rake down my side. I kick her without even trying to as I struggle to keep my head—

A yelp, and the alpha warg's body bashes into mine. I slam off a rock and ricochet back, the water roiling as it hits rapids. Something strikes my leg. I catch a glimpse of gray paws clawing at the air, a muzzle flying up, opening in another yelp and—

I'm falling. Tumbling, a torrent of water hitting my face so hard I can't breathe. I flail, but there's nothing under me as I tumble over a waterfall.

CHAPTER THIRTY-FIVE

I smack into water again, and my body plummets down, water closing over my head. My fingers brush fur. Claws scrape my bare arm. My arms and legs churn wildly, but there's nothing here except water.

I can't breathe. I'm underwater, and I can't breathe, and I don't even know which way is up. The world has gone pitch-black. When I kick, my foot brushes fur again. It's the warg, but she's struggling, too. Her nails rake my arm, and I push away from her.

My chest feels like it's going to burst. I'm panicking, clawing and kicking as wildly as the warg. Her paw strikes my cheek hard, and my mouth flies open, water rushing in as I start to choke.

As I try to get away from the drowning alpha, she smacks my back. Another blow and another. My vision blurs. Then suddenly, I see light above, and I don't know if it's real or not, but I rise toward it.

I keep swimming, and the warg keeps pushing me. I really do see light, way above, but then it dims. I keep kicking and pushing toward it, my lungs on fire.

The warg pushes harder now. Then I'm flying through the water so fast I gasp, swallowing more and—

My head breaks the surface. Air hits me, and I gasp, sputtering and heaving.

I'm still rising, though. I'm above water, my arms treading, and the warg continues propelling me upward . . .

My hands touch seaweed. Long strands running through my fingers. I pull away, but the strands wrap around my fingers even more, and it's like yanking against wire and—

One hand flies free, and I lift it, knowing what I'll see. Even when I do, my heart thuds so hard I gasp like I'm underwater again, my lungs seizing.

Two long strands of dark-green horsehair wrap around my fingers.

The ceffyl-dwr's head bursts from the water, ears first, streaming water, and then its mane, whipping, wet strands hitting my fingers and sticking. The beast rises beneath me, and I'm astride it, my hands wrapped in that sticky mane.

A bard's song crashes through my head. The tale of a maiden who spied a ceffyl-dwr on the bank. When it bent to drink, she climbed onto its back, and it plunged into the lake, mane wrapping around her hands, holding her fast as the beast dove, taking her to a watery grave.

I flail, and my hands come free, and I topple sideways off the ceffyl-dwr, plummeting into the water. Cold water. *Ice* cold. As the water closes over me, I gasp.

Then a warm, solid body pushes me up again, and this time I don't fight. I wrap my numb arms around its neck and hold tight until we break the surface and I can breathe.

The ceffyl-dwr twists to look at me, emerald eyes meeting mine with a snort of annoyance, as if to say, "Jump off again, and I'll let you drown." I blink hard, my vision still fogged. Then I make out the white blaze on the beast's nose. It's the young stallion.

I lift my hands. The ceffyl-dwr's mane rises with them, but they aren't glued to it. The strands are just weirdly sticky, and I marvel at that before shock clears from my brain, and I realize I'm astride a ceffyl-dwr. A ceffyl-dwr swimming fast through a lake. I crane my neck to see a mountain towering far to my left, the top white with snow. Behind me, there's a waterfall where the river feeds into the lake. That's what the alpha warg and I tumbled over.

As we near the shore, I try to slide off, but the ceffyl-dwr shoots from the water, and I hold on for dear life as he gallops along the lake edge, water spraying.

A flash of something pale ahead, and I remember the alpha. Then an equine scream rings out ... one that does not come from the ceffyl-dwr. The ceffyl-dwr stops so abruptly that I'm glad for his sticky mane, or I'd have shot clear over his neck. There, charging toward us, is Sunniva, her eyes alight with fury.

I scramble off the ceffyl-dwr, dropping the last few feet to land on my rear. I leap up and dart into Sunniva's path, waving my arms.

"It's okay!" I call. "I'm fine!"

She aborts her charge, swerving, and on her back Jacko sways. I lunge, ready to grab him, but he has a firm hold. Sunniva turns on the ceffyl-dwr and paws the ground, snorting.

The ceffyl-dwr stares, his eyes wide, not a single muscle twitching. He's wondering, I'm sure, at this pegasus with the strange jackalope-shaped growth on her back. But then Jacko jumps into my arms, and the ceffyl-dwr's gaze stays riveted to Sunniva. She stops pawing and snorting, and tosses her head, her roan-red mane rippling, front hooves tapping the ground in a two-step before she turns away from him with a sniff.

The ceffyl-dwr keeps staring, with a look that reminds me of when Mom would come out dressed for a ball. Dad would be there to escort her, and he'd stare just like this. When I was little, I'd whisper, "It's Mom," because he honestly didn't seem to recognize her. He'd smile and say, "I know. Isn't she beautiful?" and I'd roll my eyes and say, "She's always beautiful," and think that my father could be very silly sometimes.

That's how the ceffyl-dwr stares at Sunniva. She tosses her mane again and then ripples her wings, showing them off.

See what I have? You don't have these, do you?

In response, the ceffyl-dwr ripples his gills, which I think are a very fine feature indeed, but Sunniva only sniffs, unimpressed. She starts eating grass, as if she's forgotten the ceffyl-dwr already, but when I reach to stroke his neck, she zooms over and wedges between us to offer *her* neck for my attention.

"Thank you for looking after Jacko," I say as I pat her. Then I do the same for the ceffyl-dwr, thanking him for saving me.

There's no sign of the gray alpha. I presume she drowned. Maybe I should say I'm glad of that. I'm not. Nor can I say I'm grief-stricken. Her death means my life, and I can't regret that.

My own wounds are superficial, the worst being the cut on my leg, but that has stopped bleeding. I'll be bruised and battered tomorrow. For now, I'm fine.

I circle the ceffyl-dwr, looking for evidence of his battle with the older stallion yesterday. I find bite marks, already scabbed over. Since he isn't accompanied by the mares, I presume he didn't defeat the stallion. The older ceffyl-dwr must have backed off, like we'd hoped he would.

I wonder whether the young ceffyl-dwr rescued me because we had helped him drive off the older stallion. Honestly, though, I think he's just curious. We are a novelty he didn't get a chance to fully explore.

As I examine him, he nuzzles my shoulder a little too hard, making me back up and give him a stern look.

"You're still wondering how I'd taste, aren't you?" I say.

He blinks, the picture of equine innocence.

"You bite me, ceffyl-dwr, and I'm unleashing him on you." I point at Jacko. "And this . . ." I draw my sword enough for him to see it. "Even worse, I'll take her away." I point at Sunniva.

Of all the threats, I think the last one would be most effective. He hasn't stopped watching the pegasus. He keeps nickering and trying to touch noses with her . . . and Sunniva keeps backing away. I feel kind of sorry for him. I will feel much less sorry for him if he nibbles me.

I find a few strips of meat in my pocket. They were dried . . . before the river plunge un-dried them. I hold them out, and the ceffyl-dwr sniffs and then slurps them up. Sunniva notices and trots over, snuffling my pocket. I show her the last strip of meat. She whinnies in horror and prances off with Jacko to play.

"Okay, you two," I call. "We need to get back to the others." I glance at the ceffyl-dwr. "I have no idea what to do with you, but I suppose you'll decide that for yourself."

I look at the waterfall. It's on a hill that doesn't look difficult to climb. I have no idea how far I traveled downstream, but at least the waterway gives me a clear path to follow.

As for the others, I'm trying not to worry about them. Dain and Alianor have Malric, and they were handily fighting off the wargs when I last saw them. With the alpha gone, it should have been easy to send the beasts running.

We start around the lake. Sunniva trots along at my one side, while Jacko bounds on the other. The ceffyl-dwr follows right behind Sunniva, and if he gets too close, she kicks backward without losing a step. When one of her hooves makes contact, he decides following *me* might be wiser.

We're halfway around the lake, walking the thin strip of land between the water and the foothills of that glacial mountain. When I see white in the sky, my tired brain spends one heartbeat thinking it's Sunniva . . . who is right beside me. Then I see the wide body and my brain flips to "Tiera," and I slump, overcome by a wave of exhaustion. If we went through all this, only to have her escape the nanny gryphon and come after us . . .

The beast dips low enough to block the setting sun. It is indeed a gryphon. A *grown* one. The nanny? I want to believe that. Every bone-weary bit of my body desperately wants to believe it's the nanny gryphon, just checking on us. Then I see the dark-brown fur.

It's a huge male gryphon.

I spend two heartbeats paralyzed. My mind goes blank, as if too tired to process this, and also too tired to believe it.

No, we're fine. The gryphon won't bother me. I haven't done anything to him, and it's late summer, with plenty of game around. One human isn't worth . . .

My gaze swings to the pegasus and ceffyl-dwr with me. Either one is big enough to be irresistible prey for a gryphon.

Still, maybe he's just flying past . . .

A shriek rends the air, and I whirl to see the gryphon diving.

I spin to tell Sunniva to fly, but there's no time. She hears that shriek and lunges into a canter. I grab Jacko and run behind her, with the ceffyl-dwr on my heels. Hooves and feet pound the hard earth.

"There!" I shout.

I wave at a cave mouth, dark against the rocky foothill. I run as fast as I can, catching up to Sunniva as she hits rocky ground. Overhead, the gryphon shrieks again.

I wheel, my sword raised, and the ceffyl-dwr screams as he rears, hooves flashing. A shadow blots out the sun as the gryphon aborts his dive and pulls up short, hovering over us.

"Sunniva!" I shout. "Here!"

I veer toward the cave, calling to her as I race up the slope.

She follows, nudging my heels until I reach the ledge just out-side the cave entrance—

I stop and stare at solid rock.

There is no cave entrance.

CHAPTER THIRTY-SIX

I blink hard and then look around wildly, as if in my panic I climbed the wrong slope. I didn't. What seemed to be a cave mouth is only a shallow depression, no more than five feet deep, the falling sun casting a shadow that made it look deeper.

I pivot, but the gryphon is right there, hovering. Behind him, the lake stretches out, with no sign of any place to hide.

I hoist Jacko onto Sunniva's back and shove her as far into the shallow cave as I can. Then I block her body, my sword in hand. The ceffyl-dwr takes up position at my side.

The gryphon hovers just over the ledge, his amber eyes fixed on me. Then with a thump, he lands, and the whole ledge quivers.

I wield my sword. "I don't want to hurt you. Just leave us alone, please. You'll find easier prey elsewhere."

Inside, I'm sure he's laughing. There's a girl, barely taller than his front legs, holding a sword the length of his beak, telling him to abandon his prey. He eyes me. Then his gaze moves to the young stallion, who rears, razor-sharp hooves slashing. To Sunniva, now edging from behind me to snap her teeth at him. And finally he looks at Jacko, on her back, hissing and baring his sharp teeth. The gryphon's head cocks, as if to say, "Well, this is new."

Talons scrape the stone as he takes a step closer. His giant beak opens a little and then clicks shut. His tail whips from side to side like a cat spotting prey. He's not attacking, though. He's considering. Assessing whether we're worth the effort.

"We're not," I say. "We aren't worth it at all. There's plenty of food out there." I slash my sword in warning. "You might get one of us, but it'll come at a price."

He listens, head tilting the other way, like he's hearing someone speak a foreign language. He knows I'm communicating. I just hope my tone is firm enough to dissuade him.

I square my shoulders and keep the sword in front of me, respectful yet posing a clear threat.

"I need you to let us go," I say. "You made a mistake. You spotted a young pegasus, and she seemed easy prey. She is not."

He starts tilting his head the other way. Then he stops. Air whistles through his nose holes. Then he steps forward and stretches his head out, massive beak coming toward me, and all I can do is stand completely still, trusting that the look in his eyes is not anger. His beak is shut. He's not signaling attack.

His beak stops mere inches from me, and he inhales deeply. A rumble in his throat, and I'm wondering what—

The aerie. He smells the aerie on me.

Oh no. He can tell I've been to the gryphon nursery, and he's going to think I invaded it, that maybe I hurt one of the juveniles and—

He pulls back, and my hands grip my sword tighter. His gaze locks with mine. Sweat drips down my face. My heart hammers.

Aim for the throat. He's close enough that if he attacks, I can aim for the most vulnerable spot on his thick hide. The place where his feathers meet his mane. An artery pulses there, and I do not want to hurt this beast, but if he misunderstands the aerie smell and attacks—

He moves closer again, and my knees tremble. I grip the sword so tight that it digs into my sweat-slick fingers.

Attack. His throat is right there. You can kill him before he hurts you.

I hear the words, but it's the wrong voice. It's the voice of survival at all costs. Kill or be killed. That is the voice of fear. Under it there's another whisper, one that courses through my veins. The voice of Jannah, of my Clan Dacre blood.

He's not attacking. He's figuring this out. Let him do that. You know he's smart. Trust him to get it right.

My breath catches, but I force myself to stand perfectly still. Jacko hisses, and Sunniva grumbles, and the ceffyl-dwr tosses his head, but those are only warnings. They do not sense threat, and I need to trust *them*, too.

The gryphon sniffs me again. Up and down. When he reaches Jacko, my heart slams against my ribs. The gryphon only sniffs, though, and then gives me one more snuffle and moves back. He sits there, for what seems like forever, as sweat drips from my chin. He sits, and he considers. Then he rises to all fours and turns around, putting his back to us. His wings flutter, preparing to extend.

He's leaving. He's realized that I could not have invaded his aerie and survived. Not unless the nanny gryphon allowed it.

I exhale as those wings spread, and he gallops across the ledge, getting up the speed to launch and—

Something hits him in the back. He shrieks—a cry of shock more than pain. Shock that he'd trusted us enough to turn his back, and we attacked him. But it isn't us. It's the gray alpha warg. She's jumped from above and landed square on his back, and he plummets, the warg atop him.

I race to the end of the ledge to see them below, the warg ripping into one of the gryphon's wings, right at the base. Blood soaks the white feathers, and the gryphon shrieks in rage and rolls onto his back.

I race down the slope. That survival voice shouts that this is my chance to flee, but I run, sword raised. Behind me, both equines let out a neigh of confusion.

The gryphon is fighting a warg, and you're running toward *them?*

Jacko tears down the slope with me. I barely reach the bottom before I spot two more wargs. They leap at the gryphon as he backs away, talons and beak flashing. He grabs one warg and whips it into the rock, and I flinch, my blood running cold as I see my aunt's body again. The shock only lasts a second, though. There are two more wargs coming at a full run.

The alpha had escaped the lake and retreated into the forest to recover and regroup with her pack. Then they

— 311 —

spotted the chance of a lifetime—a gryphon out of the air and distracted.

Now they have the gryphon grounded, his wounded wing held at an odd angle. He keeps backing away, keeps retreating.

Why is he retreating? He's big enough to fight them.

The gryphon glances my way, and I understand. He's leading the wargs off. Getting them farther from us, where he'll fight while we run.

That survival voice screams that I should take advantage. Don't worry about the gryphon, he can take care of himself. But I didn't listen to it before, and I'm not about to listen to it now.

CHAPTER THIRTY-SEVEN

I put Jacko on Sunniva's back and tell her to get out of here. Then I tell the ceffyl-dwr to do the same, motioning for him to flee into the lake. He seems confused, but he'll figure it out.

The gryphon is fighting the wargs, snatching them up and whipping them aside. He doesn't have time to do more. As soon as he grabs one, another attacks, so he keeps throwing them off. They hit the ground and the rocks, and one goes clear into the lake, and when the gryphon realizes that, he shifts his battle-ground to where he can pitch them into the lake, which slows them down. They still come back, though, battered and bleeding. They will not give up as long as their alpha fights alongside them.

I know what I need to do.

The alpha is smart, darting in for the attack only when the gryphon is busy with another warg. She bites and then dances out of his reach after he throws off his latest attacker.

As she zips back from another bite, the gryphon sees me running toward her. Our eyes meet . . . and he ignores the two wargs closer to him and charges the alpha. He grabs her and throws her hard into a tree.

By the time the alpha recovers from the blow, I'm there, swinging my sword. She evades, and I barely nick her, but I manage to block her attack. We face off, circling. Out of the corner of my eye, I see another warg running at me. The gryphon tries to grab him, but two new wargs barrel from the forest and attack the gryphon.

I swing toward the warg charging me, knowing that opens me up to the alpha. As I'm turning, a dark shape slams into the charging warg. It's the ceffyl-dwr stallion. He knocks the warg to the ground, rears over him and comes down, the warg yowling as those sharp hooves trample the beast.

The alpha lunges at me. I block, and the others are forgotten as we lock into our private battle. Her teeth scrape my arm once, and I get in a few nicks, but she's too smart to come close enough for a solid blow. At a noise behind me, I half turn. My attention is still on the alpha warg, but she sees her chance and charges. That's *my* chance, and I swing hard, my blade on target—

Something smacks between my shoulders. It's another warg. I pitch forward, and I manage to keep hold of my sword and land in a roll, hitting the ground flat on my back. I raise my sword, but it's too heavy to swing from this position. I try to lever up. The new warg grabs my sword arm.

The alpha looms over me, triumph shining in her dark eyes. She paws the sword blade, as if dismissing it, mocking the human who is useless without her weapon. I quake beneath her, shivering with fear, unable to meet her gaze, my eyes half shutting as I shrink into myself. Her eyes gleam brighter. Her opponent is exactly where she wants her, cowering before the killing blow. She eases back, as if to enjoy the scene for one last moment . . . and I strike.

I slam my knee into her stomach and my fist into the bottom of her muzzle. The other warg starts in surprise, releasing his grip on my sword arm just enough for me to jerk it up, the blade catching him in the underside.

I leap to my feet and swing at the alpha. The sword chops into her shoulder, cutting deep. She tumbles back, and I fall on her, swinging and parrying and driving her toward the rock of the hillside. She's still fighting, snarling and snapping, but I have her in retreat. Then an arrow slices through a loose fold in my tunic.

"Hey, princess! Stay out of the way of my arrows!"

I grumble, even as my heart leaps. Dain and Alianor are here. A black streak blurs past me and launches at the wounded alpha.

"Rowan!" Alianor shouts. "Watch—!"

Another thump cuts her short. Two thumps, actually, in quick succession, and I wheel to see the other warg, his charge cut short by Dain's arrows as Alianor runs at him, her dagger raised.

The other warg falters. He doesn't drop. He's only injured. But when he recovers and sees me on one side and Alianor on the other, he starts backing away. That isn't all he sees either. His alpha lies motionless on the ground under Malric, her throat torn out.

The warg turns tail and runs. I glance at Malric.

"That was mine," I say.

Alianor thumps my shoulder. "You had her dead to rights. We know that. Toss the old boy a bone, making him feel better for failing in his bodyguard duties."

Malric growls at her.

"Hey, pup, don't glower at me. I was talking about him." She hooks a thumb at Dain.

Dain opens his mouth to reply when a dark shape streaks toward us. They fall back, Dain raising his bow as I cry, "Don't!" It's the ceffyl-dwr, his muzzle and hooves bloody. He trots over to me and eyes the other two. Alianor says something, but I don't hear it. I'm already jogging ahead. I find the gryphon where I left him, still fighting two wargs. The others are dead or gone.

As I run toward the gryphon, my sword raised, Dain shouts, "Princess!"

"Where did *he* come from?" Alianor exclaims. "And why is Rowan running *at* him?"

"Don't hurt him," I shout back as their footfalls pound behind me. "Just help him fight the wargs."

When the gryphon throws off one of the wargs, I charge it. So does Malric. The warg scrambles to its feet and sees us. Its gaze fixes on Malric. Its nostrils flare, and it must recognize the scent of the alpha's blood, because after a quick look around, it turns tail and runs.

Malric chases the warg just far enough to be sure it's not coming back. By then, the last warg fighting the gryphon *realizes* it's the last warg fighting the gryphon . . . and takes off.

That's when the gryphon spots Malric. He shrieks and charges, and I launch myself between them, waving my arms. Then I pet Malric, who suffers through it as slightly preferable to being chewed by a gryphon.

The gryphon backs off and shakes his head. His wings extend and then settle back as he sits, observing us.

"Your wing," I say. "It's hurt. Can I . . . ?"

I notice he's not holding it at that strange angle anymore. I ask permission to approach and bring Alianor, who trots over as unconcerned as if he were the size of a house cat. We check his wing. It's cut, but fine.

"You were faking," I say. "Pretending you couldn't fly so they'd be overconfident . . . and you could still fly away if you needed to. Clever."

"Uh, princess?" Dain says. "Why is this ceffyl-dwr sniffing me?"

"He likes you," I say as we finish checking the gryphon. "It's a sign of affection."

"And *licking* me?"

"Also a sign of affection. If he tries to take a nibble, firmly refuse, however tempting it is to let him."

"Uh . . ."

"Little ceffyl-dwr, please do not nibble Dain."

"At least you haven't named him," Dain mutters as he steps away from the overly inquisitive beast.

I check a cut on the gryphon's front talon, and he lifts it to let me look closer. "Thanks for the reminder. I'm thinking . . ." I purse my lips. "Devourer of Small Children and Cranky Hunters. Doscach for short."

Dain snorts, and I'm showing Alianor the cut when an arrow glances off the beast's shoulder, making it rear back, its talons smacking my shoulder and knocking me to the ground.

Alianor wheels on Dain, her mouth opening, but he isn't holding his bow. I scramble to my feet, running in the direction the arrow came from, shouting, "Stop! We're okay!" There, running toward us, is Wilmot with his bow raised. Kaylein is right behind him as Yvain and Swetyne follow.

"It's okay!" I shout. "The gryphon's with us!"

They slow, looking very confused, but obviously we're right beside a gryphon that is not attacking. They lower their weapons.

"Wait there, please," I call. "He'll leave soon, but Alianor and I need to finish examining his wounds, and you're making him nervous."

"We're making *him* nervous?" Kaylein says, gaping at the gryphon, twenty feet away. "Princess, I understand you want to help this beast, but I'm going to need to insist you get behind us—"

"No," Yvain says as she catches up. "The princess knows what she's doing."

"That's—that's—" Kaylein says.

"Yes, it is, and if you feel you are remiss in your duties by allowing the princess to get close to it, then may I point out that the beast is calm, and upsetting it may be more dangerous than allowing Rowan to do what she wishes."

"Yvain's right," Wilmot murmurs. "Go ahead, Rowan. We'll stay back unless we must intercede."

Alianor and I clean the gryphon's wounds with lake water. When he's ready to go, I step back.

"Thank you for your help," I say, dipping my chin.

The gryphon steps forward, and I steel myself, but his giant beak lowers over Alianor and he sniffs her thoroughly, as if committing her scent to memory. Then he sniffs me the same way, up and down, that sweet-hot breath blowing over me with each exhale. When he pulls back, I exhale myself, in relief, but then that beak swings toward me and before I can move, it knocks into my chest. It's a light knock, more of a nudge.

"I think he's telling us it's okay to leave," Alianor says.

"Or telling us *to* leave," I say. "He's sayinging thank you very much for the healing, but you can go now. Please continue going until you're off my territory."

She chuckles. "That might be it, too."

We step away, and the gryphon extends his massive wings and takes to the sky. Once he's gone, I jog to the ceffyl-dwr and stay beside him as I call Wilmot, Kaylein, Yvain and Swetyne over. Sunniva lands beside us, and I take Jacko as I explain about the ceffyl-dwr and the gryphon as quickly as I can.

Kaylein and Wilmot look at each other. Then Wilmot says, "I think we're going to need the longer version. Much longer."

Yvain chuckles and says, "So do you still doubt you have a natural gift for monsters, child?"

She's right. I have something, and it is both gift and curse. I attract monsters, which puts anyone near me in danger. But I understand them, too. I *want* to understand them, and I think that makes a difference.

For now, I only know that I have achieved what I set out to do—returned Tiera to her own kind—and that we have a very long walk ahead of us.

CHAPTER THIRTY-EIGHT

Without a raft, we have to walk the whole way home. We follow the river, and see no sign of the ceffyl-dwr herd. The young stallion sticks close, though, and I suspect that's more about Sunniva than me. I think he's just happy to find another young equine monster. Alianor insists he's in love. Whatever the answer, he stays with us and quickly learns that if he wants to make friends with Sunniva, offering her dead fish is not the way to do it.

While I keep expecting the ceffyl-dwr to wander off, I must prepare for the possibility that he won't. So every night, I work on training him not to nibble people. It's harder than you'd think, but he eventually figures out that humans *give* food; they're not food themselves. He stays with us, swimming in the river, trotting alongside Sunniva and playing with Jacko.

When we need to cross the river at one point, he insists I ride his back. After that, I ride him for a little each day.

Sunniva doesn't fail to notice that, and she doesn't fail to be annoyed by it. She's fine with me riding my mare, but this seems different, and she seems—dare I say it—jealous of the ceffyl-dwr. She's not ready for me to ride her yet—I haven't forgotten the disaster with the wyverns—but I begin to see a possibility, perhaps not too far in the future.

Yvain and Swetyne break off near Dropbear Cabin. They'll speak to their family and meet us at the castle. We continue on our long walk, our journey punctuated with tiny adventures until, finally, we are back in Tamarel and truly on our way home.

Three months ago, I rode this same route back with a wagon-bound gryphon. This time I left the castle with a gryphon . . . and return without her. That still hurts. Every day it hurts. But every day it hurts a little less, and every day I am a little more confident that Tiera is happy and will ultimately be happier than I could ever make her.

I'm also, just a little, pleased with myself for having done this. Not for having survived the voyage—harrowing as it was—but for having made a hard choice. When I first felt Jannah's sword on my back, I thought that would make me feel grown up. It didn't. This does. I did a very, very hard thing, a thing that was right for everyone else, as much as it hurt me.

Jannah always said that a royal monster hunter's life was full of excitement and adventure, but sacrifice, too. I thought she meant getting injured or losing hunter friends, but now I see there's more to it. We put the kingdom's needs above our own. Always.

When I came this way three months ago, Rhydd rode out to meet me. And so he does again, having been notified by a runner that we were on our way. He comes astride Courtois, galloping down the dirt road, dust flying behind him. Seeing him, I smile, but my insides twist a bit, too, as I realize this is how it will always be, my brother riding to greet me after a grand adventure . . . rather than riding in at my side.

Rhydd is destined to be king, and he can no longer join my adventures, no more than Mom could ride out with Jannah and Dad on theirs. I know that hurts him. It hurts me, too. We'll get through it, though. We'll find our own smaller adventures together.

I urge my steed into a canter as I hang on for dear life. Rhydd doesn't get within twenty paces of us before Courtois stops short, snorting and tossing his head, his horn glittering as he eyes my mount.

"Is that a . . . ceffyl-dwr?" Rhydd says.

I pat the beast's neck. "It is."

"You took a gryphon and returned with a ceffyl-dwr," he says as he shakes his head.

Alianor rides up beside us. "It's sibling rivalry. She tamed a pegasus, and you started riding a unicorn, so she brought home a ceffyl-dwr. Your move."

Rhydd laughs. "I think I'll stick with Courtois." He rubs the unicorn's neck. "Sorry, boy. Looks like she brought home another equine monster to share your pasture."

"If he stays, it'd be in the pond," I say.

"Oh, he'll stay," Alianor says. "He's in love." She catches Rhydd's look. "No, not with Rowan. He likes her, but his true love . . ." She gestures toward Sunniva as the pegasus lands nearby and the ceffyl-dwr turns to stare at her.

Courtois makes a noise that might be a sigh. Rhydd urges him toward us, and the unicorn approaches, head regally high. He gives the ceffyl-dwr a perfunctory sniff. The ceffyl-dwr leans forward and sniffs him back. When he opens his mouth, just a little, I tug on his mane with a sharp, "No."

"He's considering taking a bite out of Courtois," Alianor says. "Just a nibble. He doesn't mean anything by it. He's just curious."

"Uh-huh," Rhydd says. "Well, I'm sure Courtois can take care of himself with . . . does he have a name?"

"Doscach," I say.

"Don't ask her what it means," Dain says as he rides over.

"Oh, now you know I'm going to have to," Rhydd says. He asks, and I tell him, and he laughs all the way back to the castle.

We're holding a council meeting at the pond. I'm pretty sure that's a first in the history of Tamarel. Everyone wants to see Doscach, though, and everyone wants to hear my story, so I deliver it pond-side, as Doscach swims. At first, no one can take their eyes off him. As my story goes on, though, all eyes turn to me. Twenty pairs of eyes—not just the council, but everyone who could find an excuse for being here.

"And so," I finish, "I accomplished my mission. The gryphon is safely with her own kind."

"You expect us to believe this"—Heward sputters—"preposterous story?"

"I can confirm it all," Alianor says. "As can Dain. Wilmot, Kaylein and Yvain can confirm all except the gryphon aerie, though they did see us with the gryphon at the end, tending to its wounds."

"Tending to its wounds?" Branwyne snorts. "She's the royal monster hunter. She had the chance to wipe out an entire aerie of—"

"No." The voice is soft, and I have to scan the crowd to place it. Then it comes again, and I realize it's Kethan as he says, "No, Branwyne. Rowan is a monster hunter, not a monster killer. Her job is to protect Tamarel, and she accomplished that better by earning the trust of the most dangerous monsters, and learning how we might avoid trouble with them in future."

She mutters and shoots her brother a look that says she'll deal with him later. He only meets that look with a calm, steady one of his own. Kethan might be the quiet sibling, but quiet doesn't mean weak.

"She took an extra companion," Heward says. "That was clearly against the rules."

Liliath shakes her head. "You insisted on one companion to reduce the number of guards required and the cost of the expedition. It wasn't a rule, and this wasn't a trial."

Heward grumbles, but Liliath is right. Alianor is Clan Bellamy. She knows all the loopholes, and she used one.

Heward is already under investigation for the death of Tiera's mother, and while Berinon hasn't been able to prove anything, Heward is being careful, and he backs down easily here.

Mom comes forward to rest a hand on my shoulder. "Rowan achieved her goal and much more. In fact, I am going to suggest a special festival day, where our people may celebrate her accomplishments with us and hear her story firsthand." She looks at the council. "What say you?"

"I say that sounds like a splendid idea," Liliath says. The others, except for Heward, agree.

CHAPTER THIRTY-NINE

It's festival night. Mom wanted to have it while Yvain was here, so there wasn't time to pull together one of our huge festivals and give people time to travel. We hold it three days after my return. Yvain and Mom and I have been in conference all day, discussing the dropbears and other monsters that seem to be moving east from the mountains. This will be my next task: returning to the Dunnian Woods with Yvain and Wilmot to investigate. Another chance to prepare for my trials, too, and while Mom may not be thrilled with it, she understands that this is my life now.

The festival started at dusk, but it's fully dark by the time I'm ready. This is a festival in my honor, and I cannot hide behind a mask tonight.

Alianor and I prepare together, with a host of maids making us both feel like princesses. Once free, we abandon all pretense of young ladyhood to scamper through the halls and run out the side door, where I can observe the festival before my grand entrance.

We tuck ourselves into a shadowy spot near the door. Malric pads in a semicircle, eyeing the crowd. Jacko walks behind him, antlers high as he patrols. When a little girl races past without noticing us, their gazes track her as if she could be hiding an assassin's blade in her whirly-toy. Then, satisfied I am safe in this spot, they settle in, Jacko at my feet, Malric off to the side. Chikako peeps from the doorway and bobs out, giving Malric a wide berth before nestling under my long skirts.

I gaze out at a courtyard aflame with torches and bonfires. Tents sell fiery streamers and phosphorus trinkets and fireworks that light up the night sky. Laughter and song fill the air. The scent of honey cakes and sweet apples makes my stomach growl, and Alianor chuckles.

"Would you like me to grab you a treat before your speech?" she asks.

"I'm not sure I could eat before my speech," I say. "But I'll stuff myself after."

She grins. "We'll eat until our seams pop." She looks out toward the festival. "Rhydd seems to be heading over here. I might slip off for a dance, then, if that's all right."

I say it's quite fine. As she leaves to join the dancers, I notice Rhydd watching her go. I wave, and he's making his way over when someone waylays him.

"That is some dress," says a voice to my left. I turn to see Dain approaching. "It's very . . . bright."

I spin, and my dress flashes. It's red and orange and yellow, patterned after a firebird, with the skirt falling in panels, each inlaid with a fiery tail-feather eye. The top is wispy lacework entwined with dyed feathers.

"Very original," he says. "I've never seen anyone dressed as a basan before."

I huff and shove at his shoulder. Then I look at his outfit: gray leggings and a tunic, a dagger at his side and a bow on his back.

"And you're dressed like . . . a hunter," I say. "Must have taken a lot of time to put that one together."

His brows rise. "Did you miss this?" He points at the ceremonial sash around his waist. It's black-and-white, and I'm about to say he could have at least worn something colorful when I see the emblem on the end.

"A royal hunter sash," I say. "Wow. That's a really old one."

"It was Wilmot's," he says. "That's what makes it a costume. Because I'm not a royal hunter. I'm just . . . trying it on for size."

"Good." I look him in the eye. "That's your choice. No one stays with me unless they want to." I glance at Malric. "Except maybe him."

Dain's lips quirk. "He's had plenty of opportunity to wander off. He could have even had a nice alpha warg girlfriend if he wanted. He doesn't. We're all here by choice, princess."

He reaches into his pocket. "I, uh, brought you a festival gift, though, you'll, uh . . . just want to put it aside for now. It doesn't quite match your theme."

He drops a pendant into my hand, the chain dangling. I shift to catch bonfire light and look down to see . . .

"Oh!" My voice catches and my eyes fill, and he snatches it back, cursing under his breath.

"I'm sorry, Rowan. This isn't the time and—"

I take it from him before he can pocket it again. It's a gryphon's eye. Tiera's eye—amber the exact shade of hers, cut into a ring with a black stone set in the middle. It rests on a circle woven with strands of gryphon feather.

I run my finger over a feathery edge.

"Those are hers," he says. "I collected a few."

Tears fall, and I sniff them back, reaching up to rub a hand over my face before Dain catches my wrist.

"You'll ruin your makeup," he says and takes a handkerchief from his pocket to dab under my eyes, careful not to smear the face paint that completes my costume.

"I should have waited," he says.

"I'm glad you didn't." I turn around and lift my hair. "Will you put it on me?"

He hesitates. "It doesn't quite match—"

"Tonight is about her. I'd like to wear it."

He fastens the necklace, and I lay the amulet on my bodice. The amber winks in the firelight, and for a moment, it seems as alive as Tiera's bright eyes. Tears threaten again, but I smile, too, at the memory of her.

I clasp the amulet in my hand and take a deep breath, so the tears are gone when I turn to face Dain.

"Oh!" I say. "I have something for you, too."

I lift my skirt, and his gaze shoots upward so fast I swear his vertebrae crackle.

I laugh. "I'm wearing so many layers you won't even see my knees, Dain. All these layers, though, are excellent for hiding things. I always ask my seamstress to sew in pockets. I have a dagger, dried beef for Jacko, my firebird feather pen . . . and this."

Only when I lift the item—and drop my skirt—does he look at me. I hold up a knife with a small blade that springs out of its sheath.

On seeing it, Dain's eyes widen and his mouth rounds in an O. He puts out a tentative hand. "Is that . . . ?"

I touch the two buttons at once and the blade shoots out, and he smiles, a wide and genuine smile, his gaze fixed on the knife.

"I asked Berinon to make one for me and Alianor, too," I say. "On our trip, I realized the necessity of weapons we can always have on us, even if ceffyl-dwrs destroy our raft."

"I'm hoping *that* will never happen again, but yes, we can always use backup weapons. Thank you."

"I had yours done first because it has a little something extra."

I lift the blade to show etching on the handle. He squints at the etching and takes it to hold in the firelight.

Then he laughs. "A jackalope?"

"Not just any jackalope," I say, waving at Jacko.

"Uh, thanks . . . ?"

"It's to commemorate your saving his life."

"And to remind me that if I want monsters to be kind to me, I need to be kind to them?"

"I'd never say that."

He smiles. "I know, but I need the reminder anyway. The knife is beautiful. Thank you."

I'm showing him how to close it when Rhydd comes over.

"Sorry," he murmurs. "I can't seem to walk five steps without someone wanting to speak to me."

"Get used to it," I say.

"I know." He sighs, but there's satisfaction in his face, too—the pleasure that comes with knowing people already see him as more than a boy prince.

As we talk, Dain's gaze slides over Rhydd's outfit. It's as elaborate as mine, but not nearly as colorful. After a moment, he says, "Oh. You're a firebird, too. In black-and-white, the royal colors."

"Rowan wanted us both to be firebirds, but it's her night, so I chose something a little more . . . subdued."

Instead of a skirt, his costume has a long tunic of feather-like panels. It reminds me of my firebird sketches. Not as bright as my costume, but regal and striking and perfect for him.

Rhydd opens his mouth. A trumpet sounds, cutting him off, and he nods to me. "That's our cue."

Dain murmurs, "I'll go stand—"

"Uh-uh," Rhydd says. "You're on the parapet with us. Alianor, too, if we can tear her away from the dance."

"Already torn." Alianor jogs to us, skirts in hand, breathing hard from dancing. "I wouldn't miss this part." She puts her arm through Dain's as I take Rhydd's, and we proceed to the stairs to the parapet.

So many people. I've been up here for bigger festivals, with bigger crowds, but I expected tonight's to be small. Instead, I'm gazing over a sea of upturned, firelit faces.

I'm still staring when Jacko begins to climb my dress.

"Uh-uh," Rhydd says. "No head-sitting. Rowan needs to look a little more dignified tonight."

He places Jacko on the wall, and I set Chikako beside him, and the crowd cheers its approval. My cheeks heat. I've never had a problem with being in public before, but this feels different. It feels as if every eye is on me, and I'm grateful for the face paint that keeps everyone from seeing me blush.

Mom steps onto the dais and makes a short speech. Then she turns to me, and her voice seems to ring across the crowd. "And now I'll stop talking and give you what you came for. Your royal monster hunter. Princess Rowan of Clan Dacre."

Rhydd squeezes my hand. I take one step, Malric rising beside me. Then the crowd lets out a gasp, and pleasure surges through me, the certainty that they've just noticed my magnificent gown. Instead, gazes are turned upward, following a streak of white.

"Sunniva?" I sigh. "Just had to steal my thunder, didn't you?"

Rhydd chuckles as she lands, light as a cloud, on the edge of a tower. "She's not stealing. She's enhancing."

"Tell me Doscach is secured. Please."

"Very secured. He will devour no small children—or cranky hunters—tonight."

Another deep breath, and then I proceed to the dais with Malric at my side. The crowd cheers, and then *oohs* and *ahhs* as torchlight illuminates my costume.

Mom beams at me before stepping aside. I move up to the low wall semicircling the parapet. Jacko hops along it until he's near me, looking out at the crowd.

"We can do this, right?" I whisper.

He chitters, and I smile. I take one more step forward. The crowd has gone silent.

I clear my throat. "Good evening," I call, my voice as strong and steady as I can manage. "Welcome to our festival."

A cheer, and I smile and wait for it to die down.

"Normally," I say, "I'd give you a report on my recent activities, but tonight is a little different, so I'm going to do something a little different. I'm going to tell you a story."

Another cheer, and some of the tension eases from my shoulders.

"I also want to introduce you to my companions, human and monster," I say. "I'll do that after my tale, so you'll hear their parts in it first." I flash a smile over my shoulder at Alianor and Dain. "I might be the royal monster hunter, but I don't do this alone."

I face the crowd. "And now, my story. Except it's not exactly mine. It's the tale of another companion, one who was very special to me." My hand closes around the amulet. "Her name was Tiera . . ."

Monsters

a field guide

PART 2

Unicorn

You know who loves unicorns? People who've never met a unicorn. They're vicious, foul-tempered, arrogant and dangerous.

iridescent spiral horn, about two hand-lengths

at least a hand taller than a regular horse

purple or gold eyes

stocky build, thickly muscled (like a draft horse)

coat, mane, tail and feathering is snow-white, ebony-black or combination of both

UNIQUE ATTRIBUTES

A unicorn's horn is unique in its composition. It isn't bone like deer antlers or hair like sheep horns. It's as hard as diamond and as sharp as an obsidian blade. To study the material, I'll need a deceased specimen. Taking a sample of Courtois's would be wrong. Also potentially fatal . . . for me.

Dropbear

Dropbears aren't bears at all. They're marsupials. That makes them sound innocent enough. Sure, no one wants an opossum falling on their head, but it's not as bad as having an actual bear drop on you. Yet dropbears are more vicious than any bear, and they travel in packs of up to twenty. Jannah said she once found a gryphon that died holding a dropbear in its beak. There was nothing left of the gryphon but bones.

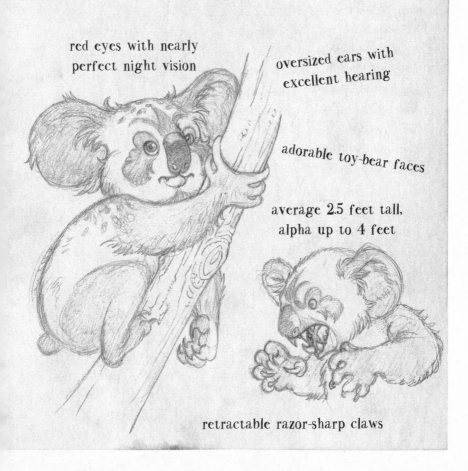

red eyes with nearly perfect night vision

oversized ears with excellent hearing

adorable toy-bear faces

average 2.5 feet tall, alpha up to 4 feet

retractable razor-sharp claws

Basan

Basans are twice as big as chickens and are considered monsters for their size and the fact that they live in the wild and are extremely difficult to domesticate.

FIRE-BREATHING CHICKENS?

Legend says that basans can breathe cold fire. Jannah believed this story began because basans can live in colder temperatures than other poultry, and they will hiss when confronted. When they hissed at people, the clouds of condensation were mistaken for cold fire.

GOLDEN EGGS?

Some stories say that basans lay golden eggs. What they really lay are huge and delicious red eggs, which are considered a delicacy in both Tamarel and across the mountains. In some areas, these eggs are worth their weight in gold, which led to the legend that basans lay eggs of that precious metal.

Chickcharney

oversized eyes fixed
in their sockets

prehensile tail,
able to grasp and
manipulate objects

undersized wings
incapable of
flight

legs often
equal
to body
length,
cannot
bend

SPINNING HEADS?

Like those of owls, a chickcharney's
eyes are fixed, meaning they need
to turn their heads to look around.
Legend says their heads can spin.
That's physically impossible, but
their owl-like spine structure
means they can turn their heads
a full 360 degrees. They just need
to turn them back again afterward.

FLY, CHICKCHARNEY, FLY!

Legend says that the first chickcharney was an owl that
stole a monkey's tail. When it tried to fly again, the tail
grabbed a tree and wouldn't let go even as the owl's legs
stretched and stretched. And so it gained a tail and extra-
long legs but lost the ability to fly.

Ceffyl-dwr

STICKY MANE

Legend says that people who try to ride a ceffyl-dwr
get trapped in the mane and pulled to the bottom of the
ocean. First, I'm not sure what kind of person would ever
look at a scary killer horse and say, "I want to ride that!"
The mane is sticky, though not like in the legends, where
you can't escape it. I would like to study what gives it
that mild adhesive quality. My theory is that there may be
minuscule suckers along the strands. My magnifying glass
reveals a coarse and bumpy structure to each "hair," but
I'll need a stronger magnifier to see better.

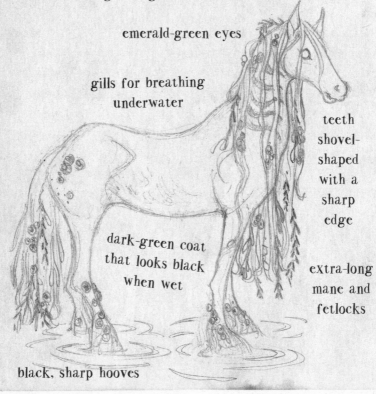

emerald-green eyes

gills for breathing
underwater

teeth
shovel-
shaped
with a
sharp
edge

dark-green coat
that looks black
when wet

extra-long
mane and
fetlocks

black, sharp hooves

Khrysomallos

WOOL COLLECTION

A khrysomallos's wings mean they can easily escape any pasture, so they can't be domesticated. Their gold-colored wool, though, makes them a prime target of poachers, who capture and shear them in the wild. The problem is that these aren't domesticated sheep, whose wool grows constantly and must be shorn. While they do shed their wool in the warmer months, they need some of their coat to survive in the colder mountains.

POACHING LAWS

To combat poaching—while permitting the collection of naturally shed wool—my ancestors made it illegal to possess more than a half bushel of khrysomallos wool. Also, any wool for sale is subject to examination, where the inspectors check for cut ends and other telltale signs of shearing.

Encantado

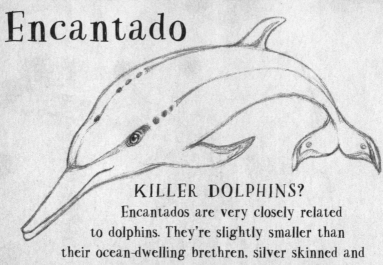

KILLER DOLPHINS?
Encantados are very closely related
to dolphins. They're slightly smaller than
their ocean-dwelling brethren, silver skinned and
silver eyed. They're also predators and scavengers who
will eat drowned humans, leading to stories of children
being lured into the rivers by these beasties. No actual
incidence of this has ever been recorded, and Jannah
believed the tales were intended to scare children out
of rivers to prevent drownings.

RIVER GUIDES
There are many stories about regular dolphins leading
humans to safety through storms, but the encantados are
excellent river guides even in good weather. Clan Hadleigh
has learned to harness their natural curiosity and rewards
them with food. In return, the encantados guide their river
craft through rapids and rough water. Other river-going
clans have attempted to capture and domesticate encantados
for this purpose, but the beasts escape as soon as they
have the chance. They have even been known to attack
and kill their captors. Clan Hadleigh understands that they
are wild creatures, who must be allowed to choose if and
when they will help.

Wyvern

THE DRAGON AND THE FOX

Legend says that once upon a time, a brave fox vixen raised her kits in a dragon's den. The fox was so small compared to the dragon that the great beast never noticed her there, scavenging from its kills and raising litters of young in its protective shadow. One day, however, the dragon flew away, leaving a clutch of eggs behind. The fox recognized the debt she owed, so she kept the eggs warm for her host. Eventually, the eggs hatched and still the dragon did not return, so the fox raised them with her own kits, and the young dragons took on the appearance of foxes, becoming the first wyverns.

Whoever invented this story clearly had no idea how biology works. Also, if dragons ever existed, they no longer do, and while it's possible that they evolved into wyverns, it's not because a vixen raised them. Admittedly, though, I still love the story.

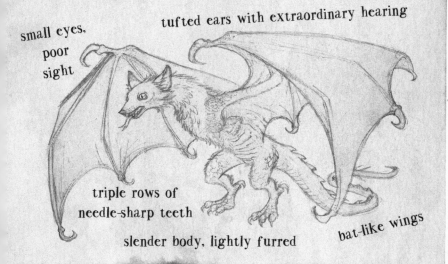

small eyes, poor sight

tufted ears with extraordinary hearing

triple rows of needle-sharp teeth

slender body, lightly furred

bat-like wings

Property of

Rowan

KELLEY ARMSTRONG is the #1 *New York Times*–bestselling author of three trilogies for teens: the Darkest Powers, Darkness Rising and Age of Legends, as well as several thriller and fantasy series for adults and three YA thrillers (*The Masked Truth*, *Missing* and *Aftermath*). She is also the author of *A Royal Guide to Monster Slaying*, the first book in a middle-grade series, as well as the co-author (with Melissa Marr) of the Blackwell Pages, a middle-grade fantasy series based on Norse gods. Visit Kelley online at kelleyarmstrong.com.